Praise for *The Lost Life*

'Carroll's prose is limpid and assured … [a] poised and beautifully burnished work. Carroll's control is masterly'
Andrew Riemer, *The Sydney Morning Herald*

'Carroll's ability to turn an ordinary moment into something sacred makes this novel a profound exploration of human desire, endurance, maturity and regret'
Bookseller & Publisher

'This novel will consolidate Steven Carroll's reputation among Australia's literati … Carroll is as much the literary ringmaster as novelist in *The Lost Life*, but remains as "rewardingly eclectic, intelligent and involving as ever"'
The Week

'[a] brilliantly envisaged novel … few novels begin with such measured elegance'
The Sunday Tasmanian

'its capacity to evoke a kind of sharp, sad nostalgia for an unlived past takes you by surprise. To enter the narrative is like entering into a slightly faded but exquisitely tinted photograph encased in gilded frame'
The Canberra Times

'this is not so much a departure as an arrival … Carroll's fiction is distinctive for the way his clean prose decelerates experience, puts aside the urgings of linear temporality, to reveal a richness that habitually evades us … his beautiful and poetically attentive novel retrieves a warm, beating heart from Eliot's haunted, stark, magnificent work of art'
Australian Literary Review

'Carroll's prose has a sublime rhythmic quality … almost as if he has sung the words on the page'
Australian Book Review

Steven Carroll was born in Melbourne. His first novel, *Remember Me, Jimmy James*, was published in 1992. This was followed by *Momoko* (1994), *The Love Song of Lucy McBride* (1998) and then *The Art of the Engine Driver* (2001), which was shortlisted for both the Miles Franklin Award in 2002 and France's Prix Femina literary award for the Best Foreign Novel in 2005, *The Gift of Speed* (2004), which was shortlisted for the Miles Franklin Award in 2005, *The Time We Have Taken* (2007), which won both the 2008 Commonwealth Writers' Prize for the South-East Asia and South Pacific Region and the Miles Franklin Award 2008, *The Lost Life* (2009), which was shortlisted for both the 2010 Barbara Jefferis Award and the ALS Gold Medal 2010, and *Spirit of Progress* (2011), which was longlisted for the 2012 Miles Franklin Award, and *A World of Other People* (2013), which was shortlisted for the South Australian Premier's Award 2014 and was co-winner of the Prime Minister's Literary Award 2014.

Steven Carroll lives in Melbourne with his partner and son.

Also by Steven Carroll

STEVEN CARROLL

forever young

To ~~few~~, ORYSIA

You've come a long
way from Hampton Arc.

Cheers,
Steve

FOURTH ESTATE

Fourth Estate
An imprint of HarperCollins*Publishers*

First published in Australia in 2015
by HarperCollinsPublishers *Australia* Pty Limited
ABN 36 009 913 517
harpercollins.com.au

HarperCollins*Publishers*
Level 13, 201 Elizabeth Street, Sydney, NSW 2000, Australia
Unit D1, 63 Apollo Drive, Rosedale, Auckland 0632, New Zealand
A 53, Sector 57, Noida, UP, India
1 London Bridge Street, London, SE1 9GF, United Kingdom
2 Bloor Street East, 20th floor, Toronto, Ontario M4W 1A8, Canada
195 Broadway, New York, NY 10007, USA

National Library of Australia Cataloguing-in-Publication entry

Carroll, Steven, 1949- author.
Forever young / Steven Carroll.
ISBN: 978 0 7322 9122 8 (paperback)
ISBN: 978 1 7430 9972 8 (ebook)
Australian fiction.
Australia – Politics and government – Fiction.
A823.3

Cover design by Darren Holt, HarperCollins Design Studio
Every effort has been made to trace and acknowledge copyright. Where the attempt has
been unsuccessful, we would be pleased to hear from the copyright holder to rectify any
omission or error.
Author photograph by Rebecca Rocks
Typeset in Baskerville MT by Kirby Jones
Printed and bound in Australia by Griffin Press
The papers used by HarperCollins in the manufacture of this book are a
natural, recyclable product made from wood grown in sustainable plantation
forests. The fibre source and manufacturing processes meet recognised
international environmental standards, and carry certification.

When I was a child, I spake as a child, I understood as a child, I thought as a child: but when I became a man, I put away childish things.

Corinthians, 13:11

My heart leaps up when I behold
    A rainbow in the sky:
So was it when my life began;
So it is now I am a man;
So be it when I shall grow old,
    Or let me die!
The child is father of the man …

William Wordsworth

Contents

PART ONE

October, 1977

1. To Put Away Childish Things

A spring wind lifts the blossoms from the trees and throws them into the sky. It is violent and comes without warning. White flowers are blasted from their branches and a cool wind carries them in flock-like formation over the park, the playing fields and the government buildings hidden among the trees. Out there the city traffic is building into peak hour, taxis are busy, birds surf the gusts of wind, and office workers, public servants and nurses from the nearby hospital look to the sky, their umbrellas ready, though everyone knows their umbrellas will be useless in this wind and if this sky comes bucketing down. The pace on the footpaths is urgent. Get where you're going and get there fast. Dead leaves left over from winter, scraps of paper and lives are tossed into the air and scattered.

The flowers are carried far from the perch of their branches and a mile away a young woman at the university, her afternoon tutorial over, pauses in the street and removes a white blossom from her hair, releasing it back into the sky, like a bird from a net; the same blossom that only moments before sat securely on a branch in a tree in the park opposite

Michael's flat — the same park, currently in uproar, that Michael has been gazing upon these last few minutes.

Overcoated people scuttle past. Cars, trams and trains make a dash for home. Out there, he imagines, Mandy will have finished her tutorial. Soon, her car will pull up in the street at the front of the flat and she will be at his door. And when she is gone, and he has told her what he has resolved to say (that at some point in the last year they had become a habit), he will sit in his lounge room alone and contemplate what he has done. But not for long. For it is not his way. He will linger on it for a few moments, then find something to do.

And towards evening, with his amplifier and guitar in the back of his car, he will drive to a flat suburb north of the city, where the land has always been cheap and which the factory owners have always favoured — the flat lands of the flat suburbs, the likes of which nurtured him and made him, with their battered milk bars, scrappy streets and vast, beer-barn hotels that bear such grand names as the International, the Arcadia and the Excelsior — where he will play for the last time with this band that, too, became a habit that has to be broken. It is a day of farewells. He didn't plan it this way, but it will happen this way. And there is a cold resolve in him that he recognises from childhood, reviving briefly the child he once was, who learnt or simply acquired a way of doing difficult things, such as saying goodbye to the idea of a happy family and realising that one day his parents *would* part and that it was better to say his goodbye before the blow fell, without too much thought. For the wise child who held his hand and guided him through difficult times is never far away.

The last gig, the last waltz, the end of something or other, should feel sad, or at least feel like one of those goodbye moments, for something will finish tonight, and the part of him that lived for music and imagined that he always would will have to move on. The old will make way for the new and fade into silence like the last dying bars of a chorus, then bow out. And so, he should feel something. But he doesn't. He will remember the goodbye to the band, the handshakes and the laughs, but he will not remember which one of those indistinguishable, grandly named beer barns he completed his last song in (or even remember what the song was).

There is only a sort of acknowledgement, a cold resolve that this inevitable day, and this inevitable night, had to come. And when he switches his amp off for the last time will he hear the sound of his youth shutting down with the click of the switch?

He turns from the view, from the park in uproar, and eyes his guitar. He has just cleaned the strings and polished it. And it shines: the body, neck, head and tuning keys. It sparkles and shines with all the promise that he doesn't believe in any more. But he remembers the days when he did. And to look at this guitar is to be touched once again by the promise that came with it. And it will always be like that. Years from now, whenever he passes a music shop and sees one in the window, he will pause and they will both nod to each other: the guitar and Michael, Michael and the guitar. I gave you once my promise, when you were young and such promises mattered. And though you have moved on I remain forever here, calling from the music-shop windows of your memory, with the same promise, fresh as the days in which you still believed.

For this, Michael knows, is no ordinary guitar. This is no cheap copy to be bought and sold or carelessly lost one careless day with neither regret nor concern. No, this is the guitar, more than all the others (at least, to Michael), that was the very sight and sound of its times. For this is a Rickenbacker. I am the jingle, I am the jangle, I am the effortless song that told you anybody could do this — that was my promise, and you believed me once. And he had. There it is, resting on a stand in Michael's lounge room. Polished and ready to play for the last time. Michael had waited all his life to buy a Rickenbacker. But, in the end, he waited too long.

* * *

One day, in his teenage years, he was walking along a street in the city. It was a Saturday morning — blue sky, bright sun, spring or autumn, he's not sure. It was still mid-morning, the street was Saturday-morning busy, and he had come here because the street contained a music shop. Guitars, mostly. But not cheap ones. Not copies. No, here you found the types of guitars that you might only ever have seen in magazines or music shows on the television, strung over the shoulders of smiling bands making the music that was everywhere. The new music, the music that always made you feel as though anybody could do this. Or if not anybody, then *you* could do this. And so he'd come to this shop just to gaze upon whatever expensive, glittering treasures it might contain. He had stopped short at the window filled with guitars to take in the spectacle, dazzled by it, eyes roving all over the display — and, suddenly, there it was. Like stumbling on the *Mona Lisa* in a cluttered window of sea-scapes and still lives. On view. Open to the world, but indifferent to the eyes of the world. The *Mona Lisa* in a city side street. A *Mona Lisa* whose eyes did not follow you but gazed into the distance, one who suffered to be gazed upon and looked ahead. There it was. A Rickenbacker. Its colours — deep reds, oranges and yellows (which the brochure he'd seen called 'sunburst') — gleaming in the music-shop window like a newly completed painting, sparkling in that spring or autumn morning, fresh and still wet.

He had never seen one before. How far had it travelled to be there? And where from? The very name of it conjured up images of faraway places. That and the promise of sound. A special sound belonging to it alone. The sound that was everywhere in his youth and that shook things up and rang true. For it is on this guitar that the songs that rang true for the first time were played. Until then the songs on the radio were your parents' songs, or songs that belonged to older brothers and sisters. Other people's songs. Theirs, not yours. And then one day he was suddenly hearing (and it was dramatic, like going to bed one night and waking to a whole new world the next morning) *his* songs. And simply to look at this guitar, as he did that distant morning and as

7

he is right now in his flat overlooking the park in springtime uproar, is to hear those songs all over again, almost all at once, like a vast jingling, jangling symphony of songs weaving in and out of each other — a distinct phrase here, a hint of another there — then merging into the sum of all its parts and forming one magnificent anthem. For the guitar and the years and the songs that it so effortlessly summons up were, and still are, all one.

And is that where it all began, the artistic life? Is that when the fatal words were first spoken: that's it, I want to do *that*? When any thought of simply waking and working and living the way the rest of the world does disappeared, when the promise the guitar offered, that *anyone* could do this, first entered his life? No, it wasn't chapel ceilings and swelling orchestras and books that you'd never pick up unless you had to because you were studying them at school that rang true and which, for the first time, made the whole life of art make sense: it was the electric jingle-jangle of this guitar and the songs that found their voice through it.

And here it is, in his flat, polished and sparkling. Not the guitar he saw that morning, but it may as well be. The same, and yet not the same. Manufactured in the same factory, Santa Ana, California, to the same design, the same specifications. Perhaps even made by the same craftsman. For his guitar, he knows, was made in 1966. And it further occurs to Michael that this is not simply the instrument upon which the songs that rang true were first played, the medium through which they were first conveyed to the likes of Michael; this is a work of art in itself. It may not hang in any of the galleries of the world, but it will not surprise Michael if one day it does. Like a bicycle seat and handle-bars calling themselves a bull's head. But this guitar doesn't *need* to call itself anything, art or otherwise.

It just *is*. In fact, it was guitars like this that smashed Art. Art with a capital 'A', Art the holy, Art the unreachably distant — except to the elect few. Guitars like this one that, in a few simple chords, dispatched those plummy-voiced custodians of Art who occasionally appeared on serious, arty television (and who spoke of Art and Civilisation as if they owned them) into mimed silence, their speeches and commentaries washed away by this tide of sound — they themselves turned into a comedy sketch, their lips still moving but their words suddenly no longer theirs; their lips suddenly mouthing the tunes that were everywhere and their eyes alight with wonder at the songs they were suddenly singing.

But, all the same, having smashed Art, this guitar may, one day, wind up in a gallery and *become* Art. That is the way the world works. That is how the *system* works — a popular phrase. It is omnivorous. It consumes everything. Nothing stands opposed to it or outside it for long — not if it sells. The shocking becomes fashionable and enters the lounge rooms of the once shocked; dead revolutionaries (and only ever dead ones) become celebrities, their cigars and berets living on long after them on T-shirts and vodka bottles; and the guitars that smashed Art one day *become* Art. It's either amusing or sad, depending on the day. Amusing because, well, it *has* to be.

Sad because it means that the age of the guitar, the guitar that shook things up, is dead, or may as well be — and won't smash anything again. But it will always have, hovering about it, the ghostly chorus of the days when it did. And those who don't even play might one afternoon enter a gallery and find, alongside famous paintings and sculptures and ancient pots, that famous guitar.

But although, with care, the guitar will always stay young, he won't. The Michael who bought the guitar a few years earlier, the Michael who waited years to buy this guitar and who waited too long, is now a different Michael from the one who first looked upon it in that distant shop window and believed utterly in its promise. And because his playing days will finish tonight, and because he will soon travel and needs the money, he will sell this guitar and it will pass into other hands.

He reaches out and brushes the strings with his fingers and immediately the thing comes to life. Like hearing the *Mona Lisa* sigh. And just as the ringing sound of the strings dies down, he sees a car pulling up in the street in front of his flat. Mandy. She has her dog with her. A big English sheepdog that she leaves in the car as she jumps out into a blast of wind and slams the door.

Mandy. They have been 'seeing' each other, as the phrase goes, for the last year. More or less. Seeing each other, but casually. That's another phrase, for there is 'casual' and there is 'serious'. Michael and Mandy are 'casual'. More or less. And suddenly he is contemplating the letter 'M' —

Michael, Mandy, Madeleine. It's been years since he last saw Madeleine's face staring back at him from the rear window of a departing taxi. But the image has remained clear. Resolutely so; it will not go. Madeleine was 'serious'. Though, he remembers, not at first. At first she was a girl he saw from time to time, as she saw him from time to time. But it wasn't serious. Then one night he looked at her and realised it was. A hand gesture, a raising of the eyebrows, a confidential glance that said this look is for you. It is impossible to pinpoint, but everything, suddenly everything, changed. That was the night he fell in love with Madeleine, knowing full well that he would be the only one to fall in love. And, knowing this, knowing that such things happen and that such moments *do* suddenly announce themselves, he has waited over the last year, more or less, for 'casual' Mandy to become 'serious' Mandy. But it hasn't happened and, he now knows, it won't. Such moments do come along and announce themselves, but rarely. And not this time. And so he has ceased to wait for it. And as he watches Mandy approach his door, the dog watching her every step too, he realises that he has just looked upon her in the same way that he has just looked upon his guitar.

* * *

Excelsior. The name, like that of the suburbs all around, contains the promise of that which it doesn't have. Like suburbs whose names ring with images of wide meadows, of eternal sunshine and sylvan valleys — when the reality is scrub and thistles, and warehouses and factories and housing estates wedged in between, crammed into a maze of streets, avenues and boulevards, each, in turn, bearing a grand name that contains the empty promise of that which it doesn't have.

Michael is sitting in the vast lounge of the Excelsior Hotel. The term used to describe these places is 'beer barn'. But even that is too quaint, for it's more like sitting in a warehouse or on a factory floor, with tables and chairs instead of machinery. The band is taking a break and he is sitting by himself, looking over the expanse of this place (and, at the same time, remembering all the other places like this that he has poured too much of his time and energy into) for the last time. He has counted the people and it didn't take long. Twenty-three. And they are spread out over the pub as if, perhaps, to give the illusion of a crowd. For a crowd brings with it the sensation of company. However anonymous the crowd might be, it is, all the same, company of a sort. In another place, in another time, those in need of the company of others, even if they didn't know them or speak to them, would seek out the comfort of a clean, well-lighted place. Be it a bar or a café. Some place small and easy to fill. But no such possibility exists here among the factories, warehouses and estates. This place is a sort of frontier. In the same way that the suburb he grew up in once was. But isn't any more. For the frontier has moved relentlessly inland — the old frontiers have become history, recorded like the rings in a tree trunk, a reminder of where

12

the limits once were but aren't any more, because Progress has moved on, creating newer and more distant frontiers of estates and factories and grandly named hotels like the one he is sitting in.

However much everybody might try to spread themselves about, this is no crowd and the scene is a lonely one. Almost like a lonely city in miniature. There is no hum of talk, no clatter and chatter within, no pleasant whining of a mandolin — only the vista of vacant eyes and lips drinking, inhaling and exhaling smoke and occasionally moving silently in speech that quickly evaporates into the air with the smoke. And, for a moment, there is the vague sensation of having landed on the moon. Playing other people's songs in other people's styles to a small gathering on the moon, which may or may not be listening. For Michael plays in a cover band, which is not the way it all started out, but is, nonetheless, the way it all finished up.

'Aren't you gonna fucking miss all this?'

It is the drummer speaking. He's new to the band, but one of those, almost like a repeat offender, who has been in and out of bands all his life. Michael didn't see him approaching, but turns to him as he sits beside him with a plate of the supper the pub gives to the band. He's drunk, very drunk. But he's always drunk and drunkenness has become a sort of normality. So, in a way, you don't think of him as drunk. His girlfriend is not far away, drunk too, and calling out for him to come back to their table because she has something for him.

'Randy!'

He hears but completely ignores her. It's not rude or insensitive, it's just their way. He drinks, she drinks. She calls out to him, he ignores her. She waits a few minutes, then calls out again. It's just their way.

'Miss what?' says Michael, eyeing the plate. 'The hamburgers or the crowds?'

The drummer looks down at his meal.

'No, not the fucking hamfucker.'

'Then what?'

'Just this whole fucking business, man. It used to be cool. Once. *I* was cool, once. We *all* were. Fucking cool.' Randy is one of the old breed who still uses words like 'cool' and 'man'. And far from being daggy, it's infectious. So much so that Michael has noticed that the word 'cool' has now become part of his vocabulary. 'Not any more. Just look at this shithole,' he says, gazing around the pub. 'I'm a good drummer, man, a good one. But does anybody give a fuck? Does anybody give a flying fuck?'

'Randy!'

'I used to be in a band once. A good band. Blues and rock — and shit we were good. And I'll give you the mail, man, I'll give you the mail now; we were gonna make it. We were that close. Fuck, we were good.'

'What happened?'

'Fucked if I know. Can't remember.' He puts his plate down. 'You never saw the best of me. But I'm still a good drummer, man. I'm still a fucking good drummer. But just look at this shithole. What am I doing here? And I keep on wondering where the fucking money goes!'

'Randy!'

Randy looks round at his girlfriend who is grinning back at him from their table with — Michael can plainly see — a wicked-looking cigarette in her hand. What, in the language of the day, is called a 'trumpet'. She beckons him with her index finger. Come here, come here Randy I've got something for you, the grin says. And Randy rises, leaving his hamburger behind on the table and sways towards her.

As Randy departs, Michael notices five young women leap from their table. It is the same five young women every time. For a song, *their* song, is now blaring out across the pub from the sound system. They do not dance when the band is playing — only sit and stare, eyes vacant. Like toys, almost, waiting to be activated. And this song is their cue, and the moment it starts they leap from their table, line up on the floor in a well-rehearsed formation and dance.

It is the same every week: their cue, this song about a place called Nutbush — which may or may not exist — and the outer limits of the place. These 'limits' of which the song speaks, Michael assumes, are its frontiers. Which would be appropriate, a frontier song for a frontier suburb.

And so they assume their positions in a line across the dance floor, the dance floor that remained empty the whole time the band was playing. The squat young woman at the head of the line, who appears to be their leader, looks to the ceiling, counting the beats, waiting for the moment in the song that will activate them. And after weeks of observing them, Michael knows the point in the song as well as she does. And he, too, is counting the beats. Then it arrives, and neither Michael nor the young woman miss their beat. Suddenly, as if having been switched on, as if receiving power from some mysterious force that transmits itself through the medium of this song and out through the speakers of the sound system into the hair and fingertips and toes of the chosen, these young women begin — suddenly they are all moving in carefully choreographed steps, and the toys are dancing.

And the whole pub, all of those who had barely registered the existence of the band, turn their eyes towards the dance floor and smiles light their faces. And what had been an expressionless assembly is now alive. They are engaged, and they, this collection that is too small to call a crowd, have discovered one another's company and unlocked the comfort they came for. They nod to each other, smile and talk. And Michael realises that, with this, something remarkable has happened. The emptiness has gone from the pub, the vastness of its dimensions has shrunk, and the place has acquired a warmth that wasn't there a few moments before. And what were previously isolated small groups and individuals have been brought together by the shared experience of these five young women dancing in choreographed unison to a song about a place called Nutbush and the limits that define it. And Michael cannot help but be caught up in this transformation, for in being brought together the twenty-three drinkers are no longer alone and a kind of happiness has entered the place. A sort of innocence has been returned to them all. For these five young women are part of their number. Drawn from them. Like children playing dress-ups and performing in someone's lounge room for grown-ups or anybody who will watch. Suddenly they are a crowd.

Then the song ends, the music fades and the toys stop dancing. And straight away, as if it, too, were part of the choreographed action, the young women return to their table and resume their places. The smiles, like the music, fade from everybody's faces, and experience becomes private once more. But something has happened, and the thing they all came for, that sense of company that tells each and every one of them that they are not alone, has entered their night, if only briefly: given to them by these five young women who transcended their silliness and became a comforting spectacle.

And when they are all done, when the evening is over and they are all leaving, amid see-yas and goodbyes, and they are walking home past the warehouses and the factories, through those empty, grandly named avenues and streets that promise all the things they do not possess, this is the part of the night they will all remember and take home with them.

As Michael rises from his chair and resumes his place on the stage, the dimensions of the pub expand, that small crowd becomes a collection of isolated groups and individuals once again, and as the band begins (the drummer looking for all the world as though he could slide off his stool at any moment), their faces take on that expressionless look they had before.

When the gig is done and the equipment has been packed away, the band gathers round Michael and he shakes each of their hands in turn. They have been together for much of the decade and in some cases the friendships go back to high school, to those days when they all heard the music that changed their lives for the first time, when they formed a band that eventually became this band and when they still believed in the promise of the music. Other members of the band are newer, because that is the nature of bands: they're always changing, and members are always joining and leaving just as Michael is now. And they all agree or silently acknowledge that this is a sad moment, and for the duration of the farewell Michael, too, feels that sadness the way he hadn't felt it earlier in the afternoon. And it is while they are all standing about (except for Randy, now passed out on the stage with his girlfriend calling out to him, 'Randy!', and telling him to get up), after having shaken hands and saying the usual things that people say at such moments, that the singer, one of the original members and the band wit, speaks up, as much to cover the silence and break the occasional shouts of 'Randy!' as anything else.

'Well then, Joyce fucking James, this is it.'

Michael doesn't say that Joyce James, fucking or otherwise, isn't exactly what he's got in mind, that he could take or leave the old Joyce fucking James, but he laughs anyway.

'You know what she'd say, the old Joyce, if she was around now? You know what she'd say?'

'No, what would she say?'

'She'd say, "I wish I'd joined a fucking band. I wish I'd bought a Rickenbacker instead of a fucking desk. I wish I had a joint. Who do you have to fuck to get a drink around here?" She'd be saying it all, the old Joyce. But look at you; you're throwing it all in to go and write your great fucking novel.'

'Who said anything about a great novel?' Michael says, arms outstretched, appealing to the rest of the band. 'It's just something I wanna do, just something I've got to do. And I never said it was going to be great. Or even fucking great.'

'Of course it will, of course it will, Mick.' They call him 'Mick', they always have. Shortened names, they're as compulsory as saying 'fuck' every third word. 'And we'll all be looking out for you. There he goes, we'll say when you're famous,' and here the whole band laughs, and Michael joins in the laughter because it's that kind of laughter, 'he used to be in our band until he chucked it all in and went off to write his great fucking novel. But we knew him when he didn't know a G string from a D string. Look at him now, our Mick, big as Joyce fucking James. A girl in every bookshop. But we knew him when he sang "Lyin' Eyes" — and we'll remind you of that if you ever go getting up yourself, pal. We knew him, we'll say, when he sang Lyin' fucking Eyes.'

They share last beers and last laughs and last handshakes. And Michael, once again, does feel the farewell in the moment, and does now feel as though he switched his youth off with his amplifier. But he also knows that once he is in his car and driving away the feeling will fade. And, in time, he will remember this last chat, but will forget which of those anonymous beer-barn pubs they said their goodbyes in. And, in time, may even forget to say 'fuck' every third word.

And when he gets to the pub door and looks back at the stage he sees the band gathered around the prostrate figure of Randy, his girlfriend having given up on trying to rouse him. Farewell my jingle, farewell my jangle, farewell my jingle-jangle days. Hello Joyce fucking James! And in the fresh, open air, he has a final laugh at that.

Tacky music from the hotel sound system follows him out the door. A small group in clothes that look ridiculous even in fashion and will look even more ridiculous once out fashion (which won't take long) passes by. Tacky music, tacky clothes, tacky decade. A tacky time to be a writer.

* * *

There is sobbing on the telephone. He had no sooner entered his flat than the telephone rang and the sobs began. They are Mandy's sobs. Distant but near. Coming down the line to him. Disembodied sobs. But, disembodied as the sobs may be, as soon as he hears them he invests these airy sobs with substance and body. Mandy's body. A great body. Mandy's face. A great face. Mandy's eyes, eyes that were always true and never played games, but which will be red from crying. Which is a shock just to contemplate because he's neither seen nor heard her cry before. She was always happy Mandy. Fun

Mandy. Casual Mandy. The Mandy who knew better than to step beyond the boundaries of the casual, because that is what they were. He was casual Michael, she was casual Mandy. And so they neither argued nor cried. Because casual doesn't argue, and casual doesn't cry. Everybody stays happy. And all those messy emotions that something more than casual might stir are never stirred, because casual is always careful never to go too deep, where all those messy emotions lie. No, casual goes out. Casual walks side by side with casual, but rarely holds hands. Casual dines, and as the night reaches its logical conclusion casual goes to bed and in the morning casually agrees to meet and do this again sometime.

But Mandy is crying. And it is something of a shock. Neither of them speaks. Mandy has called to sob. She has no shoulder to cry on. But she can, nonetheless, have her sobs registered in Michael's ears, out there in Michael's world which is no longer hers. And she doesn't speak. She doesn't even try to. She simply goes to the heart of things, to all those messy emotions that casual doesn't touch upon. Short staccato sobs, followed by long drawn-out sobs, almost musical in their delivery. But as he listens, shocked and moved by Mandy with a tenderness that is new, there is also a part of Michael that is noting that Mandy is breaking the rules.

And all the time there is a song playing in the background. The stereo is not loud, but audible. And there is a song playing, a popular song from a year or two before. And in this song a young man is proclaiming to the world or whoever will listen that he is not in love. And as Mandy's sobs continue, he finds, despite himself and a voice saying not to, that he is listening to the song as much as he is listening to Mandy. Even enjoying it. For it is a good song. And part of him is visualising the chord changes as he might play them. And it is with a jolt that he realises at some point that the sobbing has stopped and that she has asked a question.

'Are you happy?'

It is an odd question. Even a haunting one. Almost a question that a couple who parted years before might ask of each other, a couple who have long since gone their separate ways, who have accidentally bumped into each other in some unlikely place and who ask of each other, 'Are you happy?' But Michael and Mandy only parted that day. And so the question may mean many things. Are you happy? Meaning, look what you've done. I've broken the rules. I'm crying. And do you know what this sound is? This is the sound of casual saying it is casual no longer. That it never wanted to be casual in the first place. That it only ever played the part. This is the sound of casual ripping off its mask to reveal the face of serious underneath. And although you waited for casual Mandy to become serious Mandy, and although the moment never came, serious Mandy was there all the time. And these are her sobs. They have to be, because casual doesn't cry. Look what you've done. I've broken the rules. Are you happy?

And while he is contemplating an answer, and if he was honest he would say yes, he is happy, not with what he has done but because he is alone (and it has occurred to him for some time — whether it be endless hours in the cricket nets in his youth, in his old room at home, or now at his desk in a world of pen and paper — that in his heart he has always lived alone) he hears the song in the background end then start again straight away. And he realises that it is a tape, a loop of some sort. The song no sooner finishes than it starts again. And he wonders how long she's been listening to it. And no sooner has the song started again than she is crying again. Short staccato sobs, followed by long drawn-out sobs. Sobs that well up from that deep, hidden source where messiness lies. Musical in their delivery, and he realises, with relief, that he will not be required to answer the question. The sobs continue. The song plays on. And then the line goes dead.

His room is silent. Eerily so. And he knows that written into the act of Mandy hanging up the telephone is the hope that Michael will call back. That Mandy is now waiting for her phone to ring. But it will not because he will not call back. Like the sale of a guitar, these things must be done quickly and finally and without too much thought. Like ripping a band-aid from your arm: do it quickly and decisively and there is no pain. It is a trick he learnt as a child, and the child who taught him, the wise child, the old child that he was who steered him through difficult times and held him in good stead, is still there. Right beside him, holding his hand at those times when the trick needs to be recovered.

And so he replaces the telephone, rises from the couch and steps out the door onto the footpath outside, contemplating the park opposite, which earlier in the day was in spring uproar but is now still. The playing fields are hidden in darkness; lights from the government buildings just beyond them glow in the night under a clear sky of stars and a distant half-moon. Taxis drop and collect their fares, night animals descend from their trees — and the telephone suddenly rings in his lounge room, but he lets it ring. A plane passes overhead; the drone of a car engine defines its path through the winding streets of the park and fades into silence; squares of light, window eyes, here and there, snap shut. And as the ringing stops he turns back to his flat as if never having heard it.

* * *

There must have been a time when he felt it all within his grasp. A time when the music that announced itself as the music that anybody could make was at his fingertips. When his fingers would intuitively form the magic chords and the instrument would give up its jingle-jangle treasure.

There must have been such a time, but he can't really, with clarity, recall it. If the years have taught him anything (and at the age of thirty-three he has concluded that if the instrument was ever going to yield its magic it would have by now), the years have taught him that it's *not* just anybody who can make that music. You listen to a symphony and think, I can't do that. Nor do I want to. But you listen to the music that comes from guitars such as this, the one he is currently carrying in its case as he walks along an inner-city street in the late Friday sun, and you like it because it rings true. But also because you think, *I* can do that. That was the trick of this music. That was its tantalising promise: you too can do this. And all the time you couldn't. Those magic chords that your fingers ought magically to have formed remained elusive. At least, not the chords themselves, but the order in which those simple, ordinary chords could be placed (like simple words in the right order, for he read only yesterday Mr Hemingway's advice that the two-dollar words will always do the job if placed in the right order) — *that* combination of melody, chords and words has always remained elusive. The instrument hinting that it might yield its magic when all the time it was never going to because you weren't the magician it was waiting for.

And so at the age of thirty-three he has concluded that he has waited long enough. And that the moment to part with his guitar has come. He comes to a stop at the front of a music shop. It is, in fact, the shop from which he bought the guitar in the first place. A guitar shop in one of his old student hang-outs. A serious music shop that serious musicians come to — to trade and buy guitars, to try the guitars they may buy one day, or just to talk guitars, pick-ups and strings. Michael smiles, always strings. Like artists talking paints and brushes.

But now he is standing at the front of the shop, not to trade or exchange his guitar for another that may yield its promise more readily, but to sell it. It is, he knows, one of those moments — those moments that define the end of something and the beginning of something else. One of those moments that must be met without thought. Without reflection. And so he enters the shop and leaves the shop in a matter of minutes. And he walks back in the direction from which he came, only now he is not carrying the guitar any more. And never will again. And the Michael who left the shop without the guitar is another self. The old one was left inside with the guitar.

And although there must have been a time when he felt it all within his grasp, he can't recall any such moments now. I gave you my promise, his guitar had said, somewhat sadly and not blaming either of them, as Michael handed it over to the shop owner. But that was in the days when you believed in such promises. Not any more. Those days gave way to years and the years have come to this. And so, we part. Quickly and without too much fuss. Too quick for tears. No time for words. All that can come later. Then money was placed in his hand and his guitar was carried to the back of the shop. Farewell my jingle, farewell my jangle, farewell my jingle-jangle friend.

That was how it went. He entered the shop and he left the shop all in a matter of minutes, the hand that held the case now light. His arms, his head, his legs, all light too as he walks away from one life towards another, as though occupying that ill-defined time and space between incarnations.

But that other life is now waiting to be assumed. For when he was not playing in those grandly named pubs he was discovering the deeply thrilling, private world of his desk. Of pen and paper, words and stories, the lamp at midnight and, outside, the world in all its darkness. Far removed from vast pubs and echoing sound systems. That is the life that calls now. And he knows the moment is right. Had he tried earlier, and made the change earlier, the moment might not have been right and nothing would have come of it. For he would not have been ready. But the timing is right, and now he is. And there is that odd sense of loss and gain, and that exhilarating sense of not knowing what comes next, as he makes his way back to his car.

* * *

'I saw the beach tram and just got on.' Rita is staring at Michael with a look of quiet wonder in her eyes. 'I followed it right through until the end of the line and spent the day at the beach.'

Rita keeps staring at Michael as if half-expecting some sort of disapproval from him, a look that suggests his mother has gone a bit funny in the head. But he gives her no such look. Instead, he is smiling. Good. People should do this more often, the smile says. Live differently. See a beach tram and jump on it and spend the whole day at the beach instead of going to work. Of course, everything would fall apart if everybody took to jumping on the trams of their fancy. But, he muses, not everybody does. Which leaves room for *some* to. Michael has been jumping on the trams of his fancy for as long as he can remember. People *should* do it more often. For this is, he tells himself, the hardest thing in the world — to live differently and to act spontaneously. And if things fall apart, what of it? If things fall apart it's because they deserve to fall apart. He knows he's slipping into something he recognises as Lawrencespeak. Lawrencethink. And even though Mr D H Lawrence is slipping out of fashion — and fast (in fact, it will be a fall from grace faster than the devil's) — he follows the runaway tram of Lawrencespeak anyway. Yes, everybody should do this. Napoleons of industry, directors of the banking system, company heads, politicians and prime ministers should do this — jump on the trams of their fancy when they appear and just live. And if things fall apart, so be it. Let the waiters and waitresses drop their trays and follow their fancies out into the street, leaving their orders behind them and the customers to help themselves. Let the shop assistants drift away, the school teachers skip school, university lecturers and public intellectuals trail off in mid-sentence ... the taxi drivers desert their cabs, the train drivers, the tram drivers ... Ah, there's a thought. What if the tram driver jumps off somebody else's tram of fancy? What if they all did? Leaving no trams of fancy to be jumped upon? And it is while he is dwelling on this complication that Rita breaks into his thoughts.

'I just sat there looking at the ships coming in from the sea and going out to sea.'

How long was he gone? How long was he not listening? He returns, a little bit annoyed at his mother's intrusion (the way her intrusions always annoy him, especially lately, and why is that?), from this truant world he has conjured up and concentrates on Rita talking about ... what was it? Ships coming in and ships going out. Yes, that's it. He nods, as if to say, go on.

'And when there were no ships to stare at I stared at the horizon. Perhaps I bought a sandwich at some stage but I don't remember eating one. Perhaps I didn't.'

Michael has come for dinner, a rare thing on a Friday night when, she's probably thinking, he has more interesting things to do and more interesting people to see. But the fact is he hasn't. No more band. No more nights lost in the vast and vacant spaces of suburban beer barns. No more Mandy, whom, like so many of the girlfriends of his life, his mother has never met because she would always be the 'wrong' girl — like that dirt street and that dusty suburb they lived in, always bound to be a disappointment or met with disapproval. And so Mandy never met Rita. They belonged to separate worlds. And with no Mandy and no band, there is nowhere else he needs to be. No one else he has to see. He's on his own, for the time, and better off alone. In any case, he's sick of cooking for himself. So, here he is.

There is a lull in the conversation and his mother looks around the lounge room of this villa unit she now lives in, at the table, dinner finished, the plates still on the table, then to the paintings and photographs on the walls, as if, Michael can't help but think, observing somebody else's room and the trappings of somebody else's life. 'It's odd how you can stare at the horizon for so long and not get bored. I must have stared at it all day.' She swings her head back to Michael, her eyes sharp and focused. 'I'm not going to stare at the horizon any more. I've been staring at it all my life.'

She picks up a travel brochure from the small table beside her, flicks through its pages, then hands it to Michael opened at a marked page, also explaining that she has taken what she calls a sort of holiday from work. A long one.

He nods as he takes in her words, registering for the first time that something serious has happened, something a little more than jumping on the wrong tram and skipping work for the day. He stares at the brochure. It is a brochure published by a well-known travel company (with one of those solid, English names), which conducts tours to places all over the world. Just for people like Rita. The page Michael is staring at details a twenty-one-day tour of Europe. Bus and train. Rome. Florence. Paris. And so on. He looks up and she half-smiles and raises her eyebrows.

'I know, you wouldn't do it. It's not your ...' And here she pauses. 'What do you call it? ... Your thing. It's not your thing.'

'Nobody says that any more.'

'Yes they do. I heard it on the tram the other day.'

He looks back at the brochure. She is serious about this. And he is happy for her, even if her attempts to assume the language and phrases of the young are ten years out of date and momentarily annoy him.

'Truth is,' she continues, 'I'm not so sure it's my thing either. I've never liked trooping off in a gang.'

He tells her that it *is* her thing — at least, this particular thing at this particular moment. The very thing she's waited years to do. And she agrees. She knows and she

30

doesn't know what's on the other side of the horizon, she murmurs. But it's far away and full of foreign places, the very places she's yearned for all her life, where they speak the languages that migrants speak. But they won't be migrants there. They'll be home, and she'll be the migrant.

Other people, she now tells Michael, explaining her choice — families and couples — they can travel together. But even if Vic were alive and they were a couple, they would never have travelled because Vic would never have left the country. Couples can travel, and they are their own comfort. But she can't travel to these foreign places alone. And she speaks of the brochure and the tour with a slight sigh. A self-conscious one. As if giving in to a cliché. I know, I know, the sigh says, everybody laughs at you. Sheep, they call you. But how else am I to go? And she stares at him as she smooths her frock. Are you laughing? It's a stare, not a statement. And he returns the stare: no, he is not laughing. It is true, you have never trooped off in a gang; true that your dresses were always just a bit too good for the street, and that the street always disapproved, just as the gang is likely to. But how else are you to go? Indeed, how else?

As he passes back the brochure he notes, for the first time, the dates of the tour, only a few weeks away.

'Yes,' she says, following his eyes, 'not long. Why wait any longer? I've waited long enough.' And her eyes are shining as she speaks and gazes upon the brochure, almost wistfully. And besides, she continues, she doesn't have to troop off in a gang — she can give them the slip. Go her own way. As if they're not there. Not all the time, but enough of the time. And she can be a real traveller. Discover little streets and little cafés that those travellers who travel as couples or alone discover and which they call their own — their little cafés, their shops, which they take photographs of and bring home with them, images of the places they made *theirs* in a way that the gang never can.

He nods as she talks, believing her and not believing her. But as much as he feels sure that it will all fall short of her hopes (it always does; everything does because nothing is perfect), and that the gang just *won't* go away, she is happy and her eyes are shining. So he keeps this thought to himself. She has followed the tram of her fancy and she will now, finally, embark on the very journey she has dreamt about all her life.

And as he remembers the dates of this tour he notes, with a quiet relief, that he will not be there in Europe. That he will not yet have left Australia. And the obligation of showing her about foreign cities, should their paths have crossed, will not fall to him.

'I know,' she says, standing as she speaks, for he is about to leave. 'I know what they say. Sheep. If it's Tuesday we must be in … where is it again?'

'You'll be too excited to care.'

'Do you think so?'

He nods.

'At least …' she says, glancing up at him with a quiet sense of wonder at the grown Michael in front of her (who, with the beard gone and the long hair cut, is looking more and more like his father every day), and is momentarily distracted by the question of when did this happen and was she watching, was she *really* watching, and when did he become, well … complete. And with that quiet sense of wonder there is a quiet sense of accomplishment at having done it, for she always felt she was never born to be a mother, unlike all the other mothers she saw about her when she was round-bellied and walked the splayed duck walk of the mother duck. And as well there is a sense of loss that Michael now lives in a world of which she knows nothing. A world of no confidences, when once he was a torrent of them. 'At least,' she continues, picking out the spoken thread of thought from the unspoken, 'I'll be there. Finally. Who cares how? I'll be there, and that *is* exciting, isn't it?'

'Yes,' he says, nodding. 'It is.'

She then looks down at her dress pocket, fishes out a coin and shows it to Michael. And he sees straight away that it is an old penny, from the old currency. A kangaroo is leaping across a copper coin and he can even see the year stamped on it: 1957. 'I'll toss this in the Trevi Fountain.' She looks up at him, eyes bright. 'It'll be the only one there. Not many of these left now. I kept it.' She puts it back and pats her pocket.

He leaves her at the door, a yellow light fanning the doorway, the unit lighting up well in the night as all the houses of her life have The wind is back, wrenching the trees and shrubs this way and that. He waves. She waves, then steps back quickly, shutting the wind out and switching off the front light, returning, no doubt, to the coloured photographs and coloured maps of the brochure. The promised world that the tram of her fancy has led her to. The tram that everyone should jump on when the fancy takes them, but which few do.

He is standing on the nature strip at the front of his mother's unit, suddenly distracted. Something is out there. Somewhere out there in the suburban night there is an insistent slapping sound, like a gate being blown open and shut. Or a loose shutter, only the windows don't have shutters here. It's a gate. Banging back and forth in the night. No, more of a slap. A sharp, slapping sound. And as he stands on the nature strip, the inside lights of his mother's unit lit behind him, he is drawn into the sound. But why? He doesn't want to be. He doesn't like it. But it draws him in as he stands there. It is a puzzle, for a moment. What is this thing?

For with the slapping sound, a memory is forming. Two hands, two hands coming together with great force. And then the memory assembles and he sees that the two hands are those of his father. His father, drunk and enraged, is standing in front of Michael's mother in the bedroom of that house they all called home all those years ago, and he is bringing his hands together with great force. She is crying and her crying is noisy, and Vic wants her to shut up. Just shut up. And so he is bringing his hands together with great force to show her what he could do and what he might do if she doesn't just shut up.

And the noise, this slapping sound and the crying, have woken up and drawn the five- or six-year-old Michael

34

to his parents' bedroom and he stands there in the doorway observing the scene, until they both finally turn and see him, and his father stops slapping his hands together and his mother rushes to him, her eyes a mess of tears and anger and shame. That was the night the wise child invented himself. He kissed his mother good-night, said goodnight to his father, and went back to bed as if nothing had happened.

Memory awakes. The image stays, that whole world comes back, and then one image is replaced by another, and another. That's the problem with memories, one thing's always leading to another, and suddenly he's seeing three figures — his mother, father and himself — standing on that dirt street in that frontier suburb that was theirs, staring at the swaying khaki grass of a vacant paddock and waiting for the setting sun to land, ears tuned for the sound of a distant thud when it does, on a summer's Saturday night long ago and far away, that started well and ended badly, as they always did. *They're walking down the old street again ...*

A gate bangs in the night. Memory, an unwanted memory, walks again. A moment before he was standing on solid ground, now this unwanted memory kicks it out from under him. It happens like this, the past rising up out of nowhere and with no warning. Three figures assembled on a dirt street in front of a vacant paddock, lives full of longing that will never be relieved and eyes full of tears and anger and shame that will never go stare back at him, still out there on that long-ago dirt street of stick houses. Must we stand here forever on this dirt street, assembling and re-assembling night after night, going through the same bloody night time after time, with no release?

Do these things *ever* go? That slapping sound in the night, those three figures that they once were assembling and re-assembling on the old street with no release? Or are they always there, just waiting for the right scent, sight or sound to spring back into life? And why the bad memories all the time? It's not true what they say about people only ever remembering the good times. Too often you only remember the bad. And why is that? Why always those memories of his father that don't bring back the best of him, when he knows full well that the best of him was there most of the time. Those times when the ten- or eleven-year-old Michael would sit on the floor at his father's feet in their lounge room as they watched the latest American television show and say, 'Dad, I'll always sit here.' Why don't those memories come back as often as they should? Why is it so often those memories that *don't* bring back the best of his parents?

They must have been happy once, his parents. And not just sharing patches of happiness, but deliriously happy. Why not? They must, at some stage, have been deeply in love. But we never see that — our parents in love — and so those memories aren't there to bring back. We just see what comes afterwards. At best, the affection that comes after love, but not those crazy days that must have existed when they couldn't see enough of each other, or keep their hands and lips off each other, and every waking moment was spent either with each other or thinking about being with each

36

other. No, we never see that. Only the bits that come after love. And too often they're the bad bits, and they're the bits we remember.

A gate bangs in the night. Slap. A memory comes back. A bad one. It's not true what they say about only remembering the good times. The wise child he once was takes his hand. Together, they blink. The bad memories go. The slapping sound stops. The three figures on the old street disappear. There. Simple. All gone.

As he eases his car from the kerb he is once again contemplating the stolen season of his mother's day. Let the waiters drop their trays, the public intellectuals trail off in mid-sentence … The houses and units and flats of the suburb recede into darkness, oblivious of the world of truant trams that may strike the fancy of any one of them at any moment.

* * *

Later in the night Michael sits in his lounge room. Alone. The telephone is silent, a song plays softly on the stereo. He has just switched the television off. The face of Whitlam had briefly passed across the screen, as had the face of Fraser. Although it has not been called yet, he suspects there will be an election soon. And when it comes, the face of Whitlam will fade from his screen, from all their screens, for the last time. In the coming weeks, however, their faces, Whitlam's and Fraser's, will be everywhere, and soon after, these years — which have already acquired the title 'The Whitlam Years' — will officially end. And, when he thinks about it, it is like watching an explosion settle — those years, those Whitlam years, were an explosion of energy that *had* to happen. Explosive times, now all but over.

On the kitchen table is a sealed and stamped envelope with something in it that Michael wrote a few days before. A little essay of sorts, prompted by the increasingly frequent appearances of Mr Whitlam and Mr Fraser in the newspapers and on the television. A little something he did one afternoon, more an amusement than anything. But something that might, all the same, make a little money for him. So he's decided to send it to the newspaper, the one he reads, that is. So it's sealed and stamped. If they take it, well and good. Money for the trip. Beyond that he gives it little thought.

The stereo plays on and his mind drifts back from the public world of politics to Mandy, already wishing he'd done things differently or not at all, and already replaying the scene as he would now have it. The lounge-room window both reflects the room and all its contents, a ghostly reflection, and is also a dim window onto the world outside, the park, illuminated here and there by the occasional lamp, the lights of the government buildings and the black sky hanging above it all.

The view will be the same when he is not here. And not the same. Things will change, and nothing will change. The world doesn't need you, not really. Not Michael, not Whitlam or Fraser. The world just is. And it will not register his or their departure any more or less than it will a bird's or a tree's. He might even have already left. The wind that only yesterday blasted blossoms and birds from their perches and tossed them into the sky, and which returned earlier this evening, has now settled. The animals that went to ground have returned: the roving cats, stray dogs, foxes and all the little things the park plays host to that they prey upon. Things will change, and not change. The wind is resting, but will return. And the blossoms will once again be blasted from their branches, next week or next year. Buildings will go up and buildings will come down. Trees, already unstable, will be ripped from the ground by spring winds, and the possums and birds will find new homes and perches.

As he rises and turns to pull down the blind he catches his reflection in the window. Gone is the long hair, and gone the beard that he wore when beards were worn and hair was long. His hair is short now, not as short as his father's was, but not so much longer. New Wave. It is the last of those young, fashionable phrases that will ever come naturally to him. From this point on, and this will only occur to him later, if he were to talk in youthful, fashionable phrases he would only sound like his mother saying 'my thing' or 'your thing' or 'their thing'. New Wave. It is the last time he will ever be in step with fashion.

And as he stares at his reflection in the window he notes, as he has increasingly over the last year, that he is beginning to look like his father. And it's not just the looks, it's the mannerisms too. How often has he caught himself lately, sitting in that old student armchair that he can't bear to part with, legs stretched out, newspaper on his lap, his eyes vacant as he stares out the window, and said to himself: this is how my father lounged in his chair, newspaper on his lap, and stared vacantly out the window through dull afternoons like someone waiting for the real living to begin. And for that moment he *is* his father. And with that sensation comes the possibility that he is thinking his father's thoughts. And the mystery that he so often contemplated as a teenager — the mystery of just what his father might have been thinking as he gazed vacantly out the window — is solved. Probably nothing much at all, just the lingering feeling that the real living was waiting for him out there, somewhere beyond the window, beyond the neatly trimmed lawns and nature strips of a suburban street, which it may well have seemed to him was more interesting when it was dust and thistles, when their homes were unpainted stick houses, and days were either filled with dust or clogged with mud, and Bruchner's dog howled like something out of the Middle Ages.

How terribly strange to feel that you have become, however fleetingly, your father. Gone is the long hair, gone the beard. Gone that feeling that he was just himself, unique, and nobody else. A clean break, free of everything — your parents, their parents — that went before. The whole past.

Michael pulls the old, tattered blind down. His image disappears. The telephone is silent now but the memory of Mandy's sobs returns. Are you happy? Are you … The song, on a continuous loop of tape, plays on. The singer proclaiming to anyone who cares to listen that he is not in love. In a flat suburb to the north of the city in a grandly named hotel the toys will dance on without him, and when they finish they will collapse onto their seats, all animation gone from them. Until, one night, those five young women will grow out of their routine and leave the pub and never go back. New toys will come along, new bands will replace the old, old waves will give way to new waves, and young foxes will sniff the park air for the first time, everything fresh.

Michael reaches for the light switch. We come, we go. Get used to it. And the sooner the better. He lies in bed in the dark, staring at the shadows on the ceiling. Out there, deep in the suburban night, a loose gate slaps back and forth in the dark for no one. Three figures assemble on a dirt street, long ago and far away. We come, we go. And yet we never go. For there they are, always assembling and re-assembling on streets dripping with longings that will never be relieved, awaiting their moment of release. Awoken by memory. Long gone, but always there. Assembling and reassembling. Going round and round, in and out of the years, like a love song on a continuous loop. Are you happy ... Or are you waiting for the real living to come along? Are you happy, Michael, are you ... Or does that even matter? The world doesn't need you, not really. No more or less than it needs rocks and stones and trees. It just is. Even as you lie here in the dark, while out there the stars stretch out forever, it is worlding. And what does your happiness matter to it, after all?

2. Chinese Whispers

They could be a painting. In fact, Peter has the distinct feeling of sitting in one. A famous painting. Two men in their everyday clothes. Late in the last century. A tablecloth spread out on the grass — food and wine on the cloth. And a naked woman sitting beside them. Peter smiles to himself. Of course, there *would* be a naked woman beside them. The scene is set in a Paris park, after all. And this famous painting he has in mind is a work of art, after all. But his smug dismissiveness aside, he knows better. He knows what the painter was doing. He was, as a popular old student phrase would have it, demythologising the naked female body. Extracting it from mythology, where people had given themselves licence to look upon it, because it was 'nude' not naked, ideal not real — and returning it to the everyday, to a city park in the harsh glare of the midday sun. A scene made all the more shocking to the shocked eyes of the day by the fact that the two men are clothed, but 'clothed' in a way that they could almost be naked — and the woman fully dressed.

Yes, he knows all that. But he's not sitting on some lawn in a park in late nineteenth-century Paris. Rather, he's in a plain, modern flat in Canberra. He is sitting in the lounge room of one of those square blocks that pass for architecture, and there are, in fact, not one but two naked women in front of him. One, the older woman, is sitting in an armchair, legs crossed casually, smoking a cigarette as if this sort of thing happens every day, and perhaps it does. The other, a younger woman, is lounging on a couch, facing Peter, front leg stretched the length of the couch, the back leg raised for support, hand resting on her knee, as if she were, indeed, posing for a painting and Peter were the painter.

The older woman is called Beth. Elizabeth, but always Beth. And never Liz or Lizzie. Peter and his university friends (like Michael, whom he doesn't see any more, not since they went their separate ways and took their separate political paths; Peter from student radical to the conservative side of politics) all knew Beth in their university days, even though she was older and had already become a tutor by the time they arrived. They sat in on her tutorials — Peter, Michael and whoever else tagged along — and they got to know her a bit. Beth was a bright young thing — that's why she was a tutor. Then again, they were all bright young things, weren't they? She'd risen through student politics. Edited the student newspaper and eventually became a journalist. Somewhere along the line she married. Acquired a husband, someone of whom Peter has only the foggiest of memories, who at a party once ironically addressed him as 'comrade', gave him a bowl of olives, took Peter's bowl of crackers and made some comment about distribution and exchange, meaning, Peter assumed, that they should each pass them on. And that was it. Did they ever meet again? Probably not. Like all those marriages, which seemed to come and go with the explosive brevity of the Whitlam government itself, it dissolved soon after. Peter and Beth were never friends. But their paths continued to cross. And so fate (or something like it), rather than friendship, kept them in touch.

She wore overalls back then, and drank and smoked her way through tutorials. In fact, Peter is currently noting, he has rarely seen her without a cigarette in her hand. And he is also noting that she has lost her youthfulness and is starting to take on the look of Marguerite Duras in her prime. And it suits her. Not old, but no longer young. Her forehead creased, her face bearing the lines of a lifetime smoker. Yes, Madame Duras indeed.

When he first arrived in Canberra, Beth had a reputation. She was the journalist to whom all other journalists deferred. Especially the young. But the young acquired reputations of their own, stopped deferring, and at some point she started looking like yesterday's woman. Stories of drinking, getting things wrong, getting sloppy, began to do the rounds like a running popular joke. Something along the lines of 'Oh, did you hear …?' There was even talk about fits of temper, which he has never seen and doesn't believe. All the same, she was slipping, *has* slipped, and could do with a good story. And Peter has one. Which is why he is here.

He'd knocked on their door and Beth had opened it wearing a bathrobe. It's all right, she'd called from the hallway, it's only Peter. And she'd led him into the lounge room where the young woman, Trix, was lounging naked on the couch, pretty much as she is now. And as he sat down, Beth removed her robe, and so, suddenly, he was sitting in a room with two naked women. It is, he assumes, what in the language of the day is called a 'statement'. This is us, the nakedness says. We hide nothing. We go through the world naked. Two women who have chosen to live together and who hide behind nothing — not even clothes.

As Beth had lowered herself into the armchair, crossed her legs and lit a cigarette, he had been aware of the eyes of Trix upon him. Studying him. Scrutinising him. Almost waiting to pounce. They have met, not often, but often enough. And he has felt from the start, whether rightly or wrongly, that she doesn't like him. Even distrusts him. As if, on any such occasion as this, he might have come to steal Beth from her. Which she knows, and he knows, is not true. But it *might* be. Perhaps that's it — the mere possibility that it might be true being sufficient to stir distrust. For they have a past, Beth and Peter. Not much of one, but a past all the same. A past that Trix doesn't share because she wasn't there. And so when Peter visits he brings that past with him, and in so doing brings with him that implicit bond to another Beth altogether — a Beth Trix doesn't know because she wasn't there, and who is, by definition, not 'her' Beth. And so whenever he visits, he takes *her* Beth away. Perhaps that's it. Perhaps not. All the same, he's keenly aware that her eyes have not left him from the moment he sat down.

And so he is sitting in a room with two naked women — one suspicious, even jealous; the other vaguely indifferent. And it might almost be a kind of compliment —

that although they might not (in spite of their 'statement') reveal themselves entirely to the greater world, they do to him. For the moment, he chooses to take it as such.

To distract Trix from her unyielding scrutiny, or to distract himself, he looks around the room. There is a Balinese rug on the floor, photographs of the two of them in various places, Asian figures, and glassware on the sideboards, and books, books … shelves of them. And not the usual paperbacks, but a serious hardback collection, many from Beth's university days. The room is testimony of another life, a face other than the public one. The inner life, he tells himself. The one most people don't see and, again, there is almost a sense of privilege in being invited in to see it, for he has the distinct impression that they live in a self-sufficient world that neither requires nor desires the outside one. It's a poster on the wall that his eyes finally come to rest upon. It is one of those posters that, no doubt, will one day become a collector's item. A window onto an age, onto a generation, capturing its statements and beliefs. In this case, his generation. A generation that has no doubt as to the validity of its pronouncements. Harbours no indecisive second thoughts. And brushes aside all resistance with a resolve that says the matter is settled. Whitlamesque. Indeed, it is the style of the day not so much to put propositions forward, but to make pronouncements. As if it were all obvious. And objections could only ever come from fools, and to question is to pronounce yourself a fool. Whitlamesque. Does the age express itself through him or did he give such uncontradictable expressiveness to the age? In the poster a woman is lying on the ground. Defenceless, violated. It is a graphic, disturbing image. The poster reads: 'Rape is a political act'.

After a moment of contemplating the poster, Peter turns to Beth. 'Why is it political?'

She stares directly at him. 'You *would* ask that.'

He pushes on. 'It's a violent, inhuman act. But why is it political? Why does everything have to be a political act?'

Beth inhales from her cigarette. 'Because everything is. You've heard of the patriarchal society?'

'I'm a member, aren't I?'

She exhales. 'It's not a club, and you don't have to sign up. And this is not a game.'

She is eyeing him in a way that says don't disappoint me, and he has the feeling of being in one of her tutorials all those years ago and of asking those questions that automatically pronounce you a fool. *Un*Whitlamesque. How many of us become our own adjective? Whitlamesque. The word floats once more across his mind and he is reminded of why he came here in the first place. He's also asking himself if it weren't for the Whitlams of this world — not just the actual Whitlam but all the others who constitute this Whitlam generation with its unshakeable self-conviction — if it hadn't been for all that, would he ever have crossed to the conservative side of politics, when such a crossing was seen as not just a political betrayal but a betrayal of a whole generation's sense of destiny? Would he have crossed? Did he walk or was he driven? And, if so, who was driving?

It's a question he's thought about, usually a passing thought, in spare moments in airport lounges, taxis and planes. Whitlamesque. Grand. Shakespearean. Unshakeable and uncontradictable. *Is* that the way to do things, after all? If you're going to change things in such a way that they will never be the same again, change things in such a way that what was once questioned becomes birthright — never to be questioned again — if you're going to achieve this, if you're going to achieve a before and an after in a nation's life, is that the way to do it? And for the moment he's admiring of this Whitlam of theirs, the style not the politics — this Whitlam of theirs, who was once his, but isn't any more.

Beth dips her fingers into a bowl beside her and slips an olive into her mouth. And when she has finished and deposited the pip on the table beside her, she looks round for a napkin, for her hands are messy with oil, and Peter, noting her discomfort, takes a handkerchief from his pocket and passes it to her in a manner that contains the mutual familiarity of old friends and shared old times, and perhaps is even suggestive of a middle-aged couple, who can read each other's minds without need of asking. All of which, he is sure, Trix notices.

'It's clean,' he says.

Beth wipes her fingers and lips and passes it back, without so much as a thank you, because old times don't require thank yous for such things. And Trix, he senses again, is aware of all this.

By now he has ceased to notice that he is sitting in a room with two naked women. They are simply sitting and talking as people will. And as he is contemplating the question of whether he walked or was driven to the conservative side of politics, he turns back to Beth (not sure how long his silence has lasted) and, to shift the topic from rape and political acts as much as anything else, asks, 'Are you ever tempted to go back? You know, to the academic life?'

She shakes her head and pronounces somewhat biblically, 'We were what we were, but we aren't any more. There's never any point going back. There's never anything to go back to.'

At this point Trix turns to him. 'Would *you* like to go back? Do things differently?'

And it's not a teasing question, not one of those 'game' questions, but one of almost dispassionate interest. Curiosity.

'Not really.'

'"Not really",' Trix repeats, 'but you think of it?'

'Don't we all?'

'Not really.'

Peter stares at her and her eyes don't flinch. She's sharp, this Trix. There's a touch of the fox in Trix. A quick, brown, young fox.

'It's just that,' Trix continues, 'you always ask that. Well, not always, but often enough.'

Peter shrugs as if to say do I?, but doesn't speak.

'What takes people back?'

Trix rolls onto her back as she poses the question to the room. And, as she does, Peter notices Beth's eyes resting upon her. The unmistakeably tender eyes of someone in love, of someone counting her blessings and who counts her blessings every day. Eyes that the world never sees, but which Trix does and which he does now. The tender eyes of this Marguerite Duras in her prime resting upon this fox that has wandered into her life and changed it utterly. But at the same time he can't help but feel (rightly or wrongly) that there is a certain sadness in Beth's eyes, as if asking herself how long this might go on for, how long might her luck last and how long might she keep this quick, brown, young fox. And he is contemplating this as Trix repeats her question.

'Well, what does?'

Peter shrugs. Beth is still staring at her and has stopped talking, a cigarette that she seems to have forgotten smouldering in her fingers. Trix is gazing up at the ceiling, oblivious of them both.

'Is it regret about having taken the wrong path and lived the wrong life? Or is it guilt? Or is it guilty regret? What takes people back — or makes them think of going back? Some people, more than others, live in the past. Why? Nostalgia or guilty regret? Do people talk about going back because they want to rectify something or other? You know the sort of thing? One of those silly, drunken stunts,' she continues, 'like locking some poor girl out in the snow then falling asleep and waking to the tragic consequences? Or those stories where someone does something excessive, a drunken prank that goes all wrong.' She turns to him. He tries to stare directly back but his eyes keep shifting, evading hers like they do her question. 'Just a thought.' And she rolls onto her side and stares at him.

Suddenly she's like one of those deliberately playful, innocently inquisitive characters from a drawing-room comedy. And, he notes, she does it well. But at the same time there's that uncomfortable feeling of being pinned to the wall. Peter laughs the question off, but the laugh rings hollow in the room.

Trix eyes him once more, a look that says she never seriously expected a response, then rolls onto her back once again. But at the same time it's a look that says she just might have stumbled upon something, the way these games sometimes do.

The smile that came with the hollow laugh fades from Peter's face and Beth is once more mindful of the cigarette smouldering in her fingers. It is then that Trix springs from the couch, seemingly well satisfied with a good evening's work, and stands upright.

'I'll leave you to old times.'

She leaves the room and Beth follows her. She is gone for a minute, possibly less, and when she returns she is wearing a dressing gown, as if to say that without the company of her fox she feels naked. She sits back in the same armchair, now staring at Peter suspiciously. He's not one for social calls, not in this town. He doesn't call often, and when he does it's for a reason, that look seems to say.

'So, why are you here? It's certainly not to talk about old times.'

How old is she? His mind is ticking over. Early forties, thereabouts. But with the drink and the smokes she looks older, despite aquiring the weathered manner of some Left Bank intellectual. No, he corrects himself, she's actually entered that ageless zone. Her unapologetic years. Her take-me-as-I-am years. But she's not on the Left Bank and she's not Marguerite Duras. She's a journalist and she's stuck in this place with the rest of them. A journalist to whom all the others once deferred, but not any more. On the slide. In need of a little something. Just what Peter needs.

'No, I'm not here for old times. Besides,' he adds in a brisk, let's-get-down-to-business manner, brushing some imagined speck from his trousers as he does, 'I'm not too sure we shared enough of those days to call them old times, anyway.'

She sips her drink, the same scotch he has beside him.

'I've got a story for you.' He pauses. 'Would you like to hear it?'

She stares at him, saying nothing. He pauses again, a dramatic pause. A little too dramatic and too long, but still she's waiting.

'Whitlam will not lead them into the next election.'

'Pigs!'

Until now there has been a quiet air of expectancy in the room, which Beth's sudden laughter dispels.

'Is that it? They've already challenged and he won.'

'Just.'

Her laughter has subsided but there is a smile left on her lips. He returns his attention to the imagined speck on his trousers, brushing it off again.

'Well, if you don't want it ...'

The implication is clear: he can take it elsewhere.

'He led them out of the wilderness,' she begins, 'he gave us the nearest thing to a revolution that we will ever have. He's *their* mountain and ours. And, heaven knows, we have few mountains. Don't you realise what that makes him?'

He lifts his eyes from the imagined speck on his trousers to the ceiling as he speaks. 'That makes him ... an expendable hero.'

Untouchable is more what she had in mind. But as he takes his eyes from the ceiling and stares directly at her she's also got to concede that he has the air, the certainty, of someone who knows something. She may not believe it, but he does.

Of course, it's preposterous. But, big news always is. At first. Isn't that what makes a big story big? That it *is* the preposterous that becomes actual and takes everybody by surprise. How many times has she read a big story and silently proclaimed to herself, 'I don't believe it?' So, what *if*? And she's aware, as she poses the question to herself, of excitement now beginning to course through her veins with the whisky. Indeed. What if?

'They're going to lose, again. Very badly, again. Very, very, badly.'

'It doesn't look *that* bad.'

'They know better.'

Again, there's that air of absolute certainty. The calm certainty of someone who knows something. There's no flinching in those eyes. The preposterous happens. Indeed. What if? But it does raise the question of why he, Peter, a ministerial staff employee, earmarked for higher things, but not just yet, should know this. And, as if reading her mind, for he seems to be, he answers her unspoken question.

'I have my sources. From the old days. From old times. From that playground of easy uprisings … "What do we want? When do we want it?"' He smiles. 'You know, when we all marched together. When history had iron laws, and history was on our side. I was there. Remember?'

She nods, remembering that, indeed, he was.

'But you can't stay in the playground forever, and you can't stay forever Left. Can you? But I've still got my contacts. We're useful to each other from time to time. And, believe me, this is one of those times.'

'Why can't they just tell me?'

'And be shot for treason? No, they need a buffer. They need a go-between. They don't have long — one or two months? Not long, and they know it. Believe me, they're serious. But they need you. They need the papers. You start it. The others follow. And soon things write themselves. And once that starts, as we both know, anything can happen. Things take on a life of their own. And at some stage we reach that point where we don't control events any more. They control us. And the speculation gets to the point where it becomes self-fulfilling. That's what they want. These people are beyond sentiment.'

There it is again. That air of absolute certainty. The air of someone who knows something. The preposterous happens. And, slowly, the preposterous is starting to look possible.

'Can I speak to them?'

'Never.'

'Can I know who they are?'

'Absolutely not.'

'How high are they?'

'Very high.'

She pauses. 'Are things *really* that bad?'

'They think they are. And they know better than us. They went close to throwing the big man out last time, now they're moving in for the kill. This is not simply a challenge. He will be there one morning, and gone the next. It'll be a back-room job, and the back-room boys will have their way.'

'Deposed?'

'He's not royalty.'

'Isn't he?'

His eyes are fixed on her as she sips from her whisky glass then lights a cigarette. Beth, aware of him staring at her, is even a little self-conscious, asking herself if there's a trace of a tremor in her hand that lights the cigarette. Does he see it?

And as she looks back at him she can read his mind, just as he can read hers, all too easily. Once, they all looked up to you, didn't they? That's what he's thinking. Once, they all deferred to you. But that was once. It's true, she notes, it's true. Somewhere along the line they stopped. Somewhere along the line her contacts dried up — retired or turned away or died. And somewhere along the line she became yesterday's favourite. That's what he's thinking. Yesterday's favourite could do with a good story. But why should he bring it to her? Is he sentimental, and do old times count for something, after all? And can she believe him? Can she really believe him?

Every part of her professional, cautious self says don't touch it. It would be an act of faith alone. More or less. It's preposterous, but the preposterous happens. There *are* times when big stories drop in our laps. And is this one of those times? Once, when they all looked to her, she had a nose. She had instinct and her instinct was good. She acted on it, and she knew when to pounce. That was when she had confidence. Ah, confidence. So hard to get, so easy to lose. And this is a confidence game. Judgement, instinct, faith — when to pounce! Once, big decisions came to her naturally, when she took her confidence for granted. But as she got one thing wrong, then another (and as much as she told herself that sooner or later everybody gets things wrong, that everybody's human, it didn't help), slowly, under the darkness of doubt, her confidence slipped away from her. And the more they all stopped looking to her, the more it gave her the slip. Now, her nose gets confused. The senses are dulled.

But she notes again that excitement is coursing through her veins with the whisky as she raises her glass to her lips. Perhaps old times do count for something. That for all the changes we go through, the years bring with them a certain loyalty that never goes away. We forgive in old friends, even old associates, things we would never forgive in others. Perhaps old times do count and that's why he's here. For the moment she's choosing to believe this.

And, once again, she's telling herself that the preposterous happens. And if she were to start events rolling until they reached that point where people no longer controlled events but events controlled them, and everybody else followed her there — wouldn't they once again be looking to her? Just like old times.

She's not sure how long it has been since either of them spoke. But the room is not silent. For, it seems to her, it hums in the way that rooms in which things remain unspoken hum.

He rises, about to leave, and she looks up.

'It's monstrous.'

'It's politics. Sooner or later everybody's time comes round. And nobody walks when it does,' he says.

'How *could* they?'

'They've already tried. Believe me, they will again.'

'You're convinced?' she asks, with just that sense of pleading that those in need of convincing couch their questions.

'Yes.'

There it is again, that unflappable air of certainty, of someone who knows something. She walks him to the door, glancing at him in the hallway as she does, nose twitching, not exactly sure what it senses.

Smoke curls from her fingers as she returns to the armchair, to the dregs of the scotch in her glass. What if? If they do try again, right on the eve of an election? Wasn't it only five years ago that they all stood and hailed their mountain? And it was roses, roses, all the way ... Now, they're beyond sentiment. It's monstrous. But what if? The monstrous happens too.

* * *

When did it first occur to him? Maybe a week ago. A convergence of factors. Well, two of them. He doesn't believe in synchronicity, the convergence of seemingly unrelated events that would mean nothing by themselves, but together do. He likes his Jung well enough, but when it comes to synchronicity he likes him in the way that you might like a novel. Synchronicity. No, it's just coincidence dressed up as fate. Still, sometimes coincidence can look like fate. Like the convergence of those two events and the birth of an idea.

He buttons his coat as he leaves Beth's flat and strides out into the wide, deserted street. It was his first impression of Canberra, and it will be his lasting image of the place — streets with nobody on them. His flat isn't far. But he decides that a walk will be good and deliberately takes a detour past Parliament House. He crosses a park, mulling over Jung and synchronicity, and there it is. All lit up. Hovering on the dark lawns. A mirage. If he were to walk into it now, the House, at this hour of the night, all lit up, for all the world hovering on the lawns — would it really be there? Or would it dissolve on contact? Recede, then recede again. Forever out of range. Sound and light. Never really there at all.

They're in there. Late-night members, ministers and their staff. Nowhere else to go — reading papers, hatching plans. Nothing else to do. That's what the place is for. And that was how his idea came to him a week or so earlier. It was simple. Mundane. There were four or five of them, the opposition, gathered in the corridor of the House one morning. Heads down. Quiet talk — always the most dangerous. Two shadow ministers and their staff. Not just ordinary shadows and not just ordinary staff. And why did he think ... something, something is happening here? They looked up, saw him, stopped talking and moved into someone's stuffy little office.

Of course, it was nothing. But it *felt* like something. Something can *not* happen and feel like it has. You are sitting in a train and think the train is moving, when it's the train on the next platform. But for that moment you think that your train is moving — and it may as well be. If you can create the impression that something is happening, it may as well be happening. Thinking that it is — that's all that matters. You don't have to wait for events to fall into your lap for something to happen — you can create the impression that it is. And for that moment when it *feels* like it is, it may as well be. The effect is the same. The damage the same.

And if he could look at that closed, furtive group and think something was happening, why not others? It's all in the effect. So, what might they have been up to? Peter's taste is for the epic. For even though he was trained in law, he moved in the company of literature students and always read. Developed a taste for Tolstoy. Even had a cat named after him, a black beast of a thing he now fondly remembers as being as big as its name. And so when he asks himself, What? What could they have been up to?, his instinct is for the Tolstoyan. And the possibility came to him almost like inspiration. Their mountain, what if they were about to demolish their mountain? Can you create events in which you take no part? Can you script them and then watch the script come to life? If only for a while. It's a tantalising thought. One that is way beyond the dull routine of his defined tasks — and all the more tantalising for it.

It suffered the fate of all such tantalising thoughts and was soon forgotten. Until later, that same morning, when he'd looked up from his tea and newspaper in the cafeteria and seen Beth sitting two or three tables away. She was alone. And it struck him that this was a different Beth from the one he'd observed when he first arrived in Canberra. In those days, she would never have been alone. Not unless she especially wanted to be. And she didn't look, at this moment, like she especially wanted to be. No, she looked ignored. Worse, forgotten. And, surely, it was only a matter of time before her paper moved her on and gave her some women's magazine to edit. And that was when the tantalising thought returned. What if the tantalising thought and the forgotten journalist in

60

need of a good story converged and became an experiment in inventing reality? All created by an anonymous artist?

Two seemingly unrelated events — a tantalising thought and the appearance of a washed-up political journalist who just might find the thought equally as tantalising, and who just might set things in motion. Synchronicity? No. Not even fate — but fate waiting to be written.

He had nothing to lose. Especially if nobody knew. If the artist who created it all remained anonymous. And if it worked, well, success has a thousand fans: he could reveal himself to the inner circle of those who matter and his stalled career could start to move again. And so, knowing he was not the first and would certainly not be the last, impatience impelled him. But, above all, there was the sheer exhilaration of the game: he was tantalised because it *was* tantalising.

He sat watching her as if, indeed, he'd conjured her up, going over the idea until it started to take on the solidity of a plan. A plan, what's more, that just might work.

That was a week ago. And as much as he'd pushed the tantalising thought to the back of his mind, if only to test its strength and resilience, it kept returning, more insistent and more tantalising with each return.

And so now he continues his walk back to his flat, the seed planted, leaving the House, white and all lit up in the night, hovering on the dark lawns. There and not there. Real, but not. Solid, but for all its appearance of solidity giving every impression that it just might dissolve upon being touched.

Peter opens the small illustrated volume and all the familiar characters, the lush green fields and lanes, the farm and the fir trees — that whole story-book world — once more reveal themselves. Peter Rabbit is poised on the brink of adventure: the vegetable garden, the watering can, the farmer and his rake. And as that story-book world opens, so too does the past. A double-terrace student house suddenly springs to mind, and the balcony upon which they all stood, the inner-city street they looked down upon and the purple door that led them into that world the house contained, when they were story-book animals. Pussy Cat and Bunny Rabbit, Bunny Rabbit and Pussy Cat. He was Bunny Rabbit; she, a girl called Louise, was Pussy Cat. Together they had adventures. And all the doors of all the rooms in their story-book house now open with the illustrated volume and all the familiar characters look up to him from their places and nod or smile as if never having grown up or changed: Pussy Cat, Bunny Rabbit, Michael, Madeleine.

In his student days Peter had played Spanish revolutionary songs on his portable stereo in his room, and the music had drifted down the hallway along with the smells of tobacco and hash. But those revolutionary songs, of a conveniently distant time and a conveniently distant revolution, were, Peter knew even then, all part of an assumed attitude, like his way of slopping around in an old Brooks Brothers shirt and not caring if cigarette ash fell on it. The songs, the attitude, the ash on a young man's sleeve — all adding a sort of colour to him, which the girls noticed. So the Moroccan rug his father had once brought back from his travels and which Peter had nailed to his wall, the revolutionary songs and the casual attitude to expensive shirts were all part of the play-acting they all played at, Peter more than the others. And it was probably no surprise to anybody, least of all himself, when Peter lifted the needle on the Spanish revolutionary phase of his life at the same time as he stubbed out his last joint, and crossed the floor, without breaking stride, to the conservative side of politics.

It is then that Peter hears the voice of his daughter telling him to begin, and why is he waiting? And immediately the voice of his other daughter follows, asking why he is staring at the drawings for so long. One story-book world opens onto another. Doors open onto other doors. But his daughters' voices bring him back to the here and now.

They are all sitting on one of the beds in the girls' room, Peter in the middle, his daughters either side. Mobiles hang from the ceiling, posters cover the walls. It is a modestly large house, with a large garden all around it in a suburb south of the city's river where the modestly large houses are. It is the weekend. Friday night, and Peter is back home in Melbourne reading to his daughters before bed. It is story time. When he is finished, when his daughters are in their beds, he switches off the light. The faint sound of television floats towards him up the hallway from the lounge room where his wife, Kate, will be stretched out on a couch.

But instead of following that sound he crosses the hallway into his study, taking the story-book world with him.

Not so long ago, but long enough to be distant all the same, Peter and his Pussy Cat played together in a world of pop-up animals. They had adventures together. And their adventures acknowledged no end of things, no whisper of mortality, because death hadn't been invented then. Death came later. Even now Pussy Cat leans over the terraced balcony of that house with provocative innocence, like Juliet from a popular film of the time, and calls down to him in the street below. At least, that is how he remembers her.

Then their adventures stopped. Bunny Rabbit's eyes began to wander and rest upon creatures other than his Pussy Cat. One night, he walked out and didn't come back. Pussy Cat cried herself into a sleep from which she never woke, and death was invented. And once more, as he does from time to time, he sees his hand snatching Pussy Cat's medicine that night just before walking out. There were always two small bottles by her bed — one, her medicine for those days when the world was too much with her (which it was more often than she cared for it to be), and the other, the sleeping pills that gave her blissful sleep at the end of those days. And as Peter sits at his desk, the hand that was death's minister reaches out again and snatches Pussy Cat's medicine before disappearing into the night. One last jibe (for the jibes were many by the end), one last act of retribution before leaving. And all, in his mind, a prank. A bit of a laugh: that'll fix her. Did you do something,

Peter? Did you? Trix, the quick, brown, young fox eyes him with a playfully dangerous smile.

Yes, a prank, that was all it was meant to be. Just one last prank before disappearing into the night, the medicine in his pocket — with every intention of bringing it back the next morning. But when he returned late in the afternoon the next day, having forgotten all about the pills (for youth sleeps in and forgets), it was already too late. Pussy Cat, the world too much for her, had cried herself into a sleep from which she never woke. Death had been invented and Peter had invented it.

Pussy Cat's eyes now watch him as he leaves his study. They accompany him to the door, then stare back with Pussy Cat resignation as he closes it. He has not felt the eyes of his Pussy Cat upon him for a long time; it is the story-book world that has brought her back. Her eyes stare at him with resignation — or is it — accusation? Both, perhaps. And he's asking himself if he will yet see forgiveness, even absolution in those eyes. Just a prank, after all. That was all it was ever meant to be.

He closes the door and treads softly as he passes the children's bedroom. As he enters the lounge room, recorded laughter erupts from the television. Kate is laughing too and acknowledges him briefly, eyes on the screen. The garden is dark but the house is bright. Then the man on the television says something funny and they're both laughing and he slides into the armchair that is generally regarded as his.

* * *

Chinese whispers. Is this how it all works? The news. Newspapers. All Chinese whispers. Someone spoke to someone who spoke to … It is neither the lead story nor is it buried. A substantial article on the front page. And written with such authority that he almost believes it himself. Except that he knows full well that in that chain of whispers, his was the first.

The kitchen is large and bright. The Saturday-morning sun slants in through the silver birch in the garden. When Peter finishes the article he puts the paper down and looks around. Colour and light. Kate is a lawyer by day and an artist by night. The kitchen is a faithful reproduction of Monet's in his house just outside Paris. It's a sort of artwork. A pleasing arrangement of colour and shape. Others might call it kitsch — let them. He doesn't. He likes it.

But he is not thinking of the kitchen at the moment. He is contemplating the whole business of Chinese whispers and news. Facts and truth. There are facts. The world is composed of facts. And there is truth. Not to be confused.

The newspaper article he is looking at is a fact. It exists. But that's as far as it goes. It exists because of a chain of whispers, light as air, that led to the article, and his was the first whisper. The woman, Beth, to whom he whispered, chose, in the end, to believe it — and passed it on to others inside the newspaper who chose to believe it enough to print it. The article appears in the newspaper, ink on paper. A fact. But not the truth. Not yet. But should one thing lead to another, and should events arrive at the point where we no longer control events but events control us, will it, at some stage, become the truth? And if it does, will anybody care at all if it began with a whisper?

At the same time, he is surprised that the story was ever printed. Perhaps even astonished. But he shrugs. What the hell, they fell for it. And there is something thrilling in that. Some stunt! Some con. Who knows how it went — that chain of events that led to publication. Perhaps, he imagines, sipping the last of his coffee, it went like this. Of course, there are checks and balances in newspapers. Checks and balances such as, let's say, Mike and Janet. What do you think, Mike? What do you think, Janet? How good is your source, Beth? What do you think, Mike? Not sure. Do we wait? Can we? They've already tried, are they going to kill him off this time? Not just before an election. Surely not. But, what if … In the end, though, there is the editor. And the editor is human. And let's just say that this editor and Beth go back a long way (as, in fact, Beth and her editor do). And let's just say he knows that Beth needs something, that she needs *this*. And if so, did he, in the end, want to believe it as much as she did? What turns a whisper into a story? What steps in? Let's say humanity stepped in. And once humanity steps in, anything is possible. Beth explained her story to the editor and he listened, by turns disbelieving and believing. And then, at some point in their discussion, a look came over his face. A look that didn't need explanation, one that Beth read perfectly and that said: What the fuck, we've done crazier things than this, haven't we? We've done crazier fucking things than this. And what if she's right? We're in on the ground floor. What the fuck. What the fucking fuck.

He is once again aware of being the anonymous artist of the whole public play. Of scripting events to the point where the author begins to play God. Or where the two begin to resemble each other — for, at this moment, he does indeed feel like a god in his universe, everywhere in evidence, but nowhere visible. A god who blew into the air a chain of Chinese whispers. Fact, but not truth. At least not yet.

It is then that his wife, who has just finished reading the same article, looks up from the paper.

'Is this true?'

He shrugs, and she shakes her head slowly.

'It's not fair. Not right.' She pauses. 'Is it true?'

There is, he notes, troubled concern in her voice. He looks at her, curiously, knowing that, like him, this mountain, this Whitlam, was once hers too when she was younger, when everybody was younger and youth surged to the mountain — but he isn't hers or his any more. All the same, there is lingering affection in her eyes, even care.

'I don't know.'

He doesn't even have to think. The answer pops out naturally. Convincingly. But it's a lie. When he set the thing in motion he never thought of it entering his kitchen. After all, the idea was hatched in a small room in the faraway world of Parliament House. Not here. He looks around. The sun slants in through the tree in the garden, highlighting the blues, greens and yellows of the kitchen. The smell of coffee and toast lingers in the air. On the television one cartoon gives way to another. It could be a scene from a film or from television and they could all be players. He has just lied, convincingly. And naturally. The scene is credible. But one part of the scene isn't telling the truth. And does that make the whole untrue? Of course, he's making too much of things and this thought will go away before the dishes are cleared. All the same, it's a nagging thought. One that contains a shiver of guilt. Vaguely disquieting. Is this, when we start playing God and start playing around with these things, how our inventions come back to haunt us? Dismantle one part of the play and soon, whether you want to or not, you start dismantling all the other constituent parts, until the whole construction comes tumbling down. Is this what you get for playing God? Is this how it feels? And it occurs to Peter that a life spent immersed in inventions, the like of which he has just set in motion, might just eventually destroy all those things you take for granted, until you don't believe anything any more. Is this how people fall from the grace of happy living and condemn themselves to the life of the penitent judge, wandering foggy wharves in foreign cities and seeking out strangers to tell their story to?

He shrugs. It's nonsense. One of those thoughts we play around with. The sort of thing that happens in books, and usually foreign ones at that. All that matters at this moment is that it's working, it's actually working. The look of concern on his wife's face will fade, nothing more will be said, and the story, this passing topic of conversation, will leave the house as quickly as it entered.

The sound of television cartoons that has continued in the background ceases, and the spell is broken. Kate bundles the children upstairs, a walk to the local park is proposed, and the kitchen is now empty. He shakes his head, shaking himself free of the thought, then rises. The newspaper, its photographs, stories and all its sense of self-importance, is left on the kitchen table, surrounded by Monet cupboards, pantries and straw chairs. A deserted set, in between takes? Or the real thing?

* * *

If power was lying there on the streets of St Petersburg just waiting to be picked up, can the same be applied to this building and these cluttered corridors? And, if so, in what part of this place does power lie? With that group of senior members gathered at the far end of a corridor, behind that closed door, or with some harmless, anonymous-looking figure (which, Peter imagines, is the way this place sees him) who knows the power of a whisper, and knows how to set it in motion so that it multiplies into the plural?

The Monday papers, the Tuesday, the mid-week papers, the television and the radio, talked of nothing but Beth's article after it first appeared that Saturday earlier in the month. And this talk blew through the streets of the country like the October wind and, like the October wind, has now exhausted itself. The power of a whisper is far greater than he ever imagined. The denials were issued immediately and emphatically, again and again, with derision and ridicule directed at all those involved, and now the story is completely discredited and nobody believes it. But they did for a while. Or at least were ready to. So the denials and the discredited story are not as important as the fact that there *was* talk. For a moment, when it could have been true, it was as good as true. And damage was done. For a short time.

Peter is looking back on it all from the vantage point of a late Friday afternoon. The hand behind it all, the anonymous artist, watched his invention come to life with a sort of detached fascination, as if contemplating the question, and with a degree of admiration: who did this? And so all the sentimental concern he read in his wife's eyes that Saturday when the story broke, and the shiver of guilt that came with it, now forgotten, he strolls onto the steps of Parliament House in the late October sun, as absorbed with thoughts of his work, of the story and how it played out, as he might be with an intriguing tale he just read. And while part of him is saying be wary of playing God too often, young man, another part is acknowledging that he has already acquired a taste for the game. And, what's more, has a natural facility for it. That, he also recognises, is a talent that might take him places. Certainly lift him from the bureaucratic rounds that now take up his time. And a political life that has stalled can start moving again.

He's not even aware of her at first as he looks over the wide street that sweeps past with the dominant spectacle of Mt Ainslie in front of him. He finds it impossible to look upon these steps without picturing, all over again, the mountain of Whitlam standing upon them on the day he was sacked, uttering words befitting of a mountain, when half the country (the half that Peter had once counted himself among but by the time of the sacking didn't) stood shocked in the streets, threatening violence and revolution. But the shock faded and everybody eventually went back to work. And as he stands where he imagines Whitlam stood that day, more or less, he can't help wondering if, for all the drama of that day and that moment, there was some part of Whitlam that was, however momentarily, contemplating the spectacle of Mt Ainslie and asking himself if it was really a mountain at all or just a big hill. And, if so, did the mountain of Whitlam feel diminished by the question? Are all our mountains, depending on how we look at them, just big hills in the end?

It is then, lost in speculation, that he turns and comes face to face with Beth. The transformation is dramatic. And in so short a time. A middle-aged Marguerite Duras has become an aged one. All in a matter of weeks. And because he knows and she knows that any expression of concern for her would be false, he offers none. That is one game he will not play. The game of false concern. And so he greets her as he would any day. As though nothing has happened. She doesn't speak. He greets her and still she doesn't speak. She will speak, her manner says, with her eyes.

You did this thing, her eyes say. A game, was it? No, not so much a game as an experiment. And all of us your guinea pigs. You lied, and why should I be shocked that you did? I know that you lie and that it is your job to lie, but did you have to lie to *me*? And could you not have returned at least one of the calls I made or shown the slightest tremor of feeling or concern? But no, they've got you, like they've got all of us, for as long as we're useful. But I can only say these things now because my usefulness has ended. As, one day, will yours. And all those who are useful, and who use, will *become* used. It is the nature of things. And I have no desire to rehearse and repeat all that has been learnt and unlearnt over the years. You will learn that our inventions come back to us. And, when you do, the approval of fools will sting. And your achievements will ring hollow in the air like a cracked bell. This you will learn.

And for a moment, it seems to Peter, it is almost as though she is not there. Almost as though he has been silently conversing with a ghost. As though the cold shadow of a ghost has passed over him, blotting out that late October sun in all its dazzling brightness. You used me … and why am I surprised? And when she turns to leave, there but not there, it is almost as though she fades on the sound of a distant horn, and in the blink of an eye is gone.

The surprise in her eyes, that hint of the belief that old times might have amounted to something more than this, lingers on. Amused glances will now follow her, whispers, raised eyebrows and audible laughter. It will all follow her now as he knew it would. Ridicule will smile back at her from hotel bars and supermarket check-outs. And she will spend her last days in this city, once her domain, before being shifted to the inevitable gardening supplement, as the object of laughter.

He walks down the steps to a waiting taxi, looking for her as he goes, for she seems to have dematerialised. Talk blew through the capital like the October winds, and for a few days or weeks talk was truth — or could have been. The effect was the same. Damage has been done. And nobody will ever know where it started, because — and he is fully confident of this — for all the look of censure and surprise on her face, she would never disclose her source. Not Beth. Ethical Beth. She will endure ridicule and laughter, but never do that.

The taxi draws away into the quiet, deserted street. The invisible hand will stay invisible. Whisper was truth for a while, damage has been done and will be done again. That is the nature of things.

* * *

Within weeks the whole affair — which some papers called a story of betrayal as old as humanity — is forgotten. That is the nature of things. Except, even for Peter, who invented the preposterous and made it plausible for a while, it is now impossible to look at this Whitlam of theirs and not see a man looking over his shoulder. Apprehensively. And if Peter is thinking this, is it possible that others are too? Does a mountain look over its shoulder to see if the landscape has changed? To reassure itself that in a land of few mountains, the mountain of Whitlam still prevails? Or does that short time in which invention was truth linger as some sort of pursuing shadow?

Nobody knows the author of it all. There is a certain wonder in that. In the sheer anonymity of it all. Like being the hero of one of those revolutionary tales who leaves his calling card at the site of daring deeds, but whose identity is never known. Everywhere in evidence, but nowhere visible. And there is, it seems to Peter, a certain wonder in not being known that makes fame look crass. Of being, for as long as the affair and its consequences lasted, the possessor of a secret that goes to the very heart of earthly matters and activities; knowing that the vast, timeless department of human affairs we call the nature of things has anonymous agents on the ground.

But all things end. He has not only discovered a taste for the game, he has also discovered he has a talent for it. And it is a talent that will take him places, but only if those who matter know. And so a time will come when he will have to discard his anonymity and reveal his talent to the select few, but not yet.

It is cold. The capital is cold. And as he looks up from his newspaper during his lunch break at a nearby café, he sees her. Beth. And as happened on the steps of Parliament House the previous week, for a moment he doesn't recognise her. Like one of those nameless refugees you see on documentaries, fleeing one war or another, she seems to have given up her identity. Become one of the crowd, but a one-woman crowd. She has that homeless look, hunched in her overcoat as if having slept in it. Her hair, usually brushed and shaped, has settled where the wind left it. She is eyeing the cakes in the café window and he is unsure as to what sort of manner he should adopt should she enter. But she lingers at the window, eyes blank, and he wonders if she's seeing anything at all. Her face is inclined, eyes on the contents of the café's window, but she is elsewhere. She does not see him, and he has every impression that even if he were to wave she wouldn't notice.

And then she moves on. Just anybody. And he has, for a reason he can't name, the distinct impression that she's not going anywhere in particular. That she is just going. An action without an object. That her path, were it to be mapped, would have no logic. She moves on, hands plunged into her coat pockets. And it occurs to him now that she had no bag: the bag, a satchel, always strung over her shoulder, which always contained her work, was not there. And he imagines that bag dumped on a chair or table back at her flat. Not so much forgotten as abandoned. And does this explain the look of the refugee? That without her bag, the work it always contained, the very thing that has always defined her, without that, she is adrift.

She will, he tells himself, snap out of it. She is one of those who define themselves by doing. It is her nature. Always has been. And when the ridicule fades she will return to what she does and immerse herself in doing it. Her nature, he assures himself, will eventually assert itself and life will go on. All things pass. That, too, is in the nature of things.

All the same, as he rises from his table, picking up his paper and a folder of work that he meant to look at but was distracted from, he concedes that the glimpse of Beth at the window brought with it the vaguely troubling suggestion that it doesn't take much for a life to unravel.

* * *

As first he doesn't notice it as he scans the newspaper. The front page is dominated by stories about politicians and power, and all the incidental stories that follow are presented as news but aren't news at all; they fill the newspaper but everybody could quite easily get by without knowing about them. There is, he muses, when you think of it, very little news. Not really. But gradually, a small piece, a paragraph actually, draws his attention, there in the bottom right-hand corner of the third page. Doyenne Journalist Dies. Even then, he is merely curious, until he realises that the Elizabeth of this short paragraph, this doyenne journalist who has just died, is Beth. And his first response is disbelief. They've got it wrong. He saw her only last week. Bedraggled, yes. The air of a refugee or a displaced person, yes. But not dead. He reads the whole paragraph in one sweep of the eyes. Died. In the night. Forty-four. No explanation. Great loss to the newspaper world. Funeral to be announced. That's all. No details. Just a clutch of basic facts amounting to a death. His wife watches as he rises from the table. The kitchen, his surroundings, fade into insubstantiality.

'Where are you going?'

'I have to make a call.'

And he leaves, forgetting that he is still holding the newspaper, clinging to the thought, which he knows is absurd, that it's all a mistake and a phone call will clear it up. He is walking in a dream. The hallway, suddenly, like a hallway from dreams. Long, and with something sinister at the end of it. Yes, he will call someone. But who? Not Trix. Not the newspaper itself. He is now standing in his study asking himself, who? And after mentally composing a list he settles on a journalist who knows her. And he phrases it like that because he is still thinking of her in the present tense. Every part of him rebels at placing her in the past. No, not possible. He is walking in a dream and the call will snap him from it. So, hastily flicking through his book of numbers, he comes to the number he is searching for and lifts the receiver.

When he puts the receiver down ten minutes later he has the details. Enough details to give a sketch of events. And to confirm the fact that, yes, she is dead. No mistake. And, of course, he never believed there was one anyway. She died, it seems, on the Thursday night. She'd been to the bar at Parliament House. They all went on Thursday evenings. Not him; last Thursday he skipped drinks. She left, although no one seems to have seen her go, and went home to die. Just how is not certain, and Trix was away. Beth was alone. But she was taking sleeping pills. She'd started taking them recently. She never had before. Possibly unaccustomed to them. For the general feeling, he learnt as he listened, was that Beth had never intended to die. She just wanted some sleep.

After he has put down the phone he sits staring round at the room: paintings, bookshelves, desk and chair. All solid. More solid than life. Pills? Pills and sleep? Sleep and pills … Beth dead? *Dead!* He leaves the newspaper on the desk and wanders out into the hallway.

And when he walks back into the kitchen he has the feeling of both being there and not there. Of being an outsider in his own house. Of floating over things, or through them. A bit of a ghost. And the home — wife, house, window, garden, tree, lawn (needs mowing), yard — pops up around him like a pop-up world. The Van Gogh chairs, the placemats, the whole Monet kitchen — not his, but somebody else's. Beth dead! It was all a game. Wasn't it? An exhilarating one. Can you invent truth? Start a whisper and watch the whispers gather — watch as whispers become events, and events gather to the point where you no longer control them but they control you?

'Did you get through?'

He stares at his wife, eyes blank. 'What?'

'Your call. Did you get through?'

That was it. He left the room. He made a call. He gathered together certain facts that he needed to know. And now he knows them. And there's nothing more to be added.

'Yes, I got through.'

'Good.'

It's a long, drawn-out 'Good', like a morning yawn, accompanied by a smile that says, hi, good to have you back. The world is returning. He's had a shock, and a shock shakes you. Kate goes back to her book of rich reproductions. Immersed in it once more. Good, she's noticed nothing.

Pills and sleep, sleep and pills. Bunny Rabbit played a trick on Pussy Cat; Peter played a trick on Beth. Peter is naughty. Peter must run, for the eyes of Pussy Cat and the eyes of Beth — Beth dead, for God's sake! — are upon him. Peter's adventures have gone wrong and the farmer's rake is poised to come down on him at any moment. Peter must be fast, or the blow will fall. The blow will …

He is floating. A balloon. And his hands grip the back of the chair upon which he is leaning in an effort to anchor his weightless self. He contemplates the walk to the sink for a glass of water, but stays anchored to the chair, deciding that it is best to stay put for the moment. And it is then that his wife slams her substantial bound volume of reproductions shut and proposes a drive. A market somewhere. Knick-knacks. And that floating sensation, the feeling of somehow being a stranger in his own home, is dispelled as the volume snaps shut and the loud slap of the hardback covers reverberates around the room with the healthy sound of reality.

As they leave the house she throws the keys to him and he notes, with satisfaction, that the catch is clean. The keys hit the back of his open palm with a smack as his fingers close instantly around them.

He's had a shock, and a shock shakes you. But the mind and the body are back, the catch was clean. And it is good to get out; streets, trees and clouds go by. Peter is fast. The farmer lowers his rake to the ground and leans on it, watching the disappearing figure of Peter. Streets, trees and clouds go by under a brilliant spring sun. Doyenne Journalist Dies. Pills and sleep, sleep and pills … The car is noisy with music from the radio, chatter and occasional laughter. And the farmer, trailing his rake and returning to his work, recedes into the distance, but looks back over his shoulder as he goes, as if to say: I haven't forgotten.

* * *

It's a small chapel on the outskirts of the city, as these places always are. He wasn't even sure he should come, thought he might be intruding on a private affair, but old times, he eventually decided, did amount to at least this much. The act of being here a sort of duty. To say farewell to one of your number. Those who were there. All the same, he doesn't really know anybody. By sight, yes — journalists and the odd politician — but not really. And is that the husband from the marriage that came and went with all the explosive brevity of the times themselves? Maybe, maybe just nobody. But in the end, it's neither duty nor old times that brought him here — an intruder at a funeral.

No, it's that final image of her. Beth at the café window, almost as if blown there by the wind. That look of displacement, of having nowhere to go. A game. That was what it was. An experiment in invention. And he never

81

imagined for one moment that it might come to this. They play games, we play games. Everybody does, and he won't be the last to play games. It's that kind of city. It was never meant to end here. But here he is, an intruder at a funeral.

Then it all begins. The speeches, the songs that meant something in life and may mean even more in death. He looks around. It is a good turn-out. This is always the concern with a funeral. That not many will turn up. Which is possibly another reason for being here. There is a sort of responsibility in being here. To make sure that the numbers are good. For good numbers tell the world that this was a full life. One full enough to accumulate a good attendance. A meagre attendance, he can't help but think, is a kind of failure. Not by any social measure of importance. But a life ought to amount, upon departing for the last time, to something more than a meagre attendance. And not to provide a good attendance is a sort of common failure. One speech blends into another, one song into another. Then the coffin slides into the furnace and soon they are all standing.

And it is only then, as the funeral party turns into the aisle, that he catches sight of Trix for the first time. She looks pale, eyes either fixed on some distant point at the far end of the chapel or just blank. Pale, but strong, he notes. Supporting an older woman who may or may not be Beth's mother. He doesn't know. He never knew her. Old times didn't extend that far. He is standing at his aisle seat at the back of the chapel, and as she draws near Trix looks up and notices him. Her eyes immediately lose the blank look and become focused and fierce. The eyes of a strong, solitary fox, sighting her enemy in her own domain, eyes relentlessly fixed on her quarry as if the stare alone were enough to drive him away. And as she passes, she removes an envelope from her coat pocket and slaps it into his palm. Then she is gone and he is left holding the envelope — small, like those envelopes containing cards we attach to presents or which carry brief expressions of thanks or good wishes.

The funeral party, compacted into somebody's appropriately sombre sedan, departs. Small groups — tears one minute, laughter the next — gather then slowly break up and drift off. Peter and a couple of strangers are eventually left standing at the front of the chapel. And it is only then, vaguely mindful of the broken talk around him, that he opens the envelope that has been resting in his palm, and reads the note inside: 'Rape is a political act'.

Amid all the tears, the cares, the consuming duty of arranging someone's send-off so that it amounts to more than a meagre attendance and doesn't take on the look of failure, among all that she found time to write this. And all on the assumption, the chance, that he might be there.

And it is now that he clearly sees the accusation in her eyes as she passed him and thrust the envelope into his hand. You, you did this. No court will ever try you. No judge will ever pass sentence — but you know, and I know. And as he leaves the chapel behind, the note still in his hand, Trix's eyes follow him. You know, and I know. And I will never, never let you forget it.

And how did she know? Beth told her, who else? They shared such things, of course they did. And so Beth told

83

Trix. Probably that very night he visited. I've got this story, she would have said. Peter just told me. And it's preposterous, of course. The way the truth always is. But it's mine. Peter just told me. I've got this story …

Sleep and pills, pills and sleep. The eyes of Beth, the eyes of Pussy Cat, turn to him. You knew our weakness and you used our weakness. No court will ever try you, no judge will ever pass sentence. But judgement is always there in Pussy Cat's eyes, in those fleeting moments when a sight, sound or a scent stirs the past and the memory of Pussy Cat pounces; it was there in the haunted look in Beth's eyes as she stood on the steps of parliament and said: you used me. Just as surely as it was in Trix's eyes as she passed him in the chapel and thrust the envelope into his hand.

The envelope is deep in his pocket as he steers back to the city, and as much as he wants to forget about it, throughout the whole drive he's preoccupied with thoughts of what on earth to do with it. For the moment, he leaves it stuffed deep in his coat pocket, like one of those pieces of wedding cake you forget all about until months after the event. All the same, it's there. And he knows it is.

3. Mandy Is Not in Love

There's unrest in the skies. No, upheaval. Mandy lifts a white blossom from her hair and stares at it as if studying some exotic creature blown in on the wind. What faraway place has it blown in from to land in her hair? And after studying the blossom a moment longer she releases it, like a bird freed from a net, and watches as a sudden blast of air lifts it back into the unrest of the sky.

She is standing on the footpath outside the university, and all around her the trees that line the street are rioting. Leaves, scraps of paper and small birds are thrown upwards into the swirling currents that make no distinction between any of them. It's beyond a riot; it's a revolution. Everything, all manner of objects, animate and inanimate, thrown this way and that, at the whim of the wind. And which one was hers, she wonders, as the blossoms, blown in from who knows where, are swept out over the university grounds. The wind doesn't care. The sky is indifferent. Do you think I stop to count the blossoms, the wind calls. It's a revolution, you silly girl.

Mandy, who normally hates this time of year, is enraptured with the sheer sweep of the spectacle and is thinking of revolution because she has just come from her history class. She is studying revolutions and the sky this afternoon is a perfect picture of one. Everything thrown into the air by a force indifferent to the upheaval it creates. Until this year she taught at the same school as Michael. That is how they met. They are, as the phrase goes, 'seeing' each other. She has come back to university to study for her Master of Arts. Not for her teaching, but simply because she wants to. She walked out of her tutorial room, leaving behind the ferment of Russia (to be picked up next week), only to be greeted by the sky in ferment. She is now making her way back to her car.

A big English sheep-dog sits up in the front seat and barks his greeting as she approaches. The dog is infinitely patient and has done this many times. He requires only that the window be let down sufficiently to allow the air in and a soft seat to sit upon and wait. The dog knows the routine and knows that he will now receive a biscuit as a reward for his patience.

He is munching on the biscuit, almost savouring it, as Mandy pulls out from the kerb and steers the car in the direction of Michael's flat. She feels liberated, the week's study is over and now her time is her own. She and Michael have been 'seeing' each other for a year now, and as often as not she drives by his flat after her tutorials. It is something to look forward to — and she is. Perhaps, she notes, looking forward to it a little more than the definition of 'seeing' each other allows. Perhaps. All the same, she is happy. For the last year has given her a kind of happiness she has not known for a long time, having somehow gone from one unsatisfactory affair to another, usually looking back and asking herself what on earth did she ever see in so-and-so or so-and-so. But she's been happy this last year. She does not call this happiness 'love'; nobody does. At least, not the likes of Mandy and Michael. It is happiness. It is light. And she is content with that for now.

And so it is with a light heart that she turns the wheel and steers the car past the parks in riot to Michael's. Yes, she is happy. But he is going away soon and will, quite possibly, take that happiness with him. So although her heart is light, there is a weight pressing against it. But he isn't going just yet, and so she will live in the moment for these last couple of months before he leaves. Let it be enough, for Mandy has decided to take her happiness where and when she finds it. She wonders what lies beyond 'seeing' each other. Perhaps, she muses, 'knowing' each other. But that's a kind of Mandy and a kind of Michael that may exist in the future, if he comes back. Let it be. Let this happiness that comes from 'seeing' each other be enough for the moment, and the weeks before his going will be happy weeks. Besides, when he leaves, who's to say he won't come back? To her. And as she contemplates this, she knows full well that there is a part of Mandy that *would* wait. And will. He needs to go, she can see that. She almost wants him to go, so that when he comes back everything will be different. That is her hope. And, at the same time, he is a puzzle to her. You fear a lasting friendship, she says to herself, turning into Michael's street, as if addressing him. You fear a lasting friendship … How strange, how very strange, when it is what I long for. Why do you fear such things? Why is that? Why does Michael have a lock on his heart?

As she pulls up at the front of his flat she can see him, sitting on the couch, staring out the window. At first he doesn't see her — his eyes are fixed on the park — then his head turns. She can't, from this distance, see the expression on his face and if there is a light in his eyes or not. But she likes to think that he's happy that she's here. That this is what they bring to each other — and if that happy look were not there on his face it would be because she no longer brings it to him, that she has lost the knack of bringing it with her. And so she likes to think there's a light in his eyes and that she still brings happiness to him. For, as long as she does, they will stay together and 'seeing' each other may well, one day, become 'knowing' each other. It is a kind of waiting game, a kind of hope, one that she rarely acknowledges, but one that she carries with her as she steps out into a gust of wind and closes the car door, after speaking briefly to the dog, and walks towards Michael.

* * *

It is sudden. Even brutal. Michael has been speaking for two, maybe three, minutes. She's not sure. She's not sure of anything at the moment. His lips are moving but she's not registering much of what he says. Only the key words. She barely had time to sit down. He barely said hello. And then he started. And from the moment he started everything went dream-like. But it's a bad dream.

There have been times, after a strong joint, when she could have sworn somebody said something to her, but they hadn't. Could have sworn that she'd had whole conversations with someone or other who was in the room, but, all along, the conversation had taken place in her head. Reality shifts at such times, and it's shifting now. Michael is speaking but she is taking in only the key words. *Key Words*. It was a text they all had to have for Literature. A sort of dictionary that contained all the key terms they had to know — such as 'plot' and 'symbol', and phrases such as 'felt experience', and so on. All the key words you needed to get you through an exam. But the phrases 'seeing each other' and 'not seeing each other' weren't in it. It was a book that got you through a subject you were studying, but not a moment like this. She's only vaguely aware of the room, of his guitar on its stand, of what is said. The sky is rioting. There's upheaval, revolution in the atmosphere. Leaves, twigs and scraps are wrenched from their resting places and thrown into the ferment. Mandy lifts a white blossom from her hair. Mandy lifts a blossom … the sky is rioting and she looks up, eyes exultant, and watches the blossom fly from her, once again, into the ferment of the sky.

'It's over. We had fun. But it's not the fun it was. We've had the best of it. It's been good seeing each other, but we're better off not seeing each other any more.'

There is a long pause. Has he finished? His lips have stopped moving. She heard only the key words, 'seeing each other' and 'not seeing each other'. Which may have been followed by 'any more'. But she's not sure because it's all a bad dream. And she's not sure if he's finished or if it's her turn to speak, as if the two of them are enacting some little play that they've just made up. He speaks, she speaks. They both speak together. They fall silent. He speaks, she speaks. But it doesn't happen this way. As much as the roles and the conventions of a little play demand that she speak now because it's her turn, she can find nothing to say.

His lips have stopped moving. In the silence he hands her a bracelet. It's hers. He found it under the bed. Under the bed … He's staring at her and she can't take her eyes off his, because these are not his eyes. At least, not the eyes she's known this last year, not the Michael she's known until now. Not the Michael she might have been foolish enough to sometimes think of as 'her' Michael. Not the Michael she might have waited for. Been silly enough to wait for, and been happy to. No, this is a Michael she's never met before. They are hard, cold eyes. No trace of sadness. No touch of regret in his eyes or tone of voice. Just this cold stare and a sort of impatience, an angry one, that says, well, get on with it — say what you have to say, then go. No, not 'her' Michael at all, but a Michael she's never met. And, what is more, one she knows she'll never be able to reach, no matter what she says. He's beyond reach. He has gone from her, and there is only this imposter sitting in his place.

It's confusing. A bad dream. Where *is* 'her' Michael? Happy Michael. Eyes lit with the happiness that she put there. Where is he? And who, who are *you*? She looks at the door of the flat and remembers walking in that door when they first started seeing each other. Kissing in the doorway. Sinking to the floor and fucking right there. And was the door of the flat still open or closed? Who knows? Were they seen and heard? Who cares? They were a world unto themselves. There, and she's still staring at the spot, not so long ago when they first started seeing each other — *there* they had sunk to the floor and fucked where they fell. And God, it was good to fuck like that. No ritual dinner and wine and all the bullshit that comes with it. Just catching the moment in all its magnificent

surprise. No, not 'surprise'. The moment in all its 'thereness'.
'Thereness', that's it. You won't find that in any book of key
terms either. You won't because she's just made it up. The
moment was 'there' and they took it. Sank to the floor in the
doorway and fucked where they fell.

And as Mandy stares at the doorway, she's wondering
if she will ever fuck like that again. And didn't they just roll
onto their backs afterwards, still clothed (except for her
knickers, out there in the room somewhere), didn't they just
roll onto their backs and say, 'Now, let's eat!' And didn't she
say these are the best fucks ever. And did she feel, even then,
the faintest shadow of sadness fall across her as she spoke
because she knew she was right? They were 'seeing' each
other, and written into the whole idea of 'seeing' each other
was the possibility that one day they would not be seeing
each other, and that whole world of unapologetic abandon, of
sinking to the floor in each other's doorways and hallways and
having the best fucks ever, would one day become a memory.

She looks back from the door. Now that day has
come, and the hint of a shadow that may have touched her
then falls across her now and her world turns cold. As cold as
the eyes of this Michael she's never met before.

And so without speaking, not sure how long she's
even been in the flat (two, three, four, five … ten minutes?,
she has no idea how long is a bad dream?), she rises,
feeling nothing, only numb, from the chair that she can't
even remember sitting in, holding the bracelet she barely
remembers accepting, walks to the door and closes it behind

her. And she can't even remember if she said goodbye. Who was there to say goodbye to anyway? Not 'her' Michael, just this imposter.

The dog turns its eyes to her as she approaches, its eyes alight with hope and trust because it knows there's a biscuit coming. A reward for its patience. And it's only as she's driving away and the dog is munching on the biscuit with the air of a gourmet savouring a long-sought-after delicacy, that the numbness begins to melt. And as much as she might ask herself did that really happen?, she knows it did. And though it all felt like a bad dream at the time, she knows that it was one of those bad dreams that are true. And as the numbness begins to fade and feeling returns, she begins to feel the pain. Right there, in the heart, where all the love poems and love songs tell you it is felt. And she knows, too, that it is not a passing pain. This is a pain that tells her that something of significance has happened, that one of those events by which we signpost our lives has occurred. That, years from now, those five or ten minutes in which she sat speechless in Michael's flat will remain clear to her, undiminished by the years — clear, but unreal, like one of those bad dreams that happen. And as the numbness melts and the pain begins, she turns the wheel towards home.

The sky is rioting. Leaves and scraps are flung into the ferment. Mandy takes a blossom from her hair and releases it, eyes on the sky, exultant with the anticipation of seeing Michael — the evening in front of them. Such a long time ago. Another Mandy. Another Michael. Such a long time … And suddenly, as pain and memory mingle and gather in force, she turns the wheel away from home and points it towards the sea.

* * *

Mandy parks the car in the street leading down to the beach. A taxi passes, women talk idly in the doorway of the shop behind her, a gull sits on the railing of the tram stop as if waiting for its regular tram. Everything is strangely still. At some point during the drive across town the wind dropped, the riot in the sky exhausted itself, and all those leaves and scraps and blossoms fell back to earth miles from where they were lifted. Upon a different earth. Which is how it feels to Mandy. An unreal stillness. A strange calm. Another earth. Not the same one she drove through on the way to Michael's. An hour ago she was *in* the world; now she's detached, walking through another one altogether. Everything strangely calm, like the lull in a violent argument that hasn't finished yet. Strangely still, the streets, buildings, ships, looking like one of those cities that have been lost in time and which, by some fluke of nature, she has stumbled across. The numbness goes, the unreality stays. Life is a dream. A bad one. She must wake.

She opens the passenger-side door and the dog tumbles out. The dog loves the sea. He can smell it. His nose is in the air. He is impatient. But he waits, like the good and true dog that he is. And upon her instruction they cross the street and suddenly the bay is spread out in front of them.

93

A tanker is coming in, a tanker is going out. There are occasional fishing boats. But the beach, in late afternoon amber light, is deserted apart from a woman sitting on a bench and looking out to sea with a quiet longing that Mandy can feel even from where she is standing. But apart from this woman, the beach is hers.

She takes the steps down to the sand. The dog runs on. She stops near the water. The dog pauses, looking back, gentle waves breaking over its paws. Life is a dream. A bad one. She must wake. Mandy looks about. Nobody. Except the woman on the bench, who doesn't seem to have eyes for anything but the horizon.

First she removes her sandals. Then her jumper. She drops it on the sand with her shirt and her jeans, and she stands in nothing other than her bra and her knickers. And all the time the dog is looking at her with a puzzled expression on its face, as if to say, what are you doing? And she could smile, if there was a smile in her. But there isn't.

Then she walks forward. The water about her feet is cold. And as she wades further in, the first rolling wave crashes into her and almost takes her breath away. She must wake. For a moment she looks back at the beach, at the small pile of clothes she has left behind on the sand, like a pile of clothes left by someone who is not coming back. Another wave crashes against her, and she welcomes it. The dog is paddling beside her, concern on its face. And then she dives.

Her legs, strong and athletic, lift her from the sand and she dives like a fish, flying through the air. A perfect arc.

There is a splash, then bubbles, and icy water all around. Black water. A cold spring sea. And this time that icy black water does take her breath away. As well as the pain. And the bad dream. And in one magnificent moment she is alive again. A living thing. And she opens her eyes to blackness and bubbles and stays there submurged. And the cold is so enormous, so complete, so utterly exhilarating that she could just stay there in darkness and bubbles. And she doesn't know how long she stays there beneath the water. A wave passes over her, the icy water stings and she welcomes it. She is in her element. She is water. She is sea. She is a sea creature come in from the land. Come home. And she drifts in the blackness and bubbles, happy to stay in her home of the sea, until the sudden urge for air drives her upwards and she breaks the surface, taking in huge gulps of air, then stands and looks back at the beach, still gasping for breath.

She is disappointed. She is land, after all. Not some fabulous creature returning to its element of the sea, but condemned to live on land. In this other earth, this other world that doesn't feel like hers any more because Michael took it away. For a moment, love turns to hate. And at the same time she notes with a cool detachment that — there! — she's said it. Love. And all the time they'd been 'seeing' each other she'd harboured the hope that 'seeing' each other would eventually become 'knowing' each other. But, even then, she couldn't call it love. But it's all gone, whatever it was. Whatever they'd been or might have been. Washed away.

And it's then, shivering in the water, in nothing but her bra and her knickers, that her whole body is convulsed, shaken by the first of her sobs. One after another, with barely any pause in between. Deep breaths and deep sobs. Oh, it's nothing, she tells the open sky, between breaths. Don't make a fuss. Big girls don't cry, big girls don't … it's nothing. Her boyfriend told her to fuck off. That's all. It's nothing. Take any street, at any hour, and somebody's bound to be telling someone to fuck off. It's nothing. Just love. Just the end of love. And there, she's named it again. Love, love, love, love, love … say it often enough and it's just a word. She wipes the snot from her nose and stares at the dog, paddling about her, circling her, the same concerned look it had on its face as she dived into the icy water and discovered, for a few incalculable moments, the possibility of another element, still there. Then she looks up to the sky. Here I am, for God's sake, waist deep in the sea, in my bra and knickers. Only love, only love can do this. You bastard. You bastard, Michael, you bastard.

And so, shivering, her face plastered in salt and tears and snot, she wades reluctantly back to the sand. A failed fish. Back to the beach and the land, and this whole world that's not hers any more.

And that bundle of clothes at her feet that had the look of having been left by someone who wasn't coming back was, in reality, always going to be reclaimed. And it's with a relief that feels like betrayal that she feels the warmth return to her as she puts the clothing on that she shed no more than a few minutes before. The shivering eases, the sobbing has stopped for the moment. And she turns back and looks at the blue, black water, and that feeling that she could have just stayed there returns.

She picks up her sandals and trudges back across the sand to the steps and the street and the car that are all waiting for her. A life, waiting to be resumed. And as she walks she notes the woman still sitting on the bench, eyes only for the horizon, and she is impressed by her powers of concentration — if concentration is the word. For it's more a longing that won't be denied. Did this woman notice her? Did she see her — Mandy and her dog diving into the icy waters of the bay on this late spring afternoon? Was her splash heard? And, if so, is she deliberately concentrating on the horizon so as not to stare? No, if she noticed anything at all, it was litle more to her than one of those incidental events that come and go, vaguely registered and forgotten almost as soon as they are noted. Mandy, for all the world, a splash that no one heard.

She opens the passenger-side door and the dog jumps in. At the wheel, she points the car for home. The sea recedes in the rear-vision mirror — the sea, and the possibility of living in another element. But as much as she might imagine there's been some bureaucratic slip-up in the administration of the natural world, and that she's been assigned to the wrong element, there's no mistake. This one is hers — streets, yards and houses full of rooms that have lost their hope. A world that doesn't feel like hers any more.

* * *

The song ends, the song begins. Ends, begins. Begins, ends … beginnings become endings; endings, beginnings. Mandy is lying across her bed. She can feel the salt still on her skin and taste it on her hands and forearms when she wipes the tears from her eyes. It is a large rented room in a large rented house in the suburbs. Michael lives in the inner city. Mandy prefers the suburbs where the houses are larger and the dog has a yard. There is a cold mug of tea sitting on some drawers beside the bed and a small square of hash lying in its silver foil beside the tea, like the last square of a chocolate block. The distinctive scent of the hash hangs in the air and there is the stub of a joint in an ashtray. She has no clear idea of how long she has been lying there or how long the song has been playing or how long she has been crying. The well seems to be inexhaustible, the tears endless. Like the song.

It is a popular song. In it, a young man (at least, Mandy imagines him to be a young man, even a familiar one, a young man with the face of Michael singing to her) is telling either himself or anybody who will listen that he is not in love. And he is neither sad, this young man, nor expresses any sense of regret. In fact, he seems to feel nothing at all. Like a character in one of those French novels who casually kills someone with neither regret nor remorse — who seem to feel nothing at all. She is not, the young man sings, to tell her friends that they are, presumably, 'seeing' each other, and she is not to make a fuss when they do. And the picture he keeps of her is to hide a mark on the wall. They are casual. They are seeing each other.

It is not a sad song. It is worse than sad. It is like being stuck in a bad dream. At least, that's how she hears it. And somehow she doesn't have the energy to rise from her bed and end it. The fact is she is drawn to it. Wants to wallow in it — in the bad dream of the song. It's her fate. A sickness that she doesn't want to be cured of. And, staring at the ceiling, recalling Michael's face that was a face she'd never seen before (or hadn't she been watching properly and was it always there?) and recalling the Michael and the Mandy that they once were — falling to the floor and fucking where they fell — she hears (wondering if she will ever fuck like that again) the song fade, merge into silence, then re-emerge from silence to start all over again. How long has it been playing? This bad dream of a song. This song that is neither sad nor regretful, but which seems to feel nothing — like the Michael who spoke to her today. But it also occurs to her, as she eyes the small block of hash, wondering if she has the energy to roll another joint, knowing that it would bring with it blissful oblivion, that for all the singer's insistence on not being in love, he may very well be. For Mandy suddenly imagines (or likes to imagine) that he insists too much. And this very insistence on not being in love brings with it a glimmer of hope. And it is a hope that she suddenly clings to. And instead of reaching for the small block of hash, she reaches for the telephone. She has stopped crying. She is calm. She is strangely hopeful. Even happy. It's hard to tell. She can do this. And, without allowing herself time for second thoughts, she dials Michael's number.

But from the moment he answers, heavy, involuntary sobs rise up in her and fall into the mouthpiece of the telephone through which she might have spoken to him. Instead of words there are only heavy sobs, like those heavy drops of rain that signal a downpour. And within seconds she is beyond talking, and simply sits there and sobs into the phone, as the song (which she'd forgotten to switch off in her eagerness to act before succumbing to second thoughts) starts up again, a continuous loop of beginnings and endings. The tape going round and round, and Mandy's sobs as endless as the song. For what she had not anticipated was not so much the sound of Michael's voice, but the perfect picture that came instantly with the sound of his voice: the arm of the couch upon which the telephone sits, the couch by the front window of the flat in which Michael will be sitting, the table, the sideboard, the books (which she can visualise and name), the rug ending at the doorway, and the floor onto which they once sank — the whole familiar scene, in all its simplicity, comes to her in a rush that takes the words from her lips and leaves her sobbing once again. And suddenly she hasn't even got the energy to hang the phone up. And so she sits on the edge of her bed and sobs into the silence at the other end. And she knows that he is listening under sufferance and that he will listen until she either stops or hangs up. And while she has no desire to detain him any longer, she has lost the will to move.

She doesn't really know how long she sits there while the song ends and begins. But at some point the sobs stop and that curious sense of hope with which she picked up the phone returns to her, and she knows that, at last, she can speak. She can do it. And the thought that she once brought a kind of happiness to him returns to her with this confidence and she determines to ask him if there is any happiness left in him at all, and, if there is, might it still be 'her' happiness, the happiness that she knows she once brought to him. And, if so, does the Mandy and Michael that they once were still exist, still live on somewhere in the blur of the day? That is when she asks him: 'Are you happy?'

Straight away, registering the silence on the other end and the absurdity the words assumed on being spoken, she wishes she'd never said it. And as the silence on the other end lengthens, and as the song swells and that voice goes on and on, intoning to the world that it is not in love, the sobs return and the deluge begins all over again.

She can't remember hanging up the phone. But it is back in place and her hand is resting on it. Then her fingers slide from the phone towards the hash. A minute later she lies back on the bed, lights the joint and slowly, luxuriously, inhales oblivion.

At some point in the morning, at three or four, she wakes to a darkened room, the song still on its endless journey through this endless night, and finally has the will to switch it off. She returns to her bed, to darkness and silence, and waits for sleep. The darkness will turn to light, the night will end, and somehow she will get through the day.

The silence is good. She can, for the first time, see the day that has just passed with a touch of distance. Like looking back on a bad dream. For it was a day that passed in a blur, but it is impossible to see the blur for what it is while you're in it. But in the silence and the darkness, and with her head now clear of the hash, she can see the day for what it was. Time, she muses, will do its work. It always has. Distance will come. It always does.

But, for the moment, she must sleep and gather herself for the day to come. A working day just like any other — and not like any other. She studies revolutions at university: one term, France; the next, Russia. She studies them, and now she feels like she has been cast into a revolution. She *is* the clambering crowd, she *is* the order of things collapsing. Her whole body, from the suburbs of her fingers and toes to the nerve centre of the heart, is in revolt. And Mandy is swept up in the tumult. But, for now, she must sleep and gather herself for the changed life she will wake to.

Are you happy, Michael? Am I? Are we? Will we ever be? The lot of us. Can a whole generation have it so good, that in wanting it all and believing we *can* have it, we lose it all? At least, the things that matter? And will we go grumpy into that good night because we never found the thing we wanted when it was there all the time? She smiles in the darkness at the thought of going grumpy into that good night, the first light thought she's had all the long day, then slides into a deep sleep.

* * *

The market is crowded and colourful and humming with Friday-night life. Couples and families wander slowly along the stalls and she especially notices — has she ever really noticed it before? — the excitement of the children, holding their parents' hands or darting here and there among the shoppers. The children liberated from school, the parents liberated from work. Everybody radiating that air of liberation, which, on Friday evenings past, Mandy would have too. But not tonight.

The market is haunted. The ghosts of Michael (currently at his mother's for an early dinner) and Mandy, as they were when they were at their happiest, haunt the stalls. She sees them. Now here, now there. She sees them on one night in particular. One night when she'd bent forward to smell the melons at a fruit stall. She'd picked up a full, round melon and had bent forward to smell it and was just inhaling the rich, heady scent of the fruit when she felt his lips on her neck. And the two combined, the scent of melon and the sudden surprise, even the shock of the kiss, ran from her neck through her whole body, washing up, spent, at her feet.

How long had his lips rested on the back of her neck, how long had the wave taken to travel through her, how long had she held the melon to her nose? The movement of the market was frozen for those few seconds, the hum of the stalls silenced. The clock stopped. A wave of deep, unutterable pleasure passed through her. Perhaps the whole idea of seconds, minutes, hours and days is no good for such moments. No, another form of time had opened up to them. And not even another measure of time, but immeasurable time. They'd stepped out of the usual calculations of such things.

It was, she imagines, standing still and staring at the same market stall with its new-season fruit all carefully arranged, a glimpse of forever. She will go on and even grow old, living through days measured in the usual way, but the kiss will stay forever there, on the back of her neck. And the moment can never fade or be taken from her because it didn't take place in ordinary time and is not subject to time's erosion, but exists, instead, in some pocket of experience where they measure things differently. Or don't measure them at all. And there, preserved in that pocket of experience, she will always be bending forward, her nose touching the melon, inhaling its scent and being, simultaneously, surprised by the kiss.

And, even now, that wave of pleasure passes through her, not with the same unutterable intensity it did then but enough to stop her where she stands, and enough for the movement of the market around her to cease and the hum of the stalls to be silenced.

There they were and there they are. And when the wave had spent itself the world returned; movement resumed, the hum of the stalls rose from the silence and the clock started again. Just as it does now, and she looks about as if wondering where on earth she is and what brought her here. A single shopper. A young woman wandering the stalls, her bag still empty, wondering just what it is she wants, if anything at all.

She fills her bag and barely registers what she fills it with or what she's paid. There they were, there they are. The hidden laughter of children playing under the stalls rises to meet her, and as it does a pang of urgent emotion accompanies the laughter. One that she can't quite put her finger on. But it's there, all the same.

There they were, there they are. And did she know, even then — from the moment she lifted the fruit to her nose — that she could play this game of 'seeing' each other for only so long? That the kiss told her, or should have told her, that she was doing something more than 'seeing' Michael? For 'seeing' each other doesn't include experiencing the exquisite. And 'casual' is never sublime, just as 'casual' never cries. No, something had happened. But she was the only one to realise it that night and, being 'casual', kept that moment to herself and didn't, as the song says, make a fuss.

The market is haunted, and she seems to float along the stalls to the exit, leaving the ghosts of what they were behind her. But the kiss … and the memory of lifting a blossom from her hair, which automatically brings with it all the anticipation of seeing Michael — these are the things that are left to her and which stay, long afterwards, preserved by memory, forever living on in some pocket of experience where they measure things differently, or not at all.

She throws the shopping onto the front seat of the car, hears the engine rumble into life and sits, drumming her fingers on the steering wheel, watching the crowd come and go under the glow of the market lights. And when she's done, when she feels sufficiently back in the world and ready to relinquish the one that the ghosts of the market plunged her back into, she moves quickly out into the street and drives back to a rented room in a rented house to a Friday night alone and the gathering sensation that things can't stay like this.

* * *

The sky is still. The parks are no longer in riot, revolution is no longer in the air and the sudden showers have stopped. Fresh green leaves sparkle in the sun. The summer is coming. She can see it and smell it. Another summer.

Mandy is lying in bed. It is early, just after seven. The sun is bright. The room is bright, and she likes that. The curtain is partly drawn to let the light in, and she likes that too for she doesn't like to sleep in a tomb. The sun will become strong as the day gathers and on the streets people will discard their coats, car windows will be down, and a holiday atmosphere will gradually enter the last few months of the year — this morning containing a first hint of those long summer holidays that once stretched out forever. And she'd love to be uplifted by the thought of it all but she is distracted by the sound of the rubbish truck slowly making its way along the street outside. And as she lies there, covered only by a sheet, she can almost calculate where in the street the rubbish truck is. Which house, and how long it will take to reach the front of her house.

Mandy isn't normally mindful of the rubbish truck, and would normally be drifting in and out of sleep at this hour. But not this morning. It has been two weeks since she last saw

Michael. And the previous evening she came to a conclusion. That if things were to move forward, and if she were not to remain on the same continuous loop, endlessly repeating the same things until she sank into endlessly repeated days in an endlessly repeated life and eventually drowned in repetition, then things would have to change. And change starts in the smallest ways.

The previous night she bundled together all the things that were hers and Michael's. They were everyday things. Things that everybody has. There were theatre tickets with their sad dates stamped on them. Sadder still, she found she could remember all of them. Not just the plays, but the occasions themselves, even what she wore. There were postcards, the odd letter and the bracelet he'd given her. And she shook her head looking at them. So, there was a time when he wrote letters to her, sent her postcards and gave her things. The postcards were hurried, but there was a sort of dashed-off care in them. And she remembered receiving them, all of them (not many, but enough to call 'all of them'), when he went to places without her because he liked to see places alone, and, often as not, he was better off alone. Or so he said. What else was there? Oh, they went to somebody's wedding. Some friend of his. A film, here and there, a picture program that she can't even recall keeping. And the odd photograph.

It's surprising how much happens in a year, because it never seems like much at the time. No, she'd corrected herself, it *always* did. It always felt like something was happening. Something, and she'd paused for a moment, looking round the room, thinking of a nicely detached way of putting it — something uncommon. Something that just might not come again. Now she was left with the common everyday things that everybody ends up with. She'd bundled them all together and put them in a bag — along with a cassette tape that a friend had made for her, of the same song going round and round, endlessly repeating itself, proclaiming to the world that nobody was in love. All of it went into a bag. Not such a big bag, but big enough. Then she'd taken it to the rubbish bin and dropped it in.

And she knows it was all a bit of a play — bundling everything together, putting it in a bag and ceremoniously dropping the bag into the bin. Yes, a sort of performance. But who for? Herself, yes. But it has to have been for more than just her. Just as a diary is written for more than just the benefit of the diarist. There's always this imagined someone, isn't there? And so, even if someone's diary is never read there's always this imagined someone who is reading it as it is being written — and that amounts to a sort of reading. And a sort of reader. And so it is with her little performance of the night before. That little one-act play of hers — performed for this imagined someone. A way of saying, There, I'm done with you, I'm done with her, I'm done with us. Do you see?

Nor is this little performance finished. The rubbish truck is near, and as it approaches she throws the sheet back, leaps out of bed and moves to the window. She watches as the truck appears then comes to a stop at the front of her house — and because she has the front room she has a good view of the street and the whole spectacle. She can put a face to the rubbish collector himself as he leaps, almost in scripted movements, from the back of the truck to assume his role in this little play of hers. Indifference is stamped all over his face. That's good. Just another bin. Just another 'us' unloaded and ready for the tip. The bin is deposited back on the nature strip, and the collector, heedless of his audience, leaps onto the back of the truck as it moves on up the street with the last of Mandy and Michael in a small bag in the back along with all the other throw-aways. And so 'seeing' each other never became 'knowing' each other. 'Casual' never became serious, and she knows now that it was never going to.

Then the truck passes from view and she returns to her bed, the little performance concluded. The play done. A way of saying to an imagined someone — there, I'm done. Do you see?

And as she lies back in her bed she's noting how a goodbye needs that. Needs to be a sort of ritual for it to be properly done with. To be convincing. Sometimes we do things, little acts, not because we want to, but because they complete the goodbye and will look good when we remember them years later. There's *always* someone watching. So goodbyes require a little crafting, to be made just that touch untrue, in order to become true.

The sound of the truck fades. Familiar street sounds return; the squeak of a gate, birds, car doors. The world goes on. Everything starts up, once again, while the last of Mandy and Michael makes its final journey to the tip.

4. The Trams of One's Fancy

As Rita steps off her tram at the intersection, another arrives. She has travelled, from her unit, through the eastern suburbs to the city. This other tram, which arrives as Rita is stepping from hers, is going south. Through the city. It is the Number One tram and it travels all the way to the South Melbourne beach. It is a weekday morning. The city opening for business, a sight she has watched for just over thirty years: office workers, sales assistants, managers of banks, public servants, street cleaners, newspaper sellers, café owners, chiefs of staff ... the whole intricate mechanism of the city's commercial heart coming to life. And Rita, part of that mechanism. Her body, like a milkman's horse, knows exactly what to do: step from the tram, cross the street and follow the footpath up the hill, to the exclusive department store where she has worked for much of her life (four days a week, Wednesdays off). A store at which the wives of prime minsters shop, the wives of army generals and of distinguished newsreaders, and all the quietly wealthy who come to this store from the other side, the south side of the river, by taxi or car, leaving their drivers at the front to wait until the morning's transaction is completed.

And they ask Rita's advice, these wives, on coats and hats and perfumes. They ask her advice and she gives it, and the exchanges that take place are between one who knows, who possesses knowledge particular to the purchase, and those seeking to know. In this way a sort of equality is established between the wife of a prime minister and a shop assistant for the fifteen or twenty minutes it takes to acquire the required article. And this is something Rita has also noticed over the years she has worked at the store — that although money is exchanged, they don't seem to *buy*, these women; they acquire. And the articles of clothing they come for are not desired articles, but required ones. They are wealthy, these wives, but they are not frivolous, and desire stirs only the frivolous. And they all come to this store, the one that Rita's body, with the reflex and faithfulness of a milkman's horse, *should* be taking her towards.

And, as in all the mornings of her working life, this is how it would be, with neither anticipation nor misgiving. But this morning, as she steps from her regular tram, this other tram arrives as she steps off. The beach tram. And it arrives almost with a sense of urgency. Here I am, it says. I am desire. Be frivolous.

* * *

She has little memory of stepping onto the beach tram. But here she is. The tram arrived with a sense of urgency and she boarded it as if having been summoned. As though the tram were more than simply a tram. As though it were something from a strange tale in which things (chairs, balloons, steam engines) take on a sort of life. As though it could speak. And it did. Didn't it?

So, instead of crossing the street and following the footpath up to the store at which she works, she is travelling in the opposite direction on a tram that speaks. Or, at least, speaks to some. Like a messenger with a message, and an urgent one. She passes Flinders Street Station, crosses the bridge and slips into the parkland on the other side of the river, to her left. To her right is the newly completed gallery and the theatres that they call the Arts Centre. She's never been there, but she will, sooner than she thinks, when a painting of Vic's aunt, who lived in a tent on the outskirts of the city many years ago, will come to the city as part of a travelling exhibition and be displayed in this new gallery — the painting not only bringing with it memories of the whole vanished world of Vic, the young Michael and the 'them' that they were but aren't any more, but itself a remnant of that world.

The gallery recedes, the parks go on and on, and the tram veers off the main road and into a tangle of streets that was once a working-class suburb but is now moving up in the world. This is not her old suburb, but she knows it well enough. Rita, by a mix of chance and her mother's cunning, grew up south of the river. South of the Yarra. In that place which, as a consequence, is simply called South Yarra. With its twin suburb Toorak, it constitutes the wealthy side of town. The right side of town. Which explains why Rita, in the department store to which she is not going this morning, can give her advice and speak to the wives of the wealthy with a sort of equality because she grew up under the same sky in the days when the right side of town wasn't all posh. Not in the same streets as the wealthy, but near enough. And brushed with them often enough to know that the rich were different in so far as they were richer. And which explains why Vic always imagined he'd married 'up', and why she never thought about it.

The tram takes her further into this beach suburb and occasionally familiar buildings clatter by: a café that was once a hat shop here, a post-office there. And soon she is on a wide avenue and on the long, straight run that takes her down to the beach. To where the tram that speaks runs out of rail. And she must decide what to do when it does. For there is time to retrieve the morning. To tell herself that she has been frivolous enough and frivolity stops here. To arrive simply late for work as apart from not at all. And, of course, it is the right thing to do. She's had her little adventure, and it's time to go back. But as the tram shudders to a stop, a thought sighs into life. Not so much a thought as a feeling that something has happened. Something quite extraordinary. From which there is no going back. And it is then that the tram speaks for the second time. 'This tram is terminating here.' And, of course, it's not the tram speaking, but the conductor. He is walking through the tram telling those few remaining passengers that the tram is terminating. And that from here it will return to the depot. In short, that it will not be going back, and neither will Rita.

* * *

There is a comfortable bench overlooking the old Victorian pier, the beach and across the bay to the horizon. Rita has no clear idea how long she's been sitting on it. The tram that delivered her here has departed, and others have since come and gone.

At first she was drawn to the old pier, recently repainted in what she imagines to be Victorian colours, contemplating the dead feet that would have strolled and tramped and skipped along its boards on those Saturdays and Sundays off work. All once as solid and alive as she is, now underground or scattered into the air. Once strolling or tramping the pier, possibly in their best or just wearing their work clothes, bringing with them all those little and big thoughts that we carry around with us but rarely allow ourselves time to dwell on.

There's a popular phrase going about — 'dropping out' (although Michael would probably tell her that the phrase has long since ceased to be a popular one and is now old hat). She smiles to herself anyway, because that's what she's done, 'dropped out', like a hippy. Like dropping out of one of those endless circular dances — everybody, hands joined, dancing in a circle, one of those dances that people danced in other times, such as when this pier was built, and before. Going round and round, the circle holding firm, until one of the dancers breaks from it and drops out. And as she imagines an open-air, Sunday party on this very pier, and people dancing in a circle, holding hands, going round and round, she imagines one of them dropping out, and the circle closing straight away. And when this happens, when one of the dancers leaves the security of the circle and the circle closes straight away, does it ever allow the dancer back in again? For this is what she has done: she has stepped back from the circle dance, and she is now watching it.

One life, she's thinking. One life. And she's lived it all in an arc of land no more than twenty miles across. Her world. Her circle, apart from trips to the country and the occasional winter holiday to the sub-tropical north of the country, where Vic eventually moved when Michael left home and they all went their separate ways. Her world, her arc of land. And suddenly, it seems small. For her eyes have now shifted from the pier to the horizon.

She has been watching a ship coming in, a large container ship. She has been watching it slowly approach, slowly come towards her, as if about to greet her. She has watched it grow from a tiny smudge on the horizon into the recognisable shape of a ship. A foreign ship. From somewhere out there, on the other side of the horizon where elsewhere lies. And she's suddenly aware of that world out there, in a way, she concludes, that you can't be when you're in the circle dance. And as she watches this ship, wondering where on earth it might have come from, she becomes aware of another ship going out to meet the horizon.

And throughout the morning, as she sits on the bench, she sees one ship after another, at various intervals, leaving the security of the bay for the world out there or entering the security of the bay from the same world.

At some point she rises from the bench, walks to the kiosk on the pier and comes back with a sandwich and a cardboard mug of tea. Ships come and go. The sandwich is eaten. The tea is drunk. The sun passes across the sky and now sits directly above her. The day unfolds in all its detail: ships; people and dogs on the beach; mothers and prams on the pier; sea birds wheeling across the open, blue sky. But even as she watches, the scene changes, and the wind, an awful spring wind, blowing in all directions at once, is suddenly everywhere and the afternoon turns ratty. Leaves and scraps of paper are tossed into the air, and mothers and their prams turn from the pier for home. And it occurs to her for the first time all day, as she watches them, that nobody knows where she is.

What would have been her lunch hour comes and goes. The wind riots, and eventually exhausts itself. The air turns eerily still. When did that happen? The day begins to fade and the sun, sliding towards the horizon line, washes everything — the pier, the sea, the sand and those ships that come and go across the bay — with a late-afternoon amber light. She imagines the department store she did not go to today getting ready to close. And, as she does, she notices a young woman and her dog approaching the water's edge, arriving at the beach when everybody else has gone. Then the young woman sheds her clothes — her jeans, her top — kicks off her sandals and wades in. The dog follows. The world doesn't hear her splash, but Rita does. It is a distant splash, but near enough to carry. It is a cool spring day and the water looks cold. A reflexive shiver passes through her, but it's one of delight. For it is a splash of utter abandon. Oh, to make a splash like that! The splash of life. And for all the world, Rita is right there with this young woman, the crash of the dive thundering in her ears, the bubbles of the icy seawater all around her too. And she's aware, for the second time today, that something tremendous has happened. And she watches, transfixed, as this young woman wades back to the sand, the water dripping from her, utterly unconcerned by the cold, calling to her dog.

Her eyes shift to the horizon, to the slight smudge of a ship in the distance and the lowering of the sun towards the same distant point — and when she looks back to the beach the young woman has gone, but the echo of her splash carries over the sand and is still in her ears as Rita rises from the bench.

The tram does not speak to her when it arrives. It does not need to. Its work is done. The journey back passes in a blur. She steps off the tram in a city street and walks towards a travel agency she has passed numerous times before and gazed upon with curiosity and longing. The air is thickening, evening is rolling in, the travel agency's lights are on and the shop glows, like one of those night cafés in faraway places. Like one of those cafés found on the other side of the horizon, in that elsewhere from which the ships she has watched all day come, and to which they go.

* * *

The next day, when Rita leaves the department store and steps onto the footpath, it is with an odd sense of loss and gain. It is Friday evening. Just after five. The footpaths are filling, and as she turns and walks towards her tram stop, it is with that now familiar clomp of the milkman's horse at the round's end.

But she will not return on Monday. When, earlier in the day, she spoke to the manager, he was more concerned than annoyed about her absence the previous day (for Rita has rarely been absent in all the years she has been at the store), and she was touched by his concern. And so, when he asked why she was absent, she forgot about the excuses she'd dreamt up and simply told him what had happened: the tram, the beach, the whole day — not mentioning that the tram spoke, or the splash of the young woman entering the icy seawater. But she did add that she hadn't phoned in because she simply hadn't thought about it — or, if she had, had been too distracted by the day to telephone. And all of this said in a matter-of-fact manner, as though she was speaking to someone who would understand completely. No disrespect, no frivolousness. And he did understand, nodding earnestly as she told him the story of her day, like a doctor listening to a patient describe the symptoms of her sickness. And when she finished, when there was nothing more to say, he nodded again and turned in his swivel chair and stared out the window onto the facades of the nineteenth-century buildings opposite, built by gold, he may vaguely have noted, in this highly fashionable part of the city.

There was a long pause, and they both sat, drawn to the same view, in companionable silence. And when he had weighed the matter, when he had drawn his conclusion, he returned from the view and quietly told her she needed a holiday. The store needed her, the store valued her, but the store could get through the Christmas period and the weeks leading up to it without her this time. She had been with the store many years now, and the store did not forget such things. And such service. She would return, they agreed, for the new year in February, when business started up again, when all the families and all the wives of bank managers, businessmen and prime ministers returned from their beach holidays. The store would also give her a little something to go on with. They were a family, after all, and the senior members of the family would be looked after as they ought to be. And he had nodded when he said this, almost conspiratorially, as if to suggest that his days, too, were numbered, and that we should all feel the benefit of our familial ties before we pass into history and before those, less inclined to such sentiments, take over as they surely will. We have, his nod implied, earned this, at least. Hard heads and hard hearts, his tone suggested, are coming — and you and I will soon come from that foreign land of the past where they did things differently. And it will look, his whole manner implied, to those hard heads and hard hearts of the future, like an age of sentimental business.

And so here she is, free. And suddenly she's not sure about freedom. Possibly because she's never really had it before. She has always been a daughter, and a dutiful one;

a housewife and a mother, and a dutiful one; an employee, in this family of the store's staff, and a dutiful one. But she has never been herself. Whoever that is. For in being a dutiful daughter, wife, mother and employee, she'd never had to ask herself that question — who am I? — because who she was came automatically with whatever function she was performing. And this is the first lesson of freedom, that it forces upon her questions that previously had never needed to be asked. And this is why she's not so sure about it. Even fears it. And she wonders, as she crosses at the lights, if this is the case with all of us. That we talk about freedom, and long for the days when we will be free of this and that and so much more besides, but, deep down, fear it as much as we long for it. Because freedom — and nobody tells you this, and you never know yourself until you've got it — comes with a sort of weight. Which makes her smile. For if it comes with its own weight, then is it freedom, after all? Is anything?

As she approaches her stop she's more mindful of the crowd than usual. Feels both part of the crowd and no longer one of their number. And that sense of loss and gain that she experienced at the front of the store when she stepped onto the footpath returns to her. What she was, what she is, what she may be — all mingling. But she's also contemplating all those eyes around her, all those minds ticking over behind them. And that if she, as she makes her way to her regular stop, can be thinking all this, about the freedom she has suddenly been granted and of the unexpected sensation of weight that comes with it, why can't they? But from the moment she thinks it, she knows they're not. That is a view of the crowd that we are only ever granted as we leave it.

* * *

A journey begins with maps. And brochures. At least Rita's does. She's never been one for maps, but tonight she is. They are spread out over the table in the lounge room, the maps and the brochures her travel agent gave her the day before.

Michael has just left after the unusual event of a Friday-night dinner, and she traces with her fingers lines denoting motorways and railways to and from foreign places that, for her, have only ever existed in books and films and television, and with the glowing, glamorous look that you know can't be real. Which may, in fact, be better than reality. Which is why, she imagines, some people only ever travel in their minds. What do they call them? She looks around the room, to the window, the garden light and the street light beyond it out there on the road, where the restless spring wind is blowing once again, and registers, somewhere in the distance, the banging of someone's gate. Armchair travellers. Yes, that's it. Those who travel the world from their lounge rooms, never rising from their chairs. And she can understand it. This reluctance to lose these cities of the mind. For to see them, in fact, is to take their mystery from them. And to take their mystery from them means that they are no longer elsewhere, but could be just anywhere.

But that's like falling in love only in your mind, because the reality will always disappoint. She raises her eyebrows for no one. She's only ever fallen in love once, and perhaps it might have been better to leave it in the mind, like a bit of wishful thinking that never happened. Kept as a sort of plaything to be taken out from time to time and toyed with, then put back in the toy-box of dreams. That way it stays forever true. And young.

But that's not living. At least, not the kind of living that ever steps outside imagined worlds or cities of the mind. No doubt, there are those who find this living enough. Living in a world of loves that stay strong, and cities of the mind that never lose their mystery and remain forever elsewhere. She'll always rather blunder in, always rather have love go wrong: for she will always choose the experience of Vic rather than no experience at all, the experience of love gone wrong rather than never having it at all; rather have cities lose their lustre upon being touched than not touch them at all.

And that sense of freedom she had on the footpath earlier in the day returns to her. That sense of freedom and the unexpected weight that comes with it, and she's wondering if it wasn't always like that at various times in her life. When her marriage ended and Vic went north, was she more than simply 'left'? Was there freedom, too, in the anticipation of what came next? Freedom that you don't ask for. Even something to be feared. But a kind of freedom all the same. Your life is suddenly yours. You are no longer a wife and a mother, and a dutiful one. But what will you be? *You* decide.

And isn't that the weight that comes with the freedom, the responsibility of deciding — when for most of your life there was nothing to decide because the decisions were made for you? And so she has felt a sort of freedom at various times in her life, but not with such urgency as when she stepped out onto the footpath at the front of the store this afternoon, knowing that she might never step back in again. Splash!

A young woman dives into the icy seawater and the sound she makes as she breaks the waves is the splash of living. Rita runs her fingers along lines denoting motorways and railways, joining places she has only ever imagined, but will soon see. Even if it is only a twenty-one-day bus tour. And she spends the next hour tracing lines on maps, opening brochures and gazing at foreign places, at images of the great world, that 'elsewhere' on the other side of the horizon.

And when she finally lies back in her bed in the darkness, she feels, for the moment, light. Almost weightless. The momentary weightlessness of having cast off the protective layers of a routine life, built up over the years, and which now leaves her feeling like some creature without a shell. Noticeably lighter, but vulnerable to cold and wind. And the creature — say, a tortoise — is apprehensive, even puzzled for a time, until it decides that an overcoat will do just as nicely. Rita smiles. But the lightness of the moment passes and the weight returns. The night closes in. The hours of the night will tick by until she wakes to the first light of morning and the new day. And all the others that will follow. Free days. Days both longed for and feared.

5. Art

That village, across the valley, on the opposite hill, has been there for a thousand years. Amerigo Vespucci set off from there in 1491. The next year he met Columbus and later sailed for the New World, eventually giving his name, Amerigo, to the Americas. Every day tourists drive or walk through that hilltop town, which still has the look of a fortress, in search of the house where he was born and where he grew up. Others barely notice the place. History tells you he was born in Florence; the locals tell you otherwise.

Art has just finished watering his garden, set back from the road behind a high stone wall, and is standing on the side of the road looking out over the valley. The country all around is a folded quilt of valleys and hills, the even lines of vineyards stitched into them and stretching as far as he can see. But it's the town — or is it a village? — on the opposite hill that he's looking at. There must have been a time, in its thousand year life, when the very idea of a New World didn't even exist. A thought, like that world itself, waiting to be discovered. When did we start thinking of New Worlds and Old? And how old does the New World have to be before it, too, becomes Old? Or does it stay forever New? Growing old, by definition, an impossibility. And will Amerigo Vespucci always be setting out from that village across the valley, his ships moored in Seville, waiting to set sail?

There is a sudden rustle of activity in the vineyard below, on the other side of the road. Art looks down just in time to see the hind legs of a deer disappearing into the vines, the broad leaves turning yellow in the October sun. Deer, boar and birds of infinite variety inhabit these hills. And the villages and towns dotted throughout them have the unchanged look of places that have been here for a thousand years and more, and shine in the morning sun with the confident assumption that, on any morning, one of their number might easily set off for the New World and be suddenly distracted by deer, boar and birds on the way.

Art has lived for thirty years in these hills and valleys. The old mill that he moved into when he first came here and which he later bought is his home now. Others may have emigrated from the Old World to the New, but Art left the New for the Old and never returned.

That particular part of the New World that Art set sail from all those years before is Melbourne. He was born there and grew up there. But he's never been back, partly because of the sheer effort required just to get there, and partly because by the time he left, he'd already had his fill of the place and that sense of satiety hasn't diminished with the years.

For he spent the war years bottled up in that city. Bursting to break free the whole time, unable to get out. All of them, all his artist friends, all they wanted to do was get out of the place. But they were stuck there, and throughout the war they fought and drank and had love affairs and made, almost without noticing, a particular kind of art full of dark, demonic trams that seem to have leapt free of their rails, amusement parks in hell and grimy city back streets where humans and animals, with little distinction between the two, scoured the gutters — a particular kind of art that is now synonymous with those days. Although they — Art and all those friends and enemies who formed the fixed circles they moved in — never really thought of it like that at the time. Somebody once called them penguins, Angry Penguins, and somewhere along the way the name stuck. They were, somebody of high importance had once announced (in that toffy way that such announcements were made back then), the last expression of a truly regional modernism. Something like that. Although Art never thought of them as a group or anything of the kind. These things only become fixed in people's minds afterwards. At the time all they wanted to do was make art and shoot through the first chance they got.

And so they did. And so he did. All to their separate elsewheres. And here he is. And every morning after watering his garden, he leaves the pots and hanging roses and shrubs behind and strolls out to the roadside to the same view of the village across the valley, on the opposite hill, from which Amerigo Vespucci set off one morning in 1491. And he is yet to tire of it. Or the thoughts it prompts. Of Old Worlds and New. Of green mornings. And of Vespucci setting out to discover what lay beyond the seas, beyond the imagined corners of the world that no one had ever seen but which were rumoured to contain monsters and sudden falls from which no traveller returned, but, at the same time, also being distracted — this Vespucci that Art imagines, in the green morning of his greatness — by the wildlife that inhabits these hills and valleys, along the way.

When he first came here he had the dark hair and eager eyes of a young man. As well as the dark goatee beard that occasionally prompted people to liken him to a young Toulouse-Lautrec. The hair is still there, though grey, as is the beard, but nobody likens him to a young Lautrec any more. He strolls back to the house, the dripping watering can in his hand.

His studio is the mill itself. And the mill wheel is still there. The old stone walls are cool in summer, damp in winter, and smell like a cave. Canvases, large and small, finished and unfinished, some possibly never to be finished, are stacked up all around him. Some go back decades. Others to just last week. And although Art has never gone back to the town that nurtured him (and he will always think of it as a town), he has never stopped painting it — that part of the city they lived in and fought in and created in all those years before. It returns to him in dreams, in sudden moments of remembrance, and he has never stopped painting it. It is his other world now. The one he left behind. And, street by street, building by building, brick by brick, he is building up a giant composite portrait of that city and its life, of a place and a time that once existed but doesn't any more. This is his life's work. He never intended it to be, not when he first came here. No, he came to escape all that, but in the end turned back to it and somewhere along the way it became his life's work.

And when he is finished it will be so comprehensive that those who wish to do so will be able to reconstruct a vanished place and time from his paintings alone, brick by brick, building by building, street by street. A whole vanished city, a lost domain — the café with the Russian name they were always forgetting, the hatter's he lived above, the station with the yawning mouth from which the workers of the city emerged every morning and disappeared into every evening. That and all the lanes and street corners that had their moments — moments of happiness, anger, love or hate — that stuck like glue to his memory and whose clarity has never diminished over the years.

A lifetime's work. Most of which has never been seen. Not yet. And the question of how on earth you would exhibit such a portrait has not, for a long time, seemed of any great importance. In fact, there is something thrilling about the sheer impossibility of such an exhibition. A portrait so vast it may never be seen. Somehow it doesn't matter. Why should it? He works anonymously, has for years. He has no fame. His name means nothing outside these hills and valleys. What does it matter? He has long since cared.

Once he did. When he first started, stuck in that city he left and which he is now meticulously reconstructing — that city they all couldn't wait to escape, but were stuck in because of the war. The war was everywhere and everyone was stuck in one place or another. That was when he cared. When they all did. The whole bunch of them. All stuck at the arse end of the earth together and longing to be on the other side of it. And it wasn't so much fame they all craved. It was that feeling of being one of the chosen. One of the Elect.

And all their exhibitions, in hired halls, galleries, mechanics' institutes and pubs — anywhere they could get — were all a kind of shifting stage upon which the Secret Society of the Elect revealed themselves to one another. And you didn't need to ask if you were one of them, because if you did, you weren't. No, it wasn't fame or money they all cared about — fame that comes and goes, indiscriminate fame that falls upon actors, footballers and murderers alike. It was election. The confirmation that the Secret Society of the Elect had recognised one of its own — in that mysterious way that never explains itself but which governs the decisions of all secret societies — and plucked you from the crowd, lifting you into the realm of the anointed.

Saints (and Art is walking towards the large easel that dominates this cave of a studio as he ponders this), those saints on church walls all over this adopted country of his, must have felt like that; the saints who moved with the crowd, ate with the crowd and knelt with the crowd, but who, all along, in their heart of hearts, knew that they were not one of the crowd. And all the time while they ate, knelt and prayed with the crowd, they were secretly waiting, praying in their duplicitous hearts for that moment when they would be plucked from it — or knew full well in those same hearts that they already had been. So it was easy, he imagines, for the saints to weep, fast and pray with the crowd because they knew, all along, that Heaven was winking. And all their humility (and Art has always distrusted the humble, always seen humility as the first sign of duplicity)was bulldust.

And it is Art, now laying out his paints and brushes to begin the morning's work, who introduced the word 'bulldust' to the hills and valleys of the area. The word had never been spoken here before. Not in the land of Amerigo Vespucci, of wild boar and deer and infinite varieties of birdlife. But it has entered the language of the hills and valleys now. When locals, in the town and small communities around him, hear something questionable, spoken by a politician, mayor or dignitary, that they know full well to be untrue, they, more often than not, pronounce it bulldust. They know exactly what it means and they like the sound of it. They like its bluntness and its lack of that very quality it decries. And Art, for his part, loves to hear this import spoken with such natural ease and conviction, as if it were always part of the language and as if the locals had all grown up with the concept of bulldust as much as they had with Heaven, Hell and honour. And it is now in these surrounding towns, as often as not, the word that marks the end of a topic of conversation, for upon being pronounced bulldust, the subject of the conversation, whatever it may have been, is self-evidently discredited and merits no more time or breath — for one's time and breath are valuable and not to be wasted. And perhaps, Art wonders, drying his brushes, perhaps in a thousand years some variant of the word will puzzle the scholars.

No, it wasn't cheap fame they all craved back then; it was the duplicity of saints. But that was once. And somewhere along the way, from there to here, he lost the craving for all of that, like losing your religion, and one day he just didn't care any more. And so of the canvases finished and unfinished, this portrait of a vanished place and time stacked all around him, only a few have been viewed and none have ever seen the light of day outside this cave of a studio.

He is only going over all this again, the place he once called home and the thing they all once craved, because a letter arrived this morning (the postman, on a scooter, is always remarkably early) from one of those painters with whom he shared that war-time city of his birth. It was addressed to 'Artie'; that was how he knew it was from the old days. Nobody ever called him Arthur. Always Art or Artie. Except here. Here it is Arturo. Which he likes.

Sam, who sent the letter, was one of the few from those old days who did find fame. One of those who announced himself right from the start and who was plucked from the crowd by the gods of the day. And he slipped into the life of fame like one of those who always knew he was born for it. One of those who looked famous before he was. Art reads about him from time to time, for he is a regular reader of the English papers — England being where Sam went to live when fame called — and also gets news from the letters that Sam sometimes sends. Sam, it seems, is coming to the local town for a festival later in the year. It is, after all, that kind of town (Art takes the half-hour walk there most mornings after work) and always has been. And Art likes it that way. A postcard town that hosts exhibitions and is occasionally swept up by arts festivals. The kind of town that appears in travel guides and about which people write books. The kind of town in which the local café owners and shop owners speak English and French and German. For as much as Amerigo Vespucci may have set off from here in search of other lands, other lands have since come to this place.

And so Sam will visit. He will exhibit his paintings, old and new (some of which Art may well remember from the early days, since Sam keeps a private collection), and they may well talk of old times. And when they have finished they will go their separate ways, until the next letter or the next time when their paths cross again.

Art applies the paint, one part of his mind still on the lost religion of the Elect, another quieter, untouched part guiding the hand that applies the paint. Time will collapse now, from this moment when the work of the morning begins and he loses himself in it. Time will be no more, the outside world will not intrude; all will collapse and the morning will pass into infinity, until the tick-tock of everyday time eventually reasserts itself, and he will know that the morning is over. But not know just where he has been or how on earth to measure how long he was there. Only that he was there. And that something that didn't exist when the morning started now does. And he will stand back from the easel, as always, puzzled by its appearance as though wondering where on earth it could have sprung from.

And that, in the end, is how he lost his religion. The discovery that the three or four hours every morning, in which time collapsed and in which the world went away, was all he really craved; the realisation that he could win and lose fame, and win and lose it again, that he could be plucked from the crowd and thrown back into it, and not be diminished. But if he were to ever lose those three or four hours he would lose something as vital as the air that he is oblivious of breathing in and breathing out in those suspended hours that belong to another measure of time altogether and which constitute a kind of heaven.

* * *

The way there is easier than the way back. The way down is the way up. The way up … He plays with it like one of those Buddhist sayings that all too easily find their way into calendars and diaries. The walk from the mill to the town is downhill, over dirt and bitumen, interrupted by the odd car of locals and tourists. The vineyards are all around. Hills and valleys, covered in vines. Row after row. An ordered landscape. This is his regular walk. Most mornings, after work, he follows this dirt road into the town. At one point he stops and looks back to the mill house on the hill behind him. Dark clouds fill the sky, their patterns constantly shifting. But he can't stop long. It will rain. And he will have to shelter in the town until it passes. Which it will do, and quickly. Those black clouds will burst upon the hills and valleys, and soon afterwards the sky will be blue. Here clouds seem to fall out of the sky. Like a sudden burst of temper. Then disappear, almost as suddenly. He turns and continues, picking up his pace to beat the rain as a car passes. They wave, he waves back. They draw away.

There are occasional visitors to the mill. Academics and scholars. For although he has long since ceased to care about fame or the society of the Elect, the fact remains he was once *there*. And the years themselves, and the place itself, have both achieved a kind of fame now. Angry Penguins. Bright young things in dinner suits. The last expression of a truly regional modernism. Something like that. One of those critics, English, one of those who anoints the chosen, said that — for it's not Old Man Time who decides what lasts and what doesn't, it's people. People like that. Toffy types, more often than not. Of course, Art and the others never thought of themselves as a movement or a school, they were too busy getting on with things. At least, that's how Art remembers it now. It's one of those things said by someone who wasn't there. An order imposed upon days that never seemed to have any order at the time.

He passes a large villa, set back from the road behind a sweeping driveway and gardens. At first he imagined some mysterious recluse lived there. Withdrawn from the world behind stone walls and gardens. But the truth is less intriguing. A wine merchant owns the place. For the vines covering these hills and valleys are a sort of gold that re-creates itself every year and never runs out. And the older the vine, the more golden the grape. From here the road dips steeply and he braces his knees to accommodate the slope. The clouds above him are swirling in and out of each other. Heavy Van Gogh clouds. The rain is coming. He must hurry. The sound of the car containing the tourists fades away and the hills and valleys revert to silence. Silence is one of the area's defining features, for, apart from the odd car or the ring of a hammer, the air always seems undisturbed. Perhaps silence isn't the word, but it feels like silence. And never an imposing one. Rather, it is almost hypnotic. And to enter these hills and valleys, to enter the encompassing silence that falls upon them, to become the sole figure in the landscape, is to become just one more constituent part of its life — vines, wildlife and the occasional wanderer.

Then his thoughts return to the place he once called home, and to the scholars and academics who occasionally visit. For the time and place they seem to have created is different from the one Art remembers. They have created a sort of fiction. A dramatic moment, an explosive one, like steam bursting from a pressure-cooker with a shrill, insistent whistle. A gush of art that had to happen because the steam in the cooker had built to that point. And he can tell when he talks to these scholars and young painters (travelling the world in a way that Art and the rest of them had been desperate to do but never could) that there is a longing contained in their questions and they wish they'd been there too. But the fact is — like the villa set back from the road, which invites mystery and fiction — the truth was nothing like that. Not as Art recalls it. No, the truth was grimy and gritty. One day dragging into another. A sort of five-year war-time winter.

At least, these are the memories that have lasted. There were springs and summers and autumns, of course, but he only remembers the winters. The five-year winter. You had nothing else to do but create other worlds. Oh, and yes, they were close. Tight. A big family, really. Laughter one minute, at one another's throats the next. And they helped one another, more than they knew. And there was an intensity to those days that comes rarely. Perhaps even something in the air … perhaps. Be careful, Artie, he tells himself as the road evens out, or you'll start thinking like them.

Footpaths appear on the fringe of the town and the road curves round towards the central square. And as he follows a narrow street past the bus stop and the bus that connects the town to Florence, just a fifty-minute ride away, leaden drops of rain thud onto the rooftops and canvas awnings above the café tables and footpaths, and he reaches the square just in time to see its population scatter for cover.

The rain is thrilling. A lunch-time show. A spectacle. And he stands under cover entranced by the drama of the storm. They sometimes ask him, these scholars and academics who visit from time to time, if Art and the rest of them didn't all do their best work back there in that place they couldn't wait to be shot of. An annoying question. It's said very politely in the manner of speculative, academic inquiry — but you can tell that it's exactly what they *do* think — and that's when Art tells them, on the verge of pronouncing the question bulldust, that they're talking to the wrong person, usually with a grunt and a tug of the goatee beard.

It's the same (to say their best was back there, and so on), he muses, watching the downpour, as imposing drama and design on days that didn't seem to have any at the time. A picture of things that those who weren't there (and wish they were) impose upon a time and place that they've only ever read about. But to these people the question is of such importance that it almost demands to be answered in the affirmative: yes, they did do their best back then and back there. In that way the place and the time achieve a level of significance that they, these academics and commentators, have discovered, more or less, and which justifies all the time they've spent, no doubt, on their studies. The one necessitates the other. The academics study a period in the country's art, pronounce it vital, and the artists of that time achieve fame. There's something in it for everyone.

There's a reply to Sam's letter in his coat pocket, and when the sky is drained his first stop will be the post office, a short stroll away. In the meantime he sits down at a café table and is approached by the owner who wishes him a good afternoon in Italian, then continues in fluent English. He is a sort of friend and one of the reasons why Art's Italian never really improved after his first year here. He settles back in his chair looking out over the square, drenched in rain now, soon to be lit by a bright autumn sun, and smiles. This place is home now — his best measure of home being the place that you don't want to be shot of.

Whatever the city of his birth may have given him, it ceased to be home the moment he left. He left the city and the country in the same way that children eventually leave the family home, and the playgrounds, schools and sports grounds upon which they played and grew up, and never return. One morning they simply rise and leave because the day has come. And so, too, he left the place that made him, with no regrets, and never returned. Not even the odd visit. But gradually he started going back there in his mind and his work, and the re-creation of that time and that place became everything, so that, if required, that square of land that was once his city could be reassembled, street by street, building by building, brick by brick.

But it is also the reason he can never return. For that three or four hours every morning in which he is transported back there would be lost to him if he did. The two things, what was and what is, cannot exist alongside each other. The one would cancel the other out — at least he fears it would. And he would lose his three or four hours every morning: that touch of heaven.

A few years before, when this Whitlam — upon whom everybody pinned so much hope — came to power, he received letters and phone calls, urgent and joyous, telling him that he *must* return. That it was all different now. As if the whole country had just woken from a long, deep sleep and was only just discovering it was alive. Surprised by all the life it had in it, which had never been stirred, but which now was. Yes, it was all different now. He must return. It was even his duty to return. Our mountain has risen up from the flat land. Our moment is upon us. It is the only place to be.

But he didn't return. And all those old friends who wrote with urgency and joy no longer write or call. For as much as he could imagine them all dancing in suburban lounge rooms with the furniture pushed back against the walls, and at Sunday-afternoon parties in city parks, all risen from a long death-in-life sleep and responding like young animals to the life in them which they never knew was there, they nonetheless remained 'them', existing in some mythic form and in some mythic realm, in the country of his memory.

During the ten or fifteen minutes it takes to ponder all this, the rain stops. He rises from the café table, waves to the owner and they part, for fun, in basic Italian. He speaks, he knows, like a tourist — a tourist who arrived thirty years ago and never left.

The hills and valleys, by the time he walks back to the mill, have been transformed by the afternoon light. A gentle light, a glow, a quality of light he had never really seen until he first came here — and a quality of light, moreover, that made sense of all those paintings he had studied and which he had only ever seen in reproduction. It was a quality of light, he'd always assumed, that only ever existed in paintings, the way the glow in a photographer's studio only exists in the studio. Until he came here and saw, for the first time, that the paintings were true.

He is tired, and happily so, when he reaches the mill. And the house, upstairs and down, has the hushed air of a house that has been waiting for its owner to return. One that, over the years, has learnt to accommodate his routines. For Art lives alone. Best for him, best for everyone else. He was once married but he wasn't very good at it. She was blonde and, he thought, beautiful, like a Hollywood actress, and he couldn't believe his luck. They were young and they lived above a hat shop in a lane in that city far away. They painted and ate and made sophisticated love like Picasso and Dora, like Sartre and de Beauvoir. They took photographs, and over their year together compiled an album of those days. But slowly their luck ran out and they grew restless. And their restlessness took them away from each other. Every day, further and further. Until, one day, they went so far away from each other they never came back and the rooms above the hat shop that had been theirs were emptied of all the things that had been them, and somebody else moved in and made those rooms their own. Who first wandered so far away that they never came back? Does it matter now? And it was all for the good. Some people live best alone, and Art is one. He only makes life difficult for others if they come too close. And so his affairs over the years have come and gone and eventually ended with little hurt or damage to anyone. Or so he imagines.

Somewhere among all the canvases, that collective portrait of the place stacked in his studio, is a painting of the hat shop they lived over. Meticulously reconstructed from memory: the hatter's sign painted on the wall; the dark lane; the small, nineteenth-century doorway, made in the days when people were shorter; and the rooms above, one window open — the only sign that somebody lived there or once lived there being a small box camera sitting on the window sill.

The same box camera with which they compiled the album of their days, when their luck was good, until their luck ran out and they became restless and their restlessness took them away from each other.

And so, no good at marriage, he lives alone. And the affairs he's had since then have come and gone like memorable dinners, fun while they lasted. But lately, and it's a feeling that gradually crept up on him, he's beginning to think of himself as being past all that, past the kind of love and desire that make people do silly and desperate things — past all that, like watching a sport you once played but don't any more. All the same, a young woman, a Norwegian, a painter too, staying in the area, came to visit recently. And at some point in their talk, for she had come to see his work and for the conversation, because these hills and valleys can be lonely, he realised he was talking quickly. Even a little theatrically. Almost a sort of performance. And he realised he was trying to impress her. And, at the same time, realised that the young woman was oblivious to this. Soon after, she left. All she saw, no doubt, was not so much an old man as an oldish one. Thinning hair, grey goatee. Someone who might once have looked like a young Toulouse-Lautrec, but didn't any more. We forget, he muses, for our bodies grow old while our minds stay young. Or, at least, we continue to think of ourselves as young. And from time to time a young mind forgets itself and speaks from an old body.

Outside the kitchen window, downstairs in the courtyard, the birds are gathering. The cat watches. The sun

141

lowers in the sky. The shadows lengthen. Leaves, yellow and red and curled, occasionally fall. Afternoons, seasons and years have passed, in ever-repeating cycles, by this window. Watch it often enough, watch it all come and go often enough, and one day you realise that you're not just watching the cycle, you're part of it. It's a clarifying thought to Art, this confirmation that things will end then go on without him. And one that always comes to him at this time when the afternoon lengthens. And far from having a negative effect, it lifts him. Almost comforts him.

The painting of the hat shop is downstairs in the studio with all the others. He hasn't looked at it for a long time. It is one part of this jumble of things stored there. Most of which nobody has ever seen. Which, at the moment, he prefers. And when Sam comes to visit in the winter (an odd time to be visiting), should he show him? If he asks? But, then again, Sam was never one to show a great deal of interest in what anybody else was doing. Conversations with Sam were nearly always about Sam, and what Sam was doing. Which used to annoy Art, but which now suits his purposes. No, there will be little talk of what Art is up to. For Sam, he is sure, all the years in between notwithstanding, will not let him down.

Art strolls downstairs to his garden and waters the pots and shrubs in the afternoon sun. And when he is finished, he strolls out to the road, the watering can dripping the last of the water, and stands by the roadside.

In that village, on the hill on the other side of the valley, Amerigo Vespucci, the locals will tell you, was born

142

and raised. And one morning, one green morning in 1491, Amerigo Vespucci set off from that village in search of the New World, occasionally distracted, no doubt, by the wild boar, deer and infinite variety of birdlife that inhabit these hills and valleys, along the way.

PART TWO

November, 1977

6. The Last New Wave

'You've made surprising friends in high places.'

Michael has not seen Peter since their student days. The hair is shorter, the beard gone. The face a little fuller, but not much. And, no doubt, Peter observes the same of Michael. The years touch us slowly. If Michael passed Peter in the street he would know him. Besides, he has seen him from time to time in the newspapers, for Peter's legal career, his courtroom jibes, were well publicised. He was someone to watch. On the way up. He had that unmistakeable air of expectation. But you don't hear that sort of talk much now. He abandoned his legal career and not so much moved to Canberra as disappeared into Canberra, as, no doubt, countless bright young things had before him. Presumably, Michael muses, he tells himself that things have stalled for a while, and that it's only a matter of time before someone finds the right seat for him and all that expectation can become reality.

He talks briefly about Canberra, just so Michael understands that he *does* know all about high places: how the minister thought such and such and the PM thought otherwise. And how somebody senior in government will soon have to retire unexpectedly, but he can't possibly say who. Michael stares at him, saying nothing. Why has Peter contacted him after all this time? Certainly not to talk about Canberra.

It's the business of surprising friends and high places that he wants to talk about. Recently Michael wrote a story for a newspaper, the paper they all read. Even if it is dismissed as a bit left-wing for conservative readers, they still read it. For it is also considered the intellectuals' paper. Michael's story had appeared the previous week. It had simply been a writing exercise to Michael and he had sent it off not really expecting it to be printed and not really caring if it wasn't. Something to possibly make him a little money for the coming trip. Nothing more. In it he described the prime minister as the Macbeth of Australian politics. Mr Whitlam was a combination of Duncan and Banquo, and that compound ghost, Michael imagined, had haunted the prime minister from the moment he took power, so his time in office had been given over to assuaging that guilt.

But it wasn't just guilt, there was the odd matter of wanting to be respected as well. The massive victory in 1975 aside, this patrician, this Western District Macbeth, Michael speculated, couldn't shake off the disturbing feeling that the people, while endorsing him, didn't respect him, and instead believed that in seizing the crown so impatiently he had played most foul for it. He was the man who had grabbed power, rather than waiting for it to fall to him naturally, like ripe fruit. And the prime minister didn't like this, or so Michael imagined. He didn't expect to be loved, nor did he want to be. But there *was* the question of humanity and the peoples' respect for *his* humanity. For no king wants to be seen as merely good at being ruthless; that is respect of the most basic nature. The king has to live with himself, after all. And the king cares what the people think, Michael speculated, because if they think well of him for long enough, and people write about him often enough in such terms, that benevolent image of him might one day become so fixed in people's minds that it becomes the truth. The way history records you. Not what you *are*, but the way people see you. And *did* the people see the new king as lacking humanity? Or having too little humanity, in the same way as they saw the old king as having too much humanity: too much *fallible* humanity? It is a kingly concern, Michael went on to say, and one that much troubles the king because it goes to the heart of such matters as integrity and the value of one's name. And so the king, much troubled, has sought to assuage his guilt.

It seemed like an amusing enough idea, one that wedded the everyday to the timeless storyland of myth and could be told in a more or less playful way, in the manner of a speculative game — and in such a way that it became clear to the reader that the author wasn't so sure he believed it himself. It was all a sort of fiction: essay as fiction, and fiction as essay. But Michael is already discovering that the two can liberate each other by introducing that element of playful speculation to things. Of course, he never expected anybody to take it seriously, and it surprises him that Peter seems to have taken it more seriously than he did. And this, it seems, is why Peter summoned him up from the past.

They are sitting at an outdoor café on a calm spring morning in their old student area: an area that was always a sort of Little Italy, an area where the ghosts of Michael and Madeleine are forever carrying steaming pizzas back to Michael's room, and which is now, more and more, a little Europe.

'You struck a chord in surprising places.'

'How?'

'Well, inside the palace, the king is seen as having all this power, and doing nothing with it. Some of my associates like your style.'

Michael smiles. 'Meaning?'

Peter stares out across the street, watching a delivery van full of bread and pastries being unloaded. 'Meaning that, from time to time, you might like to write a few things for us.'

'What!'

Peter's gaze returns to Michael. 'Oh, just the odd speech here and there. And no names, of course. We can't have you losing your friends. But there'd be some handy pocket money for an aspiring scribbler.'

Michael shakes his head, a disbelieving smile across his face. 'I might sink to the bottom eventually, but I'm not going to start there.'

'You're not Faust and I'm not the devil. And this is no great matter.'

'No.'

Peter smiles and pulls a card from his wallet. 'Here, take this anyway.'

Michael takes it, telling himself that it'd be petty not to, and gives it a quick glance. He has never had a card and can't imagine ever having one. But here is Peter's, proclaiming him an 'advisor' in the ministry of something or other. No doubt he has acquired all sorts of entertaining small talk over time, the likes of which Michael has just heard, to be trotted out at dinners and drinks and what-not. But it must be a bit of comedown all the same, for he was once earmarked for bigger things.

Michael puts the card in his pocket, at the same time beginning to realise that you can never really be sure who is reading you or, indeed, how they are reading you. They both look out over the street in silence.

'You come back here much?' Peter eventually asks.

'Yes.'

'Nostalgia already?'

'No, I just like it.'

'Ever go past the old house?'

'Sometimes. More accident than anything.'

Peter nods, looking round. 'I've never been back.'

There is another brief silence, and Peter finishes his coffee with a slight frown.

'It's impossible to walk past,' Michael says, 'without thinking about Pussy Cat ... Louise.'

It is an aside, just a bit of thinking out loud, but Peter suddenly swings back to Michael as if having heard the tolling of some giant bell. And he could almost be waiting for the ringing to die down before he speaks.

'You think of her?'

'Of course.'

'Often?'

'Not often, but I think of her. You?'

'Sometimes.'

There is a pause, Peter seemingly engrossed with the unloading of pastries from the van.

'I know it shouldn't matter that she was beautiful,' Michael says, 'but it does.'

They were all just a bit or a lot in love with Pussy Cat; it was impossible not to be. But as much as she was born to be loved, Michael wonders if she ever was. And while part of him will always mourn the day that her body was carried from the house, there is another part that recognises that the world was always too much with her and too much for her. That in death she was safer, and that neither Peter's jibes (which he heard all too often from his room next to theirs in those last days) nor anybody else's could touch her now.

'I'll always remember that last night … sitting with her in the doorway, on the landing. She looked like she'd just been thrown into the world and landed on the doorstep. And I mean *really* thrown. Into this strange, baffling world. Eyes wide. No idea what the rules were. I tried to talk to her, but she wasn't listening. And then she said, "I've lost my pills." I didn't even realise she had pills.'

Peter is silent. The bakery van departs, a bus belches smoke into the air.

'Then she just stood up, turned back into the room and closed the door. Not a word, not a look at me, or a nod. I wasn't there. We were already in different worlds. And that was it. Goodbye Pussy Cat.'

Michael pauses, looking at the silent, withdrawn figure of Peter, just a few feet away but in another world. 'I was always just a bit in love with Pussy Cat.'

'Weren't we all.' Peter speaks like a dreamer waking from sleep. 'Weren't we all.' His eyes are vague, almost as though he's not sure whom he is talking to. And Michael wonders if Peter has understood anything he has just said, or if he has been speaking to himself, more or less, the whole time. And for a moment Peter seems to hover on the verge of saying something about Pussy Cat, the frown and the intake of breath suggesting that he is about to go on, still in that hazy zone between dreaming and waking, but he snaps back into life with one of those automatic smiles that says, well, we could go on, couldn't we, but let's leave that to another time.

He takes another deep breath and checks his watch. Then he is standing and shaking Michael's hand. And once again it's the everyday Peter in front of him, back on duty. Smiling face at the ready to meet the faces … he meets.

'The offer's still there. Don't lose the card, you never know. One of those rainy Mondays, the final notice for the power on the table — things might look different. And remember, you've got surprising friends in high places. They like your style.'

They shake hands and walk off in different directions. Michael, to the airport to see his mother off. Peter to a meeting, he says, then back to Canberra. Peter, an 'advisor', of whom bigger things were once expected. Back to the land of power, to the land of 'the minister thought this, and the PM thought otherwise'. The card is still in Michael's pocket, the prospect of a Monday morning rainy enough to make him pick up the phone too distant to contemplate.

* * *

Driving to the airport to see his mother off is a rehearsal for leaving the country. Except that he imagines that when he leaves there will be no one to see him off, which is the way he wants it. It's not some Romantic impulse to become the lone voyager setting off for distant lands. It's just a desire to slip, almost anonymously, out of the country. Like slipping away from a party without farewell: you're gone and halfway home before anybody notices, if they notice at all. There's freedom in such anonymity, like being invisible. This morning's drive, he now decides, is not so much a rehearsal for leaving as an intimation. And the closer the freeway takes him to the airport the more liberated he feels.

His mother seems somehow smaller as she leaves her suitcase at the check-in counter and walks towards him. And he eventually concludes that it's the fact that she's in unfamiliar surroundings. She's been to airports before, but not as a traveller. Only ever to see someone off. And already she has asked him a number of times what she should do now, and where does she go after that. And is there anything they've forgotten? She has already strayed from her group, the group that she will be travelling with, before they've even left — and, Michael suspects, it won't be for the last time.

What she doesn't know is that, not so long from now, she will be leading these travel tours and she will be the one to whom all the anxious questions of first-time travellers will be directed. But for the moment she's asking them of Michael. She is in his hands. Like a child asking questions, curious about the world. And is this the way things go, he muses? How they've always gone? Eventually our parents become children again and we guide them through a changed and constantly changing world like they once did, for as the world becomes more and more curious, they grow younger and younger until they are children again. The older they grow, the younger they become. The younger we all become, our children patient or impatient with us the way we were patient or impatient with them. The process has already begun, and somehow it makes her look smaller. It's her wide eyes and her questions and the trust she places in him that is doing that. She's not really smaller; the world is just becoming larger.

They sit at a café table and order coffee and tea, and she eyes the group, her party, in the distance, in the same way, Michael imagines, that she once eyed the old street. The way she eyed it and always found it unsatisfactory. No, worse

155

than unsatisfactory — a step down. If Vic had married 'up' in the world, had she married 'down'? And did it always show? And was the street always going to be beneath her? For the street read disapproval in her eyes — and in the dresses she wore, which were always too good for the street and which the street always took as a snub. And he has no doubt she has already found her travelling party wanting and unsatisfactory in the same way that the street always was. And, no doubt, the party will read this in her eyes and take it as a snub. And so it goes, on and on.

Michael looks across at them. 'Shouldn't you join them soon?

Rita looks at them dubiously, as if delaying a duty or an appointment with the wrong side of the family.

'Not yet.'

And he can't blame her. They are so clearly a travelling party, looking forward to their voucher meals, smorgasbords and hotel breakfasts, which will be all or most of what they remember when they return — the blue-vein cheese breakfast here, the hotel room and the Italian TV variety show there. At least, that's the way he's summed them up. Already. At a glance. And is it fair? Does *he* really ever remember anything much more than that himself? Isn't their talk of travel, his and his friends', always about a wonderful meal in some unassuming little country town or the view from a hotel window? Are they really any different? But the more he glances at them (and possibly through Rita's eyes), the more they have that look of, well … dependence. All looking up to the tour guide, following her about, trailing behind her like a group of school children on an excursion. But perhaps — who knows — there are other Ritas among them, who have reluctantly given up their independence too.

At the same time he's wondering if she's ever fitted in anywhere. She's never trooped off with a gang because the gang has never been worth trooping off with. She has never felt at home with them — unlike Vic, who always did. Who was always bumping into a mate somewhere or other. No, she was never at home with *them*. Only ever at home at home. With the door closed and the world of the street shut out. But at the same time there's her desire for the great world beyond the street, beyond the city and the country; the curiosity that has brought her here for her late morning flight. Here, where time means something, before it becomes a succession of time zones and calculations — of mornings departed and mornings flown into, flying from today into yesterday, depending on where you're standing.

'I'll call you from Rome. I arrive at …'

She searches her itinerary and names the arrival time there and the matching time here, and they eventually reach a formula for calculating time here and time there — and the balancing of daylight hours and night-time, of convenient and inconvenient hours to call, begins. And already, time, time that her mind and body have always responded to and by which her waking and sleeping hours have always been measured, is slipping from her. Rushing from her or rushing towards her as new time, to which her mind and body will have to adjust. And suddenly, it seems to Michael that all those scientific theories — and even the less scientific ones — start to make sense. A man sits on a riverbank observing a bend in the river. An eagle circles above. Beyond the man's view, back along the river, there is a willow tree; ahead of him, further up the river, a waterfall. But the man sees only the bend in the river in front of him, not the willow or the waterfall. Whereas to the eagle it is all one: past, present, future. Stay in a Jumbo Jet long enough though, he muses with a bit of a laugh, and you eventually become the eagle.

They go over her list, a last check of all the things she ought to have. And when they have gone over everything again, she finally stands.

'Well …'

He follows her to the group and watches as they all introduce themselves to one another. And he can see that she's smiling as she shakes hands and chats — and that she's trying. But her heart's not in it. And she looks at Michael from time to time as if to say she can't do this. But she can. And he steps back and watches the whole business see itself through.

And then it's done. When everyone is present and accounted for, their tour guide checks her watch and directs them all to the departure door. And he watches as she joins the flow of the touring party, reluctantly surrendering her independence. And at the last moment, just before disappearing through the door, she turns, checking that he is still there, and waves. And somehow she's smaller again. Like a child waving. And, although in a group, alone. She always looks alone. How does she manage that? Even fragile. And then he suddenly realises that he is all she has in the world.

And as she waves there is a hint of a smile that says, I can't do this, but … of course I can. That and a suggestion of a departing *Baaa!* I know what they'll say. Sheep. All sheep. I know what they'll say … Then she is gone and he knows without a doubt that on the other side of that door she will be in the group, but alone.

* * *

That intimation of what it will be like to slip out of the country unseen, of being liberated, doesn't diminish on the drive back, a feeling that is accentuated by having taken the day off work to farewell his mother. The hum of the airport, that sense of imminent departure and the stolen nature of the day combine to prolong the feeling. A feeling like … what? Of course, like skipping school. And because the day is his, and because he'd like to prolong that sense of departure, he doesn't drive home but back to that Little Europe where he'd met Peter earlier in the day.

The fruit and vegetable shop is quiet in the early afternoon. It is a clean shop. And orderly. In its stillness, a retreat from the world. Certain shops have that effect. And the effect they have is sometimes more important than the goods they contain. This is such a shop.

The owner stands by the cash register. Motionless. Someone else, a young woman, hovers at the back of the shop.

Michael has just entered and stopped where he now stands as if arrested by the stillness of the place and that feeling of leaving the familiar world behind and suddenly being elsewhere. The owner smiles, the curving of her lips, it seems to him, the only movement in the shop. Here, there is no need of speed. Take your time, choose thoughtfully, with due consideration given to each of the items you choose. And as foolish as it seems he could simply linger in the shop and dwell upon the goods it contains for longer than it takes for a commercial transaction to be completed.

Outside, a black spring cloud passes over the sun and sudden heavy rain falls. He will need to take refuge longer than he intended. His mother will now be flying high above blue seas or wrapped in white cloud, making conversation, doing her best, or simply reclining in her seat wondering what on earth she's doing there. He moves slowly about the shop, selecting this and that, admiring the way everything is arranged and placed. For it denotes care, and must take considerable time to arrange — only, in the end, to be meddled with by customers, whose purchases the owner must view, in some part of her (at least, so Michael imagines) as an intrusive disruption. Her arrangements requiring constant rearrangement. And he wonders if she would be content for customers to enter the shop, survey the goods on display, stand for that moment in frozen, still appreciation of the way the goods are arranged, then leave. And he thinks that if the shop could effect just such a calming stasis in people its existence would be justified. Commercial exchange, money for goods, would almost be rendered unnecessary, a mere excuse for experiencing the shop itself.

All the same, the rain has stopped, he has selected his goods and he moves slowly towards the owner at the cash register at the same time as the other customer, whom he has barely noticed until now. If they were to continue as they are they will collide at the counter, so he steps back and gestures — a wave of the hand, almost comically regal — that she should go first.

It is then that she looks up from her cane basket (which the shop provides) and everything that follows happens very quickly. Stasis gives way to sudden movement. For the young woman, whom he has barely paid attention to, is Mandy.

And although everything takes place very quickly, it also happens with such speed that speed meets its opposite — and becomes slowness. Like an accident. An accident that takes place in a split second, but which also takes place in the kind of elastic time that the sheer intensity of events stretches to breaking point, before rebounding and snapping the participants back into the measurable present where events are, in fact, taking place.

But by the time he is snapped back, Mandy has left the shop. She was there in front of him for a moment, and then she was gone. Her basket, the contents abandoned, has been left exactly where she placed it, before looking up at Michael in response to that vaguely regal gesture.

He remembers speaking her name. And she may or may not have responded with 'Hello'. He may be imagining that she spoke. She then rushed past him, her head down so as not to catch his eye (or allow him to catch hers) and ran out the door onto the footpath, disappearing into the afternoon.

The shop owner, eyes wide with curiosity, looks at Michael, not expecting an explanation, but knowing, all the same, that he is in possession of one. Her shop, over the years, has witnessed a variety of stories — happy, sad, comic, the full range of feeling — and *that* was one of them. As he is leaving, she picks up the abandoned basket then catches his eye in the doorway as he glances back, and the look says: You don't have to tell me. It's you, isn't it? You did this. She ran from my shop because of you.

And she is right. He did do this. For it was hurt that caused Mandy to abandon her basket and leave the shop as quickly as possible. And that, too, was why Mandy's eyes were fixed on the floor as she left, so he shouldn't see that hurt. So as not to confirm that he had the power to do such a thing. To hurt her. But he had. And why had he? Because 'casual' Mandy had never slipped into 'serious' Mandy, the way 'casual' Madeleine had become 'serious' Madeleine. And, in the end, was her only fault that she wasn't somebody else?

Suddenly he knows what it was to be Madeleine, who expressed her deep gratitude (and 'gratitude', as she used it, was neither light nor dismissive) for the days they'd had together all those years ago, but who also carried the weight of knowing that gratitude could only sustain them for so long. And so Madeleine, her gratitude exhausted, had left.

As Michael had left Mandy. We are left, and we leave. It is the way of things.

But as he walks towards his car, the street fresh from rain (that feeling of being liberated washed away by the events of two or three minutes before), it is simply not enough to tell himself that the weight of leaving shifts from bearer to bearer through the years, that we all leave and we are all left, and that the same story has been enacted on the same shop floor or the street corner where he is now standing, and always will be. No, it's not enough, for this is his story, her story, their story. A particular story. With a particular cause. And no recourse to eternal re-enactments, or solace in universal verities of the same story playing over and over again throughout time with only the players themselves changing, can correct this or make him feel better. For the shop owner was right. You, *you* did this. You were the cause. And it hits him with the sudden force of an illumination: a wrong has been done. He has done it. And nothing can atone for that but an act of correction.

* * *

Telephones, like the numbers you dial, change over the years, but the idea of a phone call itself remains the same — its ring stirring excitement, annoyance or dread, but never indifference. And speaking through a telephone and hearing a voice at the other end always carries with it that residual hint — from those days when it was a source of wonder — of communicating with Mars. At least, it still does for Michael, for he came from a home that showed great respect for the telephone. Even deferred to it. There was a correct way to deal with it: never speak too long, and only ever telephone for a reason. Not only was the telephone expensive, it was not invented for social calls but for meaningful communication. Social calls demeaned the whole achievement of the telephone and did not show it the respect it deserved.

Michael is sitting on the couch in his lounge room staring at the white plastic telephone perched on the arm of the couch, because he is about to call Mandy. It has been two hours since he saw her in the shop and, in that time, the need to speak to her has become more and more pressing, to the point that it now feels urgent. He *must* speak to her. And so, without further delay (for she must be home by now), he dials the number, which — and this surprises him — he knows by heart. It rings for a long time and he is convinced she is not in, but then a voice that he doesn't recognise answers, and he leaps to his feet. He asks if he can speak to Mandy, and the woman (one of those with whom she shares the house) tells him that he can't. That she doesn't live here any more. The woman's tone is light, even casual. He hadn't expected this. And, already, he can see events slipping from him — or, rather, the power to control events. And Mandy's world, which he imagined he could slip back into with a few considered words of correction, has changed while he wasn't watching. Damn! And when he asks for her new number he notices that there is an urgency in the way he asks, almost in a rush. And the woman senses this — or he imagines she does — and so she asks who is calling.

'Michael.' There is silence on the other end. 'Mandy and I used to—'

'Yes, I know. She doesn't live here any more.'

From the moment he gives his name, the woman's whole tone changes. She is now abrupt. And in response, Michael's tone, too, becomes abrupt.

'Well, can you give me her new number?'

'I don't know it.' Again, there is a pause. 'She didn't leave one.'

'Well, where is she? Can you give me her new address, then?'

'I don't know it.'

'What?' And he adds, his voice rising with the realisation that events are slipping away from him, 'She can't have just vanished!'

'I *told* you, she didn't leave a number or an address.'

'She must have. You *must* know.'

'I don't. Nobody does. Mandy left without giving one,' the woman continues, her voice rising with Michael's. 'She was upset!'

'I know she was upset.'

'*Do* you?'

'I *must* speak to her.'

'I'll pass that on.'

It is not simply the feeling that events are slipping from him that he is keenly aware of now, but also a feeling of powerlessness. That all the will in the world will not persuade this woman to give him Mandy's new number. And this, in turn, gives way to exasperation.

'I don't think you understand. I have something very important to tell her!'

'I'm sorry—'

'No, you're not!'

'I have to go.'

'But—'

'I'm sorry—'

'I have something very—'

'Thank you.'

The line is suddenly dead.

'Bitch!'

He throws the phone onto the couch and brings his hands together with great force, creating a loud, slapping sound. And with the sound he looks down at his hands, stares at them, almost in disbelief — the sound of the impact still fresh as if hanging in the air — then lets his arms fall to his side. He knows that sound. And suddenly he is asking: is this how these things not only return, but live on? And do those sudden sensations of not only being like his father but becoming his father include the best and the worst of Vic? So that, out of the blue, he is suddenly shouting 'bitch' into the air and re-enacting those very actions he witnessed as a child, but which have now become *his* actions. And is he breathing new life into old fights? Giving them new rooms to inhabit, and new tears to add to the circle game of eternal return. Michael calculates that he is, more or less, the same age now that his father was when he witnessed that scene in his parents' bedroom all those years ago, and he is left wondering, as he slumps back onto the couch, if it really is true, that there are parts of the mind that lie dormant for years, never gone, which go into a kind of hibernation, but which nonetheless have a clock, an alarm clock — and has the alarm just rung?

He looks at the telephone lying on the couch where he threw it, still emitting its mechanical buzz, and hangs it up properly. And at the same time as he is staring up at the ceiling, as if having just seen rain fall from a clear sky and asking himself where did *that* come from, he is also telling himself that it is imperative he speaks to Mandy. As if to address the hurt that he has done and correct whatever it is that can be corrected were in some small measure a way of waking up to the alarm that has just sounded. Hearing it, and not missing it. He is not in love with Mandy (the song is true of them, and it now sadly seems to be 'their' song), but he has caused hurt and harm. For her friend was right; although he knew Mandy was upset, it had not registered with him, not properly, until today. And her friend's question, '*Do* you?', was justified. He knew, but it hadn't touched him. Now it had. Besides, it is no way to leave the country, as he soon will, with a wrong uncorrected, for the weight of uncorrected wrongs travels with you. And so, for any number of reasons that will gather with the days, it is suddenly vital that he speaks to Mandy.

But how? Clearly the woman, her old housemate, knew the new number. Mandy would not have left without leaving a number and an address. But the woman, no doubt, was under instructions not to give the number or the address to Michael, should he ever call. Her loyalty, and he is calm enough now to concede this, is with Mandy. And that is right. This, as it should be, is the loyalty that friendship demands. And she would have been perfectly aware of what has happened, and her words — Mandy was upset — echo the unspoken sentiments of the shopkeeper. So there is no point calling back. The world doesn't stay still for long. In a few weeks, while he wasn't watching, it shifted.

He concludes, at the same time, that his need to correct a wrong might be driven purely by selfish motives. For if he can't correct the wrong, then the wrong stays with him. And she, Mandy, will never know that he tried. Will never be aware of his efforts. Will take his lack of recorded effort as indifference. And will think badly of him. The wrong will stay with him, even define him, and she will think badly of him ever after. Is that it? Is it about *him*, after all, not her?

Why should it matter that someone thinks badly of you? Because, he concludes, a 'you' then exists that *you* don't like. And so all your efforts are directed towards replacing the 'you' that you don't like with one that you do. There is a portrait, a picture of you out there, and while it might exist only at the moment in one person's head, it may also be shared. Has been shared, for she must surely have told her friends about the manner of their parting. So there may, eventually, be a number of people who, when they think of Michael, think of the Michael he doesn't like when, all the time, he imagines he's better than that. That the image is false. But is it? Maybe it's right, after all. Maybe he is a shit. He has acted like a shit, but somehow clung to the notion that he wasn't. So is the Michael that he doesn't like, in fact, true (and that's really why he doesn't like it) and is the Michael that he thinks he is, in fact, false? And has he always clung to this falsity? It's a mess.

And he is beginning to feel like a mess. The order of things is shifting, and the more it does the more urgent it becomes to correct a wrong. However shady the motives may be. For he is rapidly coming to the conclusion that if he can only correct some part of that wrong or have his efforts and his care registered as apart from his apparent indifference, the 'you' that he doesn't like can, in Mandy's mind, become more likeable and some semblance of the Michael that he imagines himself to be can emerge. And suddenly, he's remembering that short essay he wrote for the paper, remembering the playfulness with which he speculated on the workings of the prime minister's mind, about the guilt and the assuaging of guilt, and is asking himself if he was really talking about the prime minister at all.

He has to get out. The flat is too small. But no sooner has he locked his door and stepped onto the footpath for a stroll through the park, no longer in uproar but late spring still, than he hears the telephone ringing from the arm of his couch. Normally, he would shrug. Too difficult. But he is convinced it is Mandy. She has heard that he tried to contact her. Her former housemate phoned her, and enough of Mandy has melted to call him. And that is the sound of her call. And so he turns and rushes up the path to his front door, fumbling for the key in his haste, the telephone ringing all of the precious time that he fumbles. And when he finally opens the door and is ready to spring onto the couch and lift the receiver, it stops ringing and he thumps the arm of the couch with his fist, the telephone lifting into the air with the impact and falling to the floor. He picks it up and puts it back in its place. Silent, no longer calling. Of course. The ending was written into the whole exercise. Rushing for a tram, rushing for a telephone — it is always futile.

He closes the door again and makes his way back to the footpath. It could have been anyone. All the same, he can't shake off the conviction that it wasn't.

He paces into the park, the sun now low over the freeway behind him, the need to correct things no less imperative — in fact, more urgent than it ever was before he picked up the telephone to call Mandy and discovered that the order of things had shifted and that he could no longer control events. And it is with a sort of short-term nostalgia that he remembers the lightness of his heart earlier that day as he drove out to the airport, not so much a different part of the day as a different day altogether.

* * *

Later that evening he is staring at the television. An election is coming. The name Whitlam is inescapable. So, too, the name Fraser. As are words such as 'democracy', 'vote', 'people' and 'trust'. These, and more like them — important words, but which, when trotted out for public consumption, ring hollow — are the key words from which all sentences flow: from the mouths of politicians, in the papers and on the television. Words have been captured and harnessed and put to work like a mill horse walking round in circles, grinding out the white powder of news. The white powder of Power's words.

Michael cares about the anarchic power of words and their capacity to surprise, shock and delight. But Power, which lingers in back rooms making plans and which inhabits its chosen representatives the way the soul inhabits the body, seeks only to control them and own them and grind them into white powder. And not because it has any great love of words. Power, rather, has a deep fear of words; for words, Power knows full well, are the seeds of its making and unmaking and so Power inevitably turns them into white powder ground out by blinkered mill horses.

He is about to switch the television off when he notices, in the background, directly behind the PM (who thinks, often as not, otherwise, when his minister says such and such), the shuffling figure of Peter. His bowed head only lifting now and then to sniff the atmosphere, his nose twitching like the rabbit he once was. He is, of course, and has been for some time, one of those who harness words and put them to work in the mill house, where the life is ground out of them. Peter, who was Bunny Rabbit in the house they all

171

shared, who once played songs of the Spanish Civil War on the portable stereo in his room and who could recite them by heart if the moment arose, who talked poetry and who treated his Brooks Brothers shirts with all the casual contempt of a working man donning a top hat after the revolution; Peter, who with the rest of them was warmed on winter nights by the sound of the Italian men who sang like a heavenly choir in the public bar opposite their house, and who was stirred by songs whose words and meanings were all the more stirring for being utterly mysterious, now harnesses words and has them walking round in circles all day.

And there he is on the screen, shuffling in the background, a back-room boy not wishing to be seen, not wishing to draw attention to himself; Peter, whose work (like God in his universe) is everywhere in evidence, but who is nowhere to be seen. Until now. There he is, up on the screen. And it is, indeed, a little like seeing the face of God and realising you've already met.

Michael blinks. The image is gone. The news moves on — or is it round and round? — and new images appear and newly harnessed words are heard. And it occurs to him that for all the speed with which these news items come and go, for all the attempts of the newspapers to make their news entertaining (as everything, it seems, must be), there is a tired, repetitive look to it all. And for all the smiling faces who occupy the screen, and who chat and laugh and whose chatter and laughter is, presumably, meant to enliven and lighten the mood of all the lounge rooms in all the cities and towns across

172

the country, the image they project is that of a worn-out world trying to convince itself that it's not. And it is draining and wearying just to stare at it all. He switches the television off. The room is silent. And the silence is preferable.

When did the world grow tired, when once it was young and every day was a fresh journey into the arches of wonder and untravelled lands? How does this happen? When did everybody start looking tired and the emotions grow stale? You look like you're ready to eat the world here, somebody recently said of him, comparing two photographs of Michael (one taken in his student years, the other not so long ago), and here, the speaker went on, you look like you've had enough. When did that happen? And since when has he been better off by himself?

He rises from his old student armchair and approaches his desk, idly gazing upon the accumulated bits and pieces gathering dust upon it. And then he is staring at an earthenware beer mug, a birthday present years ago from Madeleine that he has held on to. He brushes the dust off the silver lid and reads the date. That's all there is. Just a date. No indication of who gave him this present. It could be from anyone. But it's not. And it casts its spell as it always does. Lifting that silver lid is like lifting the stopper on the very essence of those days. Days that stayed up all night and walked home in the dawn and never knew the meaning of tired, days in which those times spent on your own were lonely. But Madeleine disappeared into the great world and he never heard from her again. And sometime in the years that followed, the world started to feel tired, and being alone felt not so bad.

He yawns. It has been a long day — seeing Peter, farewelling his mother and colliding with Mandy — and now he is feeling the effect of it. Somewhere out there in the night the blinkered mill horse of Peter's art will be going round and round in circles, as this white-powder world grinds on. He runs his hand through his hair as he closes the lid of the beer mug. New Wave. Old world. Tired world. Time to go. Time to set off. A good time to be gone. Into the arches of wonder and untravelled lands, if they still exist.

A life without Madeleine. Somehow, after all this time, he still feels as though he is missing an arm or a leg. Still feels that he will one day recount to her the years he lived without her and ask, 'How did that happen?' One life, and it will pass, he knows, in the blink of an eye. We come, we go. And the sooner we get used to that, the better. The world spins on. Are you happy, are you happy, Michael? He turns away from the desk and the beer mug sitting on it, the last remembered days of Madeleine stoppered inside, and walks towards the bathroom. He brushes his teeth and spits the day out then hangs his toothbrush on the wall. The day is done: a day that started full of life and ended in weariness. The world spins on and doesn't need you, not really. It just is. And does your being happy or not happy really matter at all in the end?

* * *

The order of things has shifted, slipped from his control. To an extent, he is like a child discovering for the first time that the world is not an extension of himself. That people are not held forever on a string, to be reeled in at will. That they act independently of his desires, and that they will go their own way. And, thereby, slip from his control.

It is two weeks since he attempted to telephone Mandy. Since then the days have warmed and the summer that will soon see him leave the country is coming. He has sent a letter to the school at which Mandy teaches, saying that he has something very important to tell her and that he wishes to correct his wrong. But wants, asks, nothing more. He says that he has no intention of imposing himself on what is clearly a new phase of her life. But there has been no reply and he can't even be sure she received it.

He is currently in the city. It is a balmy Friday night, the newsstands full of election talk, and he is buying winter clothes. He is alone and this, for the moment, suits him. He can pass along the footpaths, mingle with the crowds, but stay separate. It is also, he tells himself, the way he likes to travel. No one else to blame if things go wrong. There are those who like to enter the life of a place and know it, however briefly, from the inside, with friends and companions. Michael prefers the view from the edges. It is a view of a place that the place itself rarely sees. So for the moment he is happy enough alone, buying winter clothes in summer for the winter he will soon fly into.

He has just left an army disposal store where they sell good, thick naval coats and is making his way back to his tram stop. When there she is. A little further on, walking, quite briskly, away from him. And he immediately hurries towards her. Dodging people here and there, hurrying in case she turns off the main street and slips from view only to disappear into a large store or taxi. He moves quickly, possibly even running, not sure what to say when he reaches her, but content, all the same, that he will be in a position to at least say something. Things may have slipped from his control, but chance has delivered some semblance of control back to him. She is near now, and he reaches out and touches her on the shoulder, at the same time calling her name.

'Mandy!'

And it is then that a stranger turns round, surprised, possibly even startled, by a stranger's touch.

'Oh …' He stops and the young woman recedes from him while still looking back. 'I could have sworn …'

And with this, the young woman smiles, understands the situation — and is there a hint in that smile that she'd rather it had not been a mistake, before she turns and resumes her path?

He is left standing there, the uncompleted sentence he might have spoken suspended in the air. He would have gone on to say that he is travelling soon, for who knows how long, and that he wishes to correct a wrong before he goes, for that is no way for two people to part or for him leave to this place — and that is why he tapped her on the shoulder and called her name. In the end, the wrong shoulder, the wrong name.

The odd thing is he will remember this encounter, which lasted two or possibly three seconds, too fleeting to even be called brief, for years to come. Years from this pleasant Friday night, when he thinks of Mandy and those wind-blown, topsy-turvy days in which they parted, he will also think of that young woman and wonder just who she was, what became of her and what she might be doing at any moment of remembrance. Odd, what the memory selects to file away to be recalled, especially whenever he thinks of these days. Days that saw parks thrown into windy uproar — birds, blossoms and lives tossed into the air.

The tram is crowded and when the doors open at stops along the way passengers seem to burst from it, rather than leave it. All the same, it is a happy tram — a travelling community that sheds its members and gathers newcomers as it goes. The shopping bags of coffee and cheese from the market, the warming chatter, the lights of the park through which they are passing, are each the possession of all.

He leaves the tram stop, animal sounds erupting from time to time from the zoo behind him as he strolls down the tree-lined avenue to his flat. A lion roars, a monkey screeches. The lights of the government buildings go on and off. And, out in the world, taxis collect their fares from street corners, bands are setting up on the stages of sticky-carpet pubs or in the vast beer barns of grandly named hotels, and the girl he mistook for Mandy will be out there too in some pub or café, having forgotten all about the young man who tapped her on the shoulder, only to discover that it was the wrong shoulder and the wrong face.

The early twilight that carried with it a hint of summer has faded. The night settles in over the park. Darkness fills its corners. A lion roars its discontent, then falls into silence. And, gradually, the distant hum of traffic floats across the park from the city streets and the freeway, bringing with it the sounds of the trams and taxis and cars that will take Mandy to and from her new life, the mountain of Whitlam to a public meeting, and Peter from the airport to his home; everybody rushing to and from their destinations, lives won and lives lost in living. One vast, constantly moving organism, evolving as it moves and always moving. It 'worlds', he smiles. The thing itself. It worlds. It is worlding.

7. Frankenstein's Monster

The sky has clouded over in the brief time it took to drive from the café where Peter has just met Michael to their old student house. He would normally have driven straight to the airport, but not this time. All that talk of Pussy Cat. Some days these things matter more than others. Some days they sneak up on you and spring, the way Pussy Cats do. He has only a vague idea of how long he has been here. Long enough for the sky to cloud over, long enough for the street to be winter-blank in spring. He looks up to the balcony they once sat on through summer days and nights; the afternoons reading, the drinks, the parties. And Pussy Cat, forever leaning over the railing with provocative innocence, calling out something to him below on the footpath. Here Bunny Rabbit's eyes will forever wander, here Pussy Cat's heart will forever be broken. He has not seen the house since their student days. Either by design or by destiny. And all the things that took place here, in the intervening years have remained locked away behind that door. More or less. And still there, locked away inside, is the Peter who existed then but doesn't any more — another Peter, whose actions and deeds cannot touch him now because they were the actions and deeds of someone else. Or so it seems. He sits in the car contemplating his former self as if it were a character in a book. Faintly familiar, but distant. Somebody he once knew.

He has been staring at the old front door since he parked and switched off the ignition. Still purple. Still, it would seem, a student house. And still there, directly opposite the house, the pub where, in the public bar from time to time, the Italian men who gathered there sang like a heavenly choir and kept them all warm on winter nights. And those years that intervened, between then and now, the years that marked the difference between being in your twenties and being in your thirties, seem to have gone in the blink of an eye. And as he dwells on the door, it suddenly opens.

A young woman, looking down, hair falling to her shoulders, is examining the contents of her bag. Then she is joined by a young man — long hair, jeans and well-worn coat. The two of them could be any number of the young men and women *they* all once were. Timeless students. They linger for a moment, close the door behind them, step onto the footpath and walk down to the corner with the easy strides of those with no pressing engagements. The slow, steady drizzle that has begun to fall doesn't touch them because they don't notice it.

Doors open upon doors upon … He looks up at the front room. The old room. They are still there, both of them. Sealed off from time. Louise, all tears and rage and Pussy Cat love, and Peter, with his Bunny Rabbit eyes forever wandering, on the brink of walking out — and all that once happened stands ready to happen all over again, two people standing on the brink of discovering death, caught and frozen there, just before death arrives.

He sees them, still up there, just as he sees his hand reaching out and snatching Pussy Cat's medicine bottle from her side of the bed: one last spiteful act, one last prank before disappearing into the night with every intention of returning in the morning before she even realises it's gone. But youth being youth, he forgot. And when he did return, Pussy Cat's body had already been removed from the house. And as he gazes at the house he seems to enter it and take that familiar walk up the stairs to their old room to find Pussy Cat still there. After all these years. Everything poised to be re-enacted. He winces as he waits for the blow to fall. For the farmer's rake to come down upon little Peter Rabbit. But it doesn't.

One moment Pussy Cat is a frozen figure. Oblivious of him. Seeing nothing. The next she turns to him with an all-knowing tenderness, wise beyond her years, seeing everything, and is grasping his hand before it can snatch the pills. 'Stop!' her eyes say. 'Stop now. Enough,' wise Pussy Cat says. 'You were young. Weren't we all? Weren't we all younger and older than we knew, and older and younger? Weren't we all? Silly beyond belief, and wise beyond our years. We knew everything, and nothing. Full of love and hate and goodness that we'll never have again, and spite that knew no bounds. And we did things, we all did such things.' And it is both a young voice and an older voice that is speaking to him. The younger Pussy Cat and the older one she never grew to be. 'Yes, we did things. We all did such things. But time to let go. We can't continue to blame ourselves for things we did a hundred years ago. Time to let be. Enough. Stop. Stop now.'

And Peter, sitting in his government car opposite the house, takes in every word and believes every word. He has conjured her up from the past, as he would have her, the Louise whom he needs to hear or chooses to hear. And she is right, of course she is. She is only telling him something he should have told himself ages ago. And, together, they don't so much airbrush old times as agree to close the book on them. At least, this part of old times. You have to be light to live, and too much past weighs you down. We did things. We *all* did such things. This is what she would have said. This is Pussy Cat as he would have her. For he knew his Pussy Cat better than them all, and this is what she would have wanted. What she would have wanted to say. For beneath her rage was the Pussy Cat who purred to his touch in those days when they all did such things; beneath her Pussy Cat rage was the generous Pussy Cat who would have said that the time has come to let it all be. That they could continue to blame themselves for things they did a hundred years ago only for so long. 'Yes, you used my weakness. You did. For when I told you of my medicine and my moods I handed over, in trust, my weakness. But that was then. These things pass. They must. Time to let be.' This is what his Pussy Cat would say, and this is how he would have her stand and leave. A final gift of forgiveness in her Pussy Cat eyes. A sort of absolution. Eyes that say, there, it's done, it's over, and we need trouble each other no more. For he knew his Pussy Cat better than them all.

The clouds move on, the day is slowly brightening. Peter drives away, the old student street receding in the rear-vision mirror. Let be, let be … Time does its work. These things recede like the view from the rear-vision mirror. We need trouble you no more. Enough. Let be, let be …

* * *

On that same Wednesday afternoon, while Peter is driving away from the past, which is rapidly disappearing from the rear-vision mirror as if it never existed, Love is hard at work.

Some parts of the flat are in boxes (books, mementoes and certain favourite, framed photographs); other parts are exactly as they were: records in stacks, a coat and a hat on a hook that she hasn't had the heart to remove, as if the body of Beth were somehow still inside them, and her shoulder bag, which always contained her work, on the floor directly beneath the coat where Beth last dropped it. It is, the scene Trix looks over, an odd conjunction of staying and going.

But Trix is going. For how long, she's not sure. She didn't have the strength to pack up the whole flat and sell it (which is what she'd like to do) or the heart to stay. So she's taking just those things that she needs to take and moving, in a week or so, back to Melbourne, where she was born and where she went to school, the same select school, endlessly producing and re-producing the same select circles, that all her cousins went to. Which was half the reason she left in the first place. She is, she knows, responding to a sort of homing instinct. Home, a place to repair yourself. What did someone say? Home is the place that, when you go there, they *have* to take you in. Not that she is going to the home she grew up in. No, her parents have long since separated and sold the old house. And she hasn't seen her cousins for years. No, she has friends who have a house, a large house with a spare, sunny room. And Trix, a book editor who can take her work wherever she chooses to go, will stay there in a large house, in a large room full of sunlight, for as long as it takes. She goes with few hopes and no illusions, but the thought of a large room filled with sunlight lifts her for a moment.

Then she looks about the lounge room in which she is now standing and up the hallway of the flat and it suddenly hits her without warning, as it has for weeks and weeks: this is where they lived, but don't any more. And won't again. And just when she thinks she's done with sadness she looks at the coat and the hat and the bag and another wretched wave of longing passes through her and she has, yet again, the helpless feeling of floating out of her depth and not being able to stop herself, of never having been this far out before, of being capable of nothing other than just staying afloat and riding the waves — waves that she can only assume will eventually take her back to shore. But which shore?

Even though she's not packing up the flat and selling it, she's cleaning it all the same. Making it ready for when the sheets are thrown over the chairs and tables and the couch. And it is while she is dusting one of the armchairs that she comes across a handkerchief stuffed down the side of a cushion — a white handkerchief with some sort of coat of arms in the corner, and a faint red smear across it. And she's puzzled for a moment, then she remembers. Of course. It's Peter's, and the smear of red is Beth's lipstick. For all her radical ways, Beth was an old-fashioned girl who wore the red lipstick of other times. There it is, the colour and the faint smell of Beth. And she remembers how it got there. Beth dipping her hand in an olive bowl, fingers sticky and looking for a napkin; Peter passing his handkerchief to her, saying it's clean, and Beth passing it back after wiping her fingers and lips. And Trix remembers it all because, for a moment, for a crazy moment, they looked like they could so easily have been husband and wife, so casual and yet intimate was the exchange. One of those moments of irrational jealousy that lent the moment enough intensity for the memory to linger. And here it is, the fallen handkerchief. Still here. And with the sight and scent of it comes not only another wave of sadness but anger as well. And a desire, not for revenge (for she knows exactly the tempting nonsense that he fed Beth that night and which Beth couldn't resist), but for a touch of justice — because nobody should be allowed to play with people's lives and then walk away as if nothing had happened. For, she is sure, Peter is one of those (they all are in this town) who are good at walking away, at granting themselves absolution as if nothing happened and no one did anything.

And so she sits and stares at the handkerchief, wondering what to do with it, then slowly folds it into a square and flattens it out with her palm. The fallen handkerchief has fallen into her hands. She rises and places it on the kitchen table and reaches for an envelope at the same time as reaching for Beth's address book. And there it is, where it ought to be, for Beth was methodical like that. Two addresses: the Canberra one and, because of the old times that connected them, the Melbourne address. Very convenient. And Trix knows the area, because it's her side of town — the plush side of town, the select side of town that it would be so easy to slip back into after a week of playing with other people's lives and then walking away as if nothing had happened.

Her first impulse is to write Peter's name and address on the envelope and post it — but then Peter will receive it, throw the envelope away, pocket the handkerchief and, indeed, nothing will have happened. No, best to post it to his wife.

185

Later that day, driving those few boxes of books and odd favourite things to the post office where they will be sent on to Melbourne, she drops the envelope into a post-box.

There are those who walk away and imagine they've forgotten whatever it is they want to forget. There are those who are good at that. But Love doesn't forget. Love has long and clear memories. Nor, when it chooses, does it let others forget. So while Peter goes about his duties, now back in Canberra, Love is hard at work. And love's work awaits him, although he doesn't know it yet.

* * *

The rest of Peter's week passes, light and fast. A time-devouring round of election meetings and election speeches, for the election has now been called and the first casualty is time. And when he finally settles back into his seat on the Friday afternoon flight home, his body, drained from the weight of the week's hard work, sinks deep into it. And as he stares out the taxi window a little later, speeding along the freeway through the early evening, he is just one part of the general hum of traffic that carries over the surrounding suburbs to Michael, strolling back through the park from his tram stop after tapping the wrong girl on the shoulder and speaking the wrong name.

It is a familiar scene inside Peter's house. The end of the working week. An air of liberation: the children in these warmer evenings passing from the house into the garden and back in repeated cycles; music coming from the stereo; shopping bags on the kitchen table. Kate looks up from the lounge-room couch, switches off the television and greets him, while the two children acknowledge his arrival with a quick wave on their way out to the yard. All is as it should be.

He sits with Kate on the couch, kicks his shoes off, a deep sigh indicating the measure of his tiredness, and small talk follows. All is well. But as the talk continues he notes that his wife's tone lacks the lightness of small talk. The talk is small, but the tone is not. There is reserve in her voice. She is saying one thing and thinking another. And he is contemplating asking just what that something else is, when she says: 'Oh, this odd thing arrived today.'

'Odd thing?' He is curious and mildly amused.

'Yes.'

She rises from the couch and takes a small, opened envelope from the kitchen table and drops it on his lap.

'Wouldn't you call that odd?'

He looks at the envelope. It is addressed to his wife, in writing he has never seen before. Distinctive writing. Almost like calligraphy, the way the writing of some people can look. He is puzzled, but that's all. Then he takes from the envelope what he assumes will be a letter and is suddenly staring at a handkerchief. At first he doesn't recognise the handkerchief, and then he does. It's one of his. He looks at his wife, the puzzled look acquiring a frown.

'Open it out,' Kate says.

He does so, and as he is staring at the square of what is otherwise a clean handkerchief he sees there is a smudge in one of the corners. It's not blood, but what is it?

'How do you explain that?'

He looks from the piece of cloth to his wife, utterly baffled.

'I can't.'

'What's the mark?'

He shakes his head. 'Jam?'

'No,' she says, and it's clear she has the answer, as it is also clear that she has had ample time to study the object. 'It's lipstick.'

'What?'

'Believe me. Smell it.'

He does and there is a faint, but clear, cosmetic smell.

'You wouldn't want that on your toast.'

He slumps back on the couch, staring at the handkerchief.

'So,' his wife says, returning to the original question. 'How do you explain that?'

To which he replies with exactly the same answer. 'I can't.'

And he can't explain it because he has completely forgotten how it happened. It is his handkerchief, there is lipstick on it, but he has no memory of where it may have been left or how it came to acquire the faint red smudge. He has, quite genuinely, no memory of passing the handkerchief to Beth, or of Beth wiping her fingers and then her lips before passing it back. He had, after all, much larger things on his mind. And he was, it must be said, sitting in a room with two naked women at the time. And they were discussing matters of grave political concern. The passage of a handkerchief, from one person to the other, in such circumstances, passed, more or less, unnoticed. Rated no mention in the memory's dispatches. And so may as well never have happened. And as much as there must be an explanation somewhere, neither Peter nor his wife is in possession of it. Furthermore, she believes him when he says he can't explain it because *he* believes it.

He folds the handkerchief, puts it back in the envelope and drops it on a cushion beside him, looking round at his wife when he is finished.

'Someone's having a joke.'

He goes on to surmise, quite genuinely, that he must have left it lying round the office, somebody found it and thought they'd play a joke on him. And he knows just the types who would. It's been a long, intense week. The troops need to amuse themselves occasionally. It's a joke, he says again.

'Somebody's read too many plays,' he adds, with a weary sigh.

'All the same, odd.'

'There *are* some oddballs up there.'

No, it's a joke, and he'll find out who the joker is on Monday. That's if the joker owns up.

They rise from the couch, leaving the envelope lying on the cushion. The fallen handkerchief, once more, left to be forgotten. Not worth any more of their time. They dine on take-away pizza, they doze in front of the television, they sleep and then wake up to a bright Saturday morning that finds Peter with his feet up reading the papers.

Peter rises from his kitchen chair. He is getting on with things. There is an election in a few weeks and the campaign machinery (with all its various parts, including Peter) is in frantic motion. The kitchen table is covered in Saturday's newspapers, as it always is on a Saturday morning. Kate is reading, listening to music, tracking the sounds of her children's voices, mindful of the smell of toast and contemplating the taste of jam — all at once. The mind gathers it all, discards what it no longer requires, then moves on. There is no further mention of the handkerchief, left in the corner of an armchair for weeks, and now forgotten all over again, as if never having been dropped. And that moment when Peter passed it to Beth and Beth passed it back, which Peter has completely forgotten because he had far greater things on his mind, never existed. Or may as well not have. Just a joke dreamt up by someone. A prank that he may or may not look into when he gets back to work on Monday, if he remembers.

* * *

In the middle of the following week Trix is ready to close up the flat before finally leaving. She has spent days putting things in boxes after all, for it seemed too sad to walk out and leave everything behind as it was, as if encouraging the place to believe that the old life would one day be resumed. Furthermore, the thought of walking back into the flat when she returns and being met by the museum of the old life was too sad to be contemplated. So Trix has spent days sorting things into boxes — those things like books, rugs and ornaments that can most easily be moved. She has even taken the paintings and posters down from the walls, so that the flat, with its shrouded furniture, now has the kind of spare anonymity she sought. A place that could be lived in by just anybody. A place that was once a home becomes a sort of bare outline waiting to be coloured in by others.

There is one last poster left to be taken down from the wall. A woman lies helpless on the ground. Violence defines the scene. Across the poster is the scrawled slogan: 'Rape is a political act'. And it is at this point that Love goes to work again. Its fees are owing, and Love always collects. The scene and the poster will now always be synonymous with the night that Old Times came to visit, the night that Old Times sat down in that very armchair, and, once Trix had gone to bed, fed Beth a pack of lies because Old Times knew full well that Beth was ready to believe a pack of lies. That's Old Times for you. And the more Trix stares at the poster, the more the anger that for the last week has been soothed by sorrow rises again. There are those who walk away and forget. Those whose whole lives are a succession of leavings and forgettings. Over and over again. Airbrushing the past.

Exploding with anger she tears the poster from the wall, almost ripping it, then rolls it up and seals it with an elastic band. Trix then sits on the arm of a shrouded armchair, her shaking frame slowly calming down, and looks about the anonymous room, asking herself just how far anger will go. When she posted the handkerchief a week earlier, there was an irresistible logic to the process. She was, after all, returning it. This, she knows, is different. But there is also a similar sense of destiny and logic. For if anybody deserves to have this poster now, if anybody has earned this poster, it is Old Times. And she now calls him Old Times whenever she thinks of him because she can't bear the sound of his name. More than the sound of his name, she can't bear to name him. For to name him, to call him 'Peter', is to confer a certain familiarity, even intimacy, on the connection. Like being on first-name terms with your torturer. It is both absurd and a betrayal of Love. No, he will not be Peter. He will be Old Times and have the same kind of anonymity that the room now has.

And what she called anger, she now sees as Love. What she is about to do is an act of Love. Love has fallen upon her and she will do Love's work. Who else will? If she doesn't, nobody will —and Old Times will simply walk away and forget. Airbrushing the past, yet again. Yes, she will do Love's work and Love has one more task to complete. For Love in all its ferocity has been stirred, its fees are still owing, and Love always collects.

* * *

192

Later in the day, the poster posted, Trix takes one last tour of the flat. And she knows there is a sort of morbidity to it, but a necessary morbidity all the same. She is, she knows, saying farewell. And if you don't say your farewells properly at the time when farewells are required, you will later regret that you didn't. So this is a necessary farewell, and it takes her from the lounge room to the bedroom and the spare room that served as a study. And throughout the farewell it is not only the ghost of Beth that is about, and whom she sees looking up from her work and smiling, but the ghost of herself as well. There they were, and there they will stay. Farewelled and abandoned. The 'them' that was 'us'.

The present is always receding into the past, and the past, soon enough, into the distant past. And the distant past eventually too distant to be remembered properly. And all that living that they did will survive only in the form of a few photographic images about which those who haven't even been born yet will one day ask, who was that? And it is then, with that thought, that the finality of the farewell and the weight of loss, which until then Love had borne, become too much to support, and the frame that is Trix, the frame that had borne the weight of loss without really noticing because it was busy doing things, suddenly gives way and sinks to the floor.

She is a spring, a gushing spring of tears. And the spring does not run dry. And the tears don't stop. Who knew she had so many in her? Drops as heavy as summer rain splash onto her chest and turn her T-shirt to a deep shady blue. She has cried before over the last few weeks. But not like this. This time she really does feel that she could sob up her heart. That Love is not only wrenching from her these sobs as heavy as rain, but also the very heart that once went out unconditionally to this slightly doddery, abstracted middle-aged woman with the look of a mature Marguerite Duras whom she met at a dull publisher's party, and who became her constant reference point throughout the years that followed, when distance was measured by her proximity, or lack of it. The reference point that she knew, in her heart of hearts, was the home she'd finally come to. And that very heart that she gave unconditionally she could now sob onto her lap because she can surely have no further use of it. Home was here, but home has acquired a spare anonymous look as though just anybody could have lived here — and her reference point is gone.

But all tears end. The heart stays on. And springs, however endless, will dry. And she doesn't know how long she's been on the floor, but when the storm clears she sits in utter stillness. Calm, even rested. And it is a lighter Trix who eventually rises, splashes the evidence of tears away and rinses the face that she will now take out into the street.

She drops her suitcase on the outside doormat, her carry bag strung over her shoulder, and pauses for a moment before pulling the door of the flat shut. For, as much as she may return to either sell or occupy the place again, the Trix who returns will be a different Trix and this place, whenever she looks upon it again, will be transformed by that difference. And so she lingers before pulling the door shut.

194

In the taxi to the airport she gazes at all the familiar places — not just the public ones but the private ones. She allows her exhausted frame to sink into the seat and her exhausted head to lean back and rest while gazing at the passing scene. Soon the city gives way to that vaguely European countryside that surrounds it. And she feels as if she is travelling, and it is a good feeling. And she is. Back to the place in which she grew up and which she once called home and which will take her in once more, because it has to.

* * *

They are close to the election and Peter, his work finished in the capital for the day, has just arrived home. His Friday evening arrivals are nearly always in darkness, but today he is early, and as he walks up the hallway to the kitchen in the late-afternoon light he has that feeling of being freed from relentless routine. Of skipping off from school early. But the feeling evaporates the moment he opens the kitchen door and sees his wife sitting at the table, a puzzled, even inquisitorial, look on her face.

She holds a tea cup in one hand and points to a poster, flat on the table, with the other.

"This arrived today.'

The moment he looks at it he recognises it and, in that instant, also remembers the handkerchief — passing it to Beth and Beth passing it back — and knows exactly what is going on. But his face shows none of this. He simply stares at it, as if seeing it for the first time.

'What is it?' Kate asks.

'It's a poster.'

'Yes, but *what* is it?'

'Who sent it?'

'Don't know.'

'Why not?'

'There's no return address.'

'A note?'

'No.'

'It's an old poster,' he says, casually picking it up and examining it. 'Don't you remember them?'

'Of course I do, but what is it doing here?'

He shakes his head, releasing the poster as he does.

'I don't know.'

'*Don't* you?'

He ignores the question. 'This is somebody's idea of a joke.'

'If it's a joke, somebody's got an odd sense of humour.'

'What else could it be?'

'I've had time to think about that. I've been looking at it and I've concluded a few things. The handkerchief and the poster were sent by the same person. Same handwriting. And it's *not* a joke.' She shifts in her seat, and an impatient, can-we-dispense-with-the-silly-games tone enters her voice. 'What's more, it assumes one of us knows what it all means.

And it's not me. So,' and she turns to him, her face hard, shaking her finger at the poster, 'what *is* this?'

As he stares at her he reads, in her face, the obvious conclusion. The conclusion she *would* reach. You've had an affair, haven't you? You had an affair, and now the affair is over. And this is what happens when affairs end. Somebody gets nasty.

It is then that she repeats herself. 'What *is* this?'

'I don't know.'

'Peter!'

Her voice echoes about the kitchen.

'I don't.'

She stares directly into his eyes and holds them.

'Oh, yes you do. Yes, you bloody well do! Don't go dragging your grubby little lipsticked handkerchiefs into this house! And don't fucking well lie to me!'

She hardly ever swears, and the effect is thunderous. Still, he shakes his head.

'I'm not responsible for every oddball who sends oddball things in the post.'

They fall silent, neither looking at the other. He can not, of course, tell her what is happening. Somebody else might, but not Peter. So he doesn't tell her that, yes, he knows what the two objects mean and he knows what the story they tell is. No, not an affair. That could possibly be explained. But not this. Not at the moment. For it is the story of an experiment born of a stalled career and a talent for, even a delight in, the thrill of game-play: an experiment in manufacturing truth.

Of throwing out into the world not so much a lie as a fiction, of watching the blinkered mill horse grind fiction into fact and turn it into the white powder of news. And, for a few weeks, that is exactly what happened. And he, Peter, the author, sat back and watched, god-like, from a distance. For a time, the experiment was a success. Then it all went wrong, because the mill horse was older, more troubled and more fragile than he realised. And events very quickly reached the point where he could no longer control them and all that was left for him to do was walk away, as if the experiment never existed.

Somebody else might tell all of that to his wife, but not Peter. For someone's death is at the end of the tale. And death is more final than the end of any affair. And to bring all this up is to bring into plain view a Peter that his wife never knew existed, one with a degree of duplicity and cunning well beyond that of any average, bumbling adulterer. And so he shakes his head. He is not responsible, he says once more, for every oddball who gets it into his or her head to send oddball things in the post.

She shakes her head, eyes staring directly at him.

'No, there's sense in this.'

'Why?' he says, trying to smile casually.

'Because there *is*!'

Once again, the last syllable echoes about the kitchen and she rises abruptly from her chair and walks to the window, staring out at the garden.

He looks at her, then back at the poster lying on the table.

'What shall we do with it?'

She says nothing for a moment, only stares out the window, then speaks without turning.

'We could put it up on the wall.'

'*What?*'

'Bound to be a conversation piece.' She continues staring out the window. No point looking into his eyes, she may well have concluded, because there's nothing to look into. 'There's a space over there that's made for it,' she says, pointing to one of the kitchen walls. 'There's almost a touch of destiny to that, don't you think?'

He says nothing, staring from the poster to the wall, and imagining it there every morning. She continues, not waiting for an answer to her question. 'I think it would lighten the wall up. A little bit of controversy among the peasant chairs. Nothing like a political statement to stir things up.'

And with that she goes out to the garden shed and comes back with a hammer and tacks. Taking the poster, she hammers it to the wall for which it was destined, then steps back admiringly.

'Yes, *that's* it.' She turns to him, smiling coldly. 'Don't you think?'

She glances at the clock and, with no further comment, leaves the room to collect the children from school. And when she is gone, when he has the room and, indeed, the entire house to himself, his first impulse is to tear the thing down from the wall. But, of course, he can't. He has pronounced it oddball. Somebody's idea of a joke. In short, of no significance. And to tear it down, as he would dearly love to do, would be to pronounce it a matter of significance after all. Significant enough to be torn down. For to tear it down, which she may well be expecting him to do — the whole business of pinning it up to the wall being an exercise in getting to the truth of the matter; that there is a story here, and he, Peter, knows what it is — would be to admit as much, and amount, more or less, to an admission of guilt. And, of course, talk would follow. And he doesn't want that.

* * *

It is still there today as it was the day before and the day before that. Up there on the wall. And it looks set to stay, after entering the house like some stranger come in off the street with an intriguing tale. For the poster has taken up residence on the wall and as much as you might choose to ignore it, you can't. Not Peter, nor anybody else who enters the kitchen.

Is this how it happens? Is this how our inventions turn back on us? An experiment in manufacturing the truth, a joke, a serious game, if you like, goes wrong because serious games do get serious, except we never look beyond the game when we start it — and the very idea of truth itself suddenly starts to look shaky, and all those truths you take for granted start to shake too. Is this how it happens?

Another man might simply tell his wife what happened, and all would be well. But not Peter. Besides, would all be well and as it was before? For in unveiling the truth of the matter, he once again recognises, he would also be unveiling a shady side of himself; worse than shady, a portrait of himself that she may not recognise or may even be disgusted by. A portrait of someone capable of things she hadn't thought were in him. A portrait of Peter that renders him, at best, a shady puzzle; at worst, somebody she doesn't know and has never known — inevitably posing all sorts of awkward questions, leading to answers, leading to questions, leading to … until everything gets messy.

Is this how it happens? Is this how our inventions turn back on us — and how the house starts to shake? And once the house starts to shake, does it eventually come tumbling down? For something has been lost, something subtracted from the structure that the structure badly needs if it is to stay up. And it is not love, for the house can stand without love. Or desire, or laughter. The house can stand well enough without all of them. No, something else is gone. Something more basic than that, the loss of which is there to be read in her eyes when she looks at him, imagining grubby little affairs and motel liaisons and heaven only knows what else; there to be heard when she speaks the short, sharp sentences that she now offers as conversation, saying the necessary things that need to be said. But only those things that need to be said. And all accompanied with the look that says: You know, and you're not telling. The look that says: Don't call this somebody's idea of a joke. When, all the time, it *was* a sort of joke. The joke that failed to laugh.

And this is what happens. This is how it all turns back on us, like Frankenstein's creaking monster. Yes, something is gone — that collection of necessary assumptions upon which the house sits. For it is the foundation of trust that has been taken away, and the house now sits on questions.

The house can well stand without love, desire, laughter and all the rest of it. But not without the foundation of trust. And not just the house, but everything. The bridge that crosses the river and joins the two halves of the city will not be crossed, because it might fall down. The train will not travel because none will board it in case it crashes. And none will ride the fairground ferris wheel because it might topple over. No, take away the foundation of trust and you take away the very centre of things. The cornerstone itself. Not just of home, but everything: the city out there, the house on Capital Hill, the whole bloody world. And Peter is reminded of this every day when he looks up at the poster.

The French kitchen is still the French kitchen, the colours still glow in the morning sun. But they don't glitter. Not now. Not today.

In spite of all this, if Peter trusts anything right now, he trusts that this awkward moment will pass. Time will do its work the way time always does. Hours will collapse into days and days into weeks. Questions, once urgent, will lose their urgency. The present will recede like the view from a rear-vision mirror into a half-remembered past, before being completely forgotten or re-invented by time. A past will emerge, airbrushed of its awkwardness. Until, one day, they will all wake to a world where none of this happened. Or may as well not have.

If there is one thing Peter trusts right now, it is this. And when it all comes to pass, when the past is forgotten or has been re-invented by time, somebody will look up at the kitchen wall one day and ask what that ugly thing is doing there and the poster will come down. And when that happens they will all walk away, the poster on the wall will be replaced and, in time, there will be nothing left to remember and nothing will have happened.

He rises from the kitchen table, the Sunday papers under his arm. His wife neither responds nor looks up. The voices of children and occasional laughter inhabit the garden. The French kitchen is still the French kitchen. The house is shaken, but the house will settle.

In his study he opens the papers. The mountain of Whitlam and the rock-face of Fraser stare back from the desk like some abstract portrait of the times. The election will come and go. And the scandals and the issues and the minister who said such and such and the PM who thought otherwise will fade into the past and eventually be forgotten. All will pass and all will continue. If he trusts anything right now, he trusts this. It is the way of things, and things will have their way.

8. Mandy's Silence

How did this happen? What was the order of events? A hike. Time in the country, away from everything. Friends had suggested it, with the best of intentions. They were thinking of her. And because they were thinking of her, and because their intentions were good, she agreed. Even though she was not excited by the idea, she could see they were. It was all for her. Poor Mandy, who had broken up with her Michael and whose misery had gone on for weeks now. For too long. Enough, her misery needed distraction. It was never said, but that was the thinking. So she went along. Carried by the current of positive feelings and good intentions, which eventually led here.

Mandy is sitting up in a hospital bed. There is a full moon, and through the window she has a good view over the tree-lined street outside and on to the university. The hospital is quiet and even the occasional buzzing sounds coming from the beds and the soft shuffle of nurses' feet padding up and down the corridor seem part of that quietness. Voices, too, are distant and vaguely comforting. And the dimmed lights of the ward, somehow blue, it seems to her, cast a dreamy film over everything, like the moonlight on the streets and the university outside.

How did it happen? What was the order of events that led here? They were walking, a morning hike up into the hills. She was chewing chocolate and nuts and sweat was pouring down her neck, arms and legs, and it was good to be out walking in the country. She wasn't so much happy as indifferently calm. Each step up into the hills, and the effort required to take each step, drawing her further into that blissful indifference. Nothing mattered. She was a tree, she was a passing bird, she was a fallen branch. She was just one other thing in a forest of things. And whatever she may have felt, the lingering sadness and anger of those last minutes with Michael floated free of her and she became part of this indifferent forest in which the passing bird feels neither joy nor sorrow, the fallen branch no despair. And the further she climbed up into the hills the more those things she may have felt, and which had weighed heavily upon her until now, floated free of her and she was left with this calm indifference. She was things. And things were her.

Then a large rock appeared in front of them. There it was, like some guardian of the hilltop, saying, thus far and no further — a giant rock pushing up through the soft, mossy ground. And it was obvious to all that they would have to go around this rock. But as they were calculating the best way round the rock without incurring its displeasure, someone suggested they simply pass over the face of the rock and continue. As if there were no rock. And for no particular reason, everyone agreed. Such was the feeling of adventure they had all come to feel. And what's an adventure without a touch of daring? She remembers following the others, climbing the rock face and almost reaching the top where her friends sat calling her up and urging her on. And then her foot slipped and she ran out of memory.

She fell, but she has no clear memory of falling, only the memory of realising she was about to. Although at the time she must have said to herself, I am falling, I will land. She fell, she landed, and the fall stopped here. That was the order of events. She tumbled from the face of the rock, incurring its displeasure, onto this hospital bed where she now sits in dreamy blue light, gazing at the moonlit trees of the street outside and the dark shapes of the university buildings.

Her head aches. A dull ache. As well as her shoulders and hip, but nothing more. No great pain. Just this dull ache. Above all, she is aware of a sort of suspended feeling. Of floating. As if the blue light surrounding her is outer space and she is sitting in a space capsule passing through it. Safe. In a sort of crib. There are voices, distant and indistinct. And the soft, padding feet of the night-duty nurse in the corridor. Then footsteps approach.

She looks round from the windows and sees a young man in a white coat and a nurse standing beside him. He smiles.

'How's the head feeling?'

'Bit sore. But not much.'

'And the hip?'

'Same.'

'You had a fall.'

'I remember.'

'You were knocked out.'

'I don't remember that.'

He smiles. 'You wouldn't.'

He then goes on to explain that they have done all the tests they needed to do and that all is well. No damage. A big knock on the head, though, and that head will ache for a while yet. Along with the hip. So, all things considered, she's a lucky girl. Could have been worse. Then he drops that white-coat smile and his face turns serious. 'So, that's all good news. But ...'

The coincidence of the word 'but' and the sudden change in his expression concern her, but not overly. She is floating through blue space in an invisible capsule. And it is with mild concern that she waits for the pause to pass and for him to finish the sentence.

'But,' he continues, 'I'm afraid you've lost the baby.'

'What!'

Everything stops — voices, shuffling feet, occasional buzzing for the nurses. There is just this silence. In the blue semi-light, her eyes are wide as she stares at the doctor.

'Baby?'

He nods. He is young and this is clearly awkward.

'You didn't know?'

She shakes her head.

'I'm sorry,' he says.

She continues slowly shaking her head. 'Baby? How can that be?'

He looks at her, carefully choosing his words before speaking.

'It was tiny. About six weeks or so.'

Her head stops shaking and she looks at him, blank-eyed. 'A baby?'

Her head falls back onto the pillow. There is nothing more to say. And even if there were, she has no desire to go on. And then she's remembering that last night at Michael's, not long before he broke it off. That last night, which, of course, she never thought of as their last night. Only now does she think of it like that. That last night, when they had fucked and fucked and fucked, like two people do when they first meet — or when they are parting. That must have been it. They had fucked and fucked, and neither of them had so much as thought of being careful, or of taking precautions, because when you fuck like that you don't. And she on that night (which she knew full well, but threw caution to the wind) as fertile as the Nile Delta. That must have been it. *Must* have. The young doctor is telling her something. Something about rest and seeing her in the morning, but she is barely aware of his words. Baby? There for six weeks or seven — now gone, and she never knew. How can that be? Was she so absorbed in her own misery that she wasn't even aware of her body? Unaware that her body was talking to her while her mind was going round and round with the same thoughts, too absorbed in her misery to listen.

The doctor is speaking but she hears only the sound of his voice. It is soft, like the distant voices of the night staff and the padding of their feet along the corridor. She is suspended. She is floating. In a capsule. Far away. The world is distant, spinning in space under a silvery moon. Small and far away. And she is floating through space gazing upon a distant earth.

* * *

A life comes and goes in six weeks or so and nobody knows. And it's not so much the brevity of the life, the short passage from birth to death, that she can't shake off. It's the fact that nobody knew. We're born alone and die alone — nobody else can do either of them for us. But, in between, we seek the comfort of company, so that we are not alone. But to be both born and to die, and for nobody to know, is to be alone at the beginning, the end and in between. A lifetime of loneliness, however brief it may be. For, just one person knowing, Mandy is sure, makes all the difference. Or would have. Affection may, after all, transmit itself — perhaps as a hand gently rubbing the belly. It is a comfort, she is convinced, an act of care that is surely registered by that six- or seven-week-old life growing inside her. But to Mandy, more important than this, is the simple fact of knowing. Knowing confirms the existence of someone or something. You *are*! Your existence is registered, and you are no longer alone. But not to be known at all, to be born and die and for no one to know, is to bear the kind of loneliness that no one or nothing should be asked to bear. For it is infinite loneliness, loneliness that is never broken. And it's the weight of that loneliness that now presses down on Mandy as she lies in her bed, gazing vaguely out the window to the trees green in the morning sun, taking in the hum of the traffic, while the world goes on oblivious of what has happened.

There is a television above the bed. Whitlam appears for the midday news. But the volume has been turned down and, while his lips move, no sound emerges. What of it? Casual Mandy is no longer casual Mandy and will never be casual Mandy again. Not that she was ever casual Mandy in the first place. It was a way of being in the world that she just fell in with because Michael wanted it. But it was never her. It was him, it was them. The whole they-world she fell in with. But never again. Never again will she just fall in with what 'they' want. All is now changed. And it will never be the same again.

And while she is contemplating those six weeks or so of infinite loneliness, she is also recalling those moments at the market just after she'd broken up with Michael when the memory of the melon's scent, the exquisite kiss, stopped her where she stood. That night when she was also, more than she would usually be, aware of the presence of children, darting here and there, along aisles laden with fruit and vegetables and wedges of yellow cheese, aware more than she would usually be of the hands that held their hands and guided them through the crowd, for the world is big and they need a guiding hand while they grow into it. And, at the same time, she is contemplating the possibility that, in some unacknowledged part of her, she *did* know. And if she did, was that infinite loneliness of the baby broken after all? And did the baby know, in ways that only the infinitely young and wise can?

Whitlam disappears from the screen. As he will soon disappear from public life. Five years ago they danced in parks and lounge rooms with the chairs and tables pushed back and drank in restaurants to the mountain of Whitlam. Now the mountain is withdrawing, with the sound turned down.

And it is then that her housemates arrive. Her fellow hikers, those who carried her and walked her down the hill to the car and the ambulance that eventually brought her here. And she sits up and is suddenly in the midst of conversation. Having to talk, when all she wants to do is drift through space. But she can't. So she is saying things such as yes, she is well. Nothing wrong. She will be leaving tomorrow or the day after, and they tell her that they are happy to hear it and that it will be good to see her back home. And that the dog will be pleased too. And then she remembers, of course, the dog. And with the mention of the dog and the house and the yard, it seems that an image of a distant life and a distant self assembles around her. And she knows instantly, gazing at her friends, at their shining faces and familiar voices, that it *is* the past. A past life to which she will not return. It is one of those instant decisions from which, she knows, there is no going back. But she doesn't tell them, not yet. Just as overnight she has resolved not to tell them about the lost baby who came and went and of whom nobody knew. Or did she realise, after all, in some part of her that knew before her mind did? Perhaps. She has resolved not to tell anybody. Not them, not Michael. It is enough, now that *she* knows. She has resolved to keep it to herself. To keep it in her care, the lost life that came and went.

Her friends leave and, it seems, take her former life with them. Casual Mandy, who was never casual and will never be casual Mandy again. And who will never just fall in with what 'they' want ever again. And nobody will know of this life that flowered for six weeks or so. Not her friends. Not Michael. Had the baby lived, were it still alive, she would tell Michael, and she would hear what he said, and read in his eyes what he thought. But not now. She will keep it in her care, think of it from now on and forever as hers and hers alone, and visit it each day with flowers of care, this small, well-tended grave that is her secret.

* * *

She is contemplating the glow of the fresh vegetables at the back of the shop and wondering why it is that they lift her heart in ways that it has not been lifted lately. These greens, yellows and reds of the new season vegetables — the green luminous, the red shining as if the colour itself had only just been invented. And each year they return, all these fruits and vegetables, as if each new year were their first.

And it is not only the new season vegetables and fruits that lift her, it is the shop itself. Outside it is an unruly spring day. Wind, rain and sun. But inside, soft string music playing in the background, the shop is a retreat, a world unto itself. She discovered the shop in her undergraduate years and has been coming here since. Not just for the wonders it contains, but for the care with which everything is arranged. For it is an ordered world, everything in its place. A glimpse of how the world ought to be. Each item so carefully arranged that it is almost a travesty to select any one of them and thereby disturb the arrangement. But, slowly and carefully, she begins to fill her basket, noting as she does not only this lifting of the heart but the power of the shop to soothe.

She has been coming here for years, introduced the place to her friends, and to Michael. She is aware of the woman who owns the shop standing by the cash register, still and calm, like this little world she has created. And she knows the woman well enough to nod to and smile at, and the woman returns her nods and smiles in a way that says, I know you. And I have watched you change since you first came here. But their knowledge of each other has never gone beyond that. And Mandy likes it that way. For it is almost as though the spell that the shop casts would be broken should they become more familiar. The familiarity, she imagines, that takes things for granted.

And so she slowly fills her basket, vaguely aware of the shop owner patiently waiting at the front counter. And she also becomes aware of another presence in the shop. A shadow almost. Someone has entered the shop. It is raining outside. How long has it been raining? She continues, slowly and carefully, placing her selections in one of the baskets the shop supplies, her back to the shadow.

Mandy left the hospital over a week before, or was it more? She's not sure. She is not teaching (she has time off) and has lost track and has since left her home and found a new one. Amazing how quickly you can find a house when you really want to. So it was all very fast. Which was good. It kept the mind occupied. No time for thinking. And all for the best. For to go back to the old house was merely to go back to the old life. As if nothing had happened. But something had and has, and there is no old life to go back to. She now has a house to herself in the suburbs. And she is, for the time being, content with that.

And it is then, her selection complete, the basket filled, the shower outside passed, that she turns, and, vaguely aware of this other presence in the shop, moves to the front counter.

Then all is movement and disruption. And she is hurrying along the footpath, wet from the rain, and turning into a laneway so that she is no longer visible on the footpath and cannot be followed. She's not sure at what point the shadow turned into Michael, but she looked up from her basket and he was there. Her selection of vegetables was complete, the shower outside had passed, she moved to the front counter — and now she is hurrying along the laneway.

Did they speak? Probably not. What, after all, was there to say? We had this gift and we never knew. This gift was given to us. And now the gift is gone. And whoever 'we' were has gone with it. There is nothing to be done and nothing left to say. And do not take this, my sudden exit and my downcast eyes, as hurt. For I am now beyond hurt. Once, when casual Mandy became serious Mandy and realised she had been all along, she cried on the telephone for you. Just as she cried unheard tears all night for you. But now she cries for something gone that is neither her nor you, and of which she will not speak because the time for telling you has passed. What we cannot speak about we must pass over in silence. Your precious Mr Wittgenstein. And yes, I know what he really meant. I know all that and I don't care. I will read it my way. Once, there might have been cause to tell you; now all that's left is silence. A gift came and a gift went and nobody knew. And is that not a picture of infinite loneliness? To say any of the usual meaningless things would be a betrayal of everything that has happened. So you see, Michael, Mandy said nothing because nothing is better. Because when there is nothing left to say the only thing left is silence.

At the end of the laneway she turns and looks back, but there is no one there. No shadow pursuing her. Just the wind and the tumbling dark clouds above.

* * *

'She doesn't live here any more.'

Mandy's friend, with whom she shared the house until recently, is speaking on the telephone. Mandy is standing in the lounge room listening to the call, holding a few odds and ends she forgot in the move. It is a few hours after she encountered Michael at the shop, and she has come by to collect a reading lamp and a pair of blue jeans left on the clothes line — jeans she bought one Friday night with Michael in that world of Friday nights past when she was another Mandy.

'No,' her friend says, glancing at Mandy with a raised eyebrow, 'we don't know where.'

Mandy nods. Yes, that is the correct answer. You don't know where I am. I've gone. Disappeared into silence.

'No,' her friend continues, 'we don't have an address.'

Her friend listens a little longer, eyebrows rising and lowering as she listens. 'Yes,' she says, 'I'll pass that on.'

She pauses and listens. 'She didn't leave one.'

As the call continues it is clear to Mandy that it is becoming heated, and her friend's voice is rising with the heat. At one point she can even hear Michael's voice, harsh and loud.

'I don't. Nobody does. She was upset!' There is a short pause and her friend adds, '*Do* you?'

Then her friend says she is sorry, adds a thank you, and suddenly hangs up. She nods to Mandy as if to say, there, that is taken care of.

'Pass on what?' says Mandy.

'It doesn't matter,' her friend replies with knowing protectiveness.

No, Mandy thinks, it doesn't matter. She's right. It's too late for these things to matter. Too late for these things to ever matter again when once they meant so much. They belong to another time. A younger time. The time for such things has passed, and she notes that at some point over the last few weeks she has ceased to think of herself as young. No longer young in that way that you see no end of things and all that is new in the world (the latest music, the latest sayings, the latest fashions) comes to you first, and everybody else is either older or old. And there is infinite time for mistakes that the next day can redress, and you don't look upon someone else and inwardly remark upon their youth because *you* are youth. But a few weeks ago, watching a group of students meeting outside the university cafeteria before rushing off together in that unmistakeable way that tells you they are also setting out on the great adventure of life, she did exactly that — inwardly remarked upon their youth. They'll tell you it's a shadow line, the transition from being young to not being young any more. That it creeps up on you and, one day, you're not young. Or at least you don't think of yourself as young. And perhaps it does work like that — perhaps the realisation had been creeping up on her over time, unnoticed, and perhaps observing that group of students outside the cafeteria was simply the moment it pounced. Then again, perhaps it all happens in an instant. One moment you are young; the next you are not — and the line, however shadowy, is traversed in the blink of an eye.

What was it that Michael wanted passed on to her? She'll never know. It doesn't matter. The time when such things mattered has gone. Her friend is right. And as they part at the door, Mandy promises to ring the next day. As she says this she notes that there is concern in her friend's eyes. A concern that says, you've had a fall. And, by a fall, she means a lot more than a tumble from a rock.

* * *

Later that evening, sitting on the front porch in her new house, she is once again dwelling on that moment of movement and disruption that marked her exit from the shop — and the words that were never spoken and never will be. The yard, in this outer suburban house where no one would think of looking

217

for her, is large. An expansive lawn and fruit trees. And now a wide, clear, starry sky above. She sits in silence. This thing has come and gone and nobody knew. Only Mandy and a white-coated young doctor who, no doubt, has forgotten all about it by now. And so the knowledge of this short life is hers alone. She has made that life hers. And she now draws it to her and enfolds it. Calm as the Buddha. Calm as the lone figure in the desert. She cradles it in silence. Wise eyes, in all their six-week wisdom, stare back at her. Eyes that know infinity. And what it is to come and go, and for no one to know. And as she cradles it, she gazes out over the lawn and the street and the starry night. Rocking, ever so slightly, back and forth. Oh, good silence. True silence. Stay. Do not fail me. Do not fail me, for I will hold fast to thee and live in thy silence. For from thee, good and true silence, will come the words your Mandy longs to hear. For this mighty silence *will* break, that she trusts, but only after it has run its course, and the pure and true words Mandy longs to hear, new and cleansed by silence, will carry to her even into this world of infinite loneliness she has chosen to inhabit: You are beautiful, more beautiful than you know, have you never been told? And I will not harm you. Or hurt you. But love you. And when she hears those words she will know that the mighty silence has run its course and broken.

* * *

The following week her friend delivers a letter. It is from Michael, and Mandy sighs. And she sighs again when her

218

friend has gone and she can read the letter alone. It is a letter that expresses regret. A wrong has been done, and while it cannot be undone, it can, at least, be addressed. It is also a letter that expresses a desire to meet and a request that she ring — and includes his telephone number. As if she may have forgotten it. And the odd thing is that when she looks at the number she realises it has acquired a certain unfamiliarity. A number from the past, from the recent past, that she may well have forgotten had his letter not prompted her memory. She places the letter on a table (the house still has that sparsely furnished, recently occupied look, which she likes) and gazes out the window onto the garden.

Once upon a time she would have given anything and everything to receive such a letter. Now it doesn't matter. There is a story she read recently. A man finds a letter from his mistress stuffed into a book he happens to pick up in his study — the story is set in the previous century in a faraway country where they use such words as 'mistress' and 'lover', as apart from this milk bar world where no one does. After a year together this man has grown tired of his mistress and he reads this letter — which has been secretly stuffed into one of his favourite books so that he *might* find it — with inevitable weariness. She wishes to meet him at the garden shelter where they always meet. He closes the book, sealing in the letter, and realises that he will *have* to meet her, noting also the bothersome need of having to climb over a garden wall to get to the shelter. But when he arrives at the garden shelter that evening she is not there. And he waits until it is apparent that she will not come and then he returns to his room where he opens the book and re-reads the letter. And, as he reads it, noticing for the first time the faded white paper, he realises that it is an old letter. And he remembers instantly that he had been delirious with expectation when he first received it — this letter summoning him to her — and that, when he rushed to meet her that evening, he *leapt* that garden wall.

So, too, the letter from Michael. Once upon a time, she, too, had leapt that garden wall. Hadn't they all? Desire expressed as love, love expressed as desire, knows no impediment. And walls are for leaping. But not now. And whereas once she would have moved heaven and earth for just such a letter, she puts it aside, placing it on the lounge-room table. For not only has the time when such things mattered passed, so too has the time for sadness.

That was another Mandy. A younger Mandy. Not the Mandy who looked up from a newspaper one morning recently in a cafeteria, noted the glowing youth of a group of students on the footpath outside, and knew, in an instant, exactly what the observation meant.

So, it seems, love and youth have fled. The dog wanders in from the yard onto the porch to reassure itself, she likes to think, that she is all right. And why not? She's all the dog has. So where does love flee to? Does it withdraw to some place quiet, like this porch upon which she now sits, to think things over? To sit and think and marshal its powers so that it may fall upon you again some day or night when you least expect it, and visit you with words you have long waited to hear, but hold out only faint hope of hearing because you no longer think of yourself as young? And, in not being young, think of yourself as too old for love's adventures as well? But are words of love still out there, after all, just waiting to be spoken when this mighty silence she has chosen to inhabit breaks and when she least expects them, and from unexpected lips? Words born of silence, simple and new. You are beautiful. More beautiful than you know. Have you never been told? And I will not harm you. Or hurt you …

She walks back inside, the dog following her, keeping a good eye on her, and picks up Michael's letter from the lounge-room table. And, without re-reading it, she takes it to the kitchen and drops it into the bin. She will not reply. There is nothing to say. Love has fled. Fled to some silent place to mull things over and to marshal its powers.

* * *

A few weeks later, at the end of the month, her friend from the old house calls and says there is an election-night party at a mutual friend's house, casually mentioning, as an aside, that an old chum has come to stay in the room that was once hers. She hopes Mandy doesn't mind. She adds that she doesn't know why their friends are having a party. There will be nothing to celebrate. But they have all decided that the occasion should be marked. That the night their mountain withdraws from the landscape ought to be given due attention and acknowledged properly.

But Mandy is not sure about a party. She is withdrawn and would like to continue her withdrawal quietly. As, perhaps, would the mountain. If only he could. And so she says this but her friend presses her and Mandy relents with a 'maybe', delivered with the tone of a 'probably not'. And her friend, for the moment, is satisfied with this, choosing to interpret her maybe as a yes, and concludes the call by saying that she will see her then, that they all will, all her friends.

When Mandy hangs up the telephone she notes that there was care and concern in her friend's voice. And that it was an awareness of this concern that led her to relent with a 'maybe'. She also notes that it is fitting, that it is somehow right, that the election and the party come at the end of the year. As though everything that has happened over the last few months might also end with the year itself.

The house is silent. The dog is stretched out on the porch floor beside her, and the rich scent of flowers open to the moon and stars floats across the garden, from all the gardens, towards her. Summer is coming to the suburbs. Soon, fountains of water from garden sprinklers will shower lawns and children alike. And in the evenings, while she sits in this very spot with the dog at her feet, the smell of a suburb in summer, water on bitumen and concrete and lawn, will rise into the night air, along with orange moons, laughter, squeals and the revving of panel vans.

9. If Our Children Should Ever Ask …

The square is smaller than she imagined. On film it is large enough to drive a Cadillac onto, but she can't imagine where they'd park one now that she's here. Even the fountain itself looks smaller. But isn't that always the case? The further you are from something the grander it looks; the closer you get the smaller things become.

Rita is sitting at an outdoor table of a small restaurant on a square in Rome. A famous square. It is late evening and there are few people about, and the staff, no doubt, are anxious to pack up and go home, but she's travelled a long way to be here, bringing with her images of vast open squares and grand fountains, and so she stays on after she has finished, after the dishes have been cleared from the table, except for a half-glass of wine, which she toys with while looking out over the square and the jets of water springing from behind god-like statues.

Rita has given her group the slip, and she knows it won't be the last time. But she had to come here. She told herself from the first that she must. And so she sits alone at a table for two, studying the Trevi Fountain. This is almost the whole reason she's come to Rome. To sit at one of these little tables. And, even though it is cool, she insisted upon an outside table because that is the way she's always imagined it. Film and life, life and film. They never match, although she's probably been trying to match them all her life. Earlier in the day the square was jammed with tourists and she could barely see the fountain. Now, the square, apart from the occasional couple or group wandering on and off into the night like extras on a set, is all hers. And as much as she thinks she's arrived at the wrong fountain, that this can't be it and she's made a mistake, she knows this is it. Just as she knows that a little over twenty years before, three young American actresses parked a Cadillac in the square and made wishes by the fountain.

She saw the film in the local hall in the old suburb, the hall that converted into a picture theatre on Wednesday and Saturday nights. And she remembers walking home afterwards along the dirt streets and dirt footpaths (not really footpaths, just a path of trampled grass) of a suburb in the throes of being born, still hovering between a farming community and the suburb it would become: a mixture of weatherboard stick houses and old stone farmhouses. And, as much as Vic would never leave the country (and never did), she promised herself that she would go there someday, to those places where films shown in wooden halls took you, before she was too old, while wishes and promises still meant something. And so here she is. And she can still picture the Cadillac for she has seen the film since and the images have remained clear. And she can still see the three young women, the actresses (any one of whom she might have imagined herself being) standing just over there on that bright summer morning a little over twenty years before, tossing their coins into the fountain. And she can imagine the wishes they never spoke of.

Now the two worlds have finally converged — the world of small wooden community halls converting into picture theatres twice a week and bringing Roman fountains to the dirt streets and stick houses that would, one day, become a suburb, and that world of Roman fountains itself. And so it is not a moment to be given passing acknowledgement but one to be lingered over. A lifetime of dreaming has gone into this moment, and the restaurant staff, restless as they are, can wait a little longer. The single woman at the table for two has a communion to complete as sacred and as holy as any vow whispered in a church. Two worlds have converged. I told you I'd come and here I am. A promise is a promise. And her words fall upon the statues as do the fountain's endless showers. But you're not what I expected. I'm not disappointed; don't imagine that. No, you could never disappoint. You are the Trevi. I told myself that first night I saw you that I'd come, and I have.

The cool autumn air is turning cold and she shivers as she calls the waiter. She is almost finished. Almost. It is a moment to be lingered over and certain things must be done properly. And so when the waiter stops at her table, she takes a small camera from her bag, hands it to him and smiles, saying please. And he smiles back at her, for as much as she has delayed his departure from work, his heart goes out to this lady of a certain age who sits alone and has no one to take her photograph. No one to record the moment apart from a waiter whom she has never met before and will never meet again.

He steps back, holds the camera up, and Rita smiles. And she gives her smile everything, but she knows it's not enough. For it's a smile with the twinkle gone out of it, like

Vic's laugh in his later years, the boom still there but the life gone out of it. And she knows that when she finally sees the photograph that, as much as she gave her smile everything, her eyes will have that slightly lost, lonely look that the eyes of ladies of a certain age have, who sit alone at restaurant tables in foreign places. And, of course, she is the only one at the table and everyone who sees the photograph will conclude that the waiter, for the moment, obliged and doubled as her companion. And as much as she tried not to make it a lonely smile, she is sure it is. All the same, perhaps something of the accomplishment of the moment comes through too. That she kept her promise, and that she is here. And as much as she contemplates another shot, she knows that she gave that smile everything and that she hasn't got another one in her. Not right now.

The waiter hands back the camera and she pays the bill, then rises, and he helps her with her coat, for his heart goes out to the woman who sits alone and smiles bravely for the camera.

The waiter watches, happy his evening is finally over, as Rita walks across the square to the fountain, knowing exactly what she is about to do. Rita nods and waves her thanks to him as he disappears into the restaurant, then turns to the fountain, its water spurting and showers tumbling onto statues for her benefit alone, it seems. You are Trevi. I said I'd come, and I have. She then takes the coin from her wallet, a 1957 penny with a leaping kangaroo that she has kept for years just for this occasion. And as she stares at it she realises

226

she is about to lose it. There is an unexpected pang and she's puzzled because she's not sure just what that pang means. Did she never expect to be here, and did she never expect to part with it? But the moment demands that she does. And she will. And it's as she is about to throw it into the fountain that the ghostly voice of one of those young American actresses calls out to her — at once echoing round the makeshift wooden interior of that community hall that doubled as a picture theatre as well as all around the empty square in which she now stands. 'No, no,' this voice is saying urgently, imploringly, 'you have to turn around; throw the coin over your shoulder.'

And so, responding to that voice, Rita turns around, her back to the fountain. Then she holds the coin up, and not so much with a wish, but conscious of the whole ritual being an act of homage, she tosses the coin over her shoulder and waits, picturing the arc of its course, the kangaroo's final leap, then hears a tiny splash in the night. And, tiny as it is, it is once again the splash of life that she hears. And the image of a young woman and her dog diving into the icy waters of the bay returns to her. She walks closer to the fountain, contemplating the coins — golden, silver and copper — glittering at the bottom under the lights, wondering where hers might have landed. The only one of its type, now indistinguishable from all the others. Each coin a wish — apart from those coins, like her own, that were more an act of homage. You are Trevi. I said I'd come, and I have.

She wanders back to her hotel — up the incline, through the narrow streets that she imagines a Cadillac could only just pass along — the realisation slowly settling on her that although she came to the square alone, she has, nonetheless, made that table, the waiter, the photograph, the square and the fountain her own, in the same way that travelling couples find their own cafés and restaurants and return home pronouncing them 'theirs'.

* * *

They're not so bad. She could even get to like them. And they happily let her go her own way. Bank clerks, public servants, farmers and more. They've formed groups and each group is currently deciding where it will go during their free time the next day. They have their maps of the city and their guide books, and they are curious. And, although she goes her own way whenever she can, she could almost get to like them.

Rita is standing in the lobby of the hotel and the touring party she is travelling with is gathered at different tables. They nod and smile when she enters and she nods back. She is talking to the concierge because she wants to know what time it is at home. After some calculation, he tells her it is seven o'clock in the morning. Early. But, she decides, not too bad. It's a work day and Michael should be up and about anyway. Rita will be his alarm.

There is a line of telephone booths just off the lobby and the concierge directs Rita to one of them. It will be expensive; she cannot afford to take long, and so must choose her words carefully. And, as she dials, she resolves to speak like a talking telegram. But when Michael answers, she babbles. And she talks into the phone far more loudly than she really needs to, as though the telephone were just some toy and she really had to shout to be heard on the other side of the world. And after saying, 'It's me, I'm really here,' she adds: 'I've done it.'

Michael, sleepy and possibly grumpy, asks what? What has she done?

'Been to the Trevi Fountain.'

She has tossed her coin in and it now rests at the bottom of the fountain with all the others. The only penny among them. Until they clear the fountain out and the old coins, the old wishes, make way for the new. And, she adds, her voice carrying beyond the booth into the lobby, it was all so much smaller than she imagined. Or perhaps the fact that she imagined it so grand made it inevitably smaller. And, once again, she understands why armchair travellers stay in their armchairs. All the same, she wouldn't have missed it. And she then realises she's lost track of time and that every shared thought is expensive. She will have to hang up soon and her link with the only thing she has in the world will be broken. And, at the same time, she's recalling those days when she wouldn't let him out of her sight or her reach, when the hand that held his was hers, and the grip stayed tight while he was little and the world was big and he grew into it. Grew into it to the point that he eventually went out into the world alone, as he was always going to — and now she calls him from the other side of it. But the hand that held his will always be holding on, no matter the distance.

She will, she says, call from Florence, in a few days. They exchange goodbyes. Except they don't say goodbye. And when she's hung up and she's looking out over the lobby, at the groups now breaking up, she can't recall how they said it. Not goodbye. Nor farewell. Nothing final. Possibly a 'see you'. Something that implied they were separated by suburbs and minutes, rather than countries and days.

After the call she smiles to some of the group then takes the tiny lift up to her room, remarking to herself as the lift door closes that it was more likely to have been 'talk soon' rather than 'see you' that were their parting words.

You pay extra to have a room to yourself, and Rita has. And, whereas the old street would have taken that as a snub, the group with which she is travelling doesn't. She sits by the window. The room is small, and the view, onto a narrow street, is nothing special. But she stays there, sitting at the window, taking in the hanging baskets on the balconies, the rendering falling off the walls here and there, and the late sounds of the street itself: scooters, voices and, not far away, the imagined splash of a coin in a fountain.

* * *

She has traced the bus and rail routes so often that she almost feels as though she is travelling along a map rather than the real thing. For, sometimes, you can stare at a map for so long that you cease to think of these places as real. Just dots on a page. The bus winds down through the hills ... the bus winds down ... It has been a long journey along freeways, with detours to small towns, stops and traffic hold-ups, and she is tired. She stares out the window at the passing trees and fields and villages. Then, as they emerge from a tunnel of overhanging autumn branches, Florence is suddenly spread out beneath her. It *exists*! She smiles and sits up. And soon they are in the heart of it, watching their bags being unloaded into the hotel lobby and receiving their room keys.

After lunch a tour guide calls them together in the foyer and Rita, with the group, takes the short walk up a cobbled street to the Duomo. And again, as she steps out into the street and sees the famous dome in the near distance, she smiles to herself. It exists.

The summer holiday crowds have long gone from the streets and the area around the Duomo itself. She has a good view of the Baptistery and the Gates of Paradise. Her guide book tells her that these doors must be seen, and should be lingered over. And it even gives her a brief biography of the artist who made them. Ghiberti. She may or may not have heard the name before. Now she has, and she also knows that it took twenty-seven years of his life to make them.

She lingers in front of them, undisturbed by summer crowds. It's the least she can do. From time to time she looks back at the bell tower and the cathedral, glowing orange and white against a blue sky, and feels sorry for those armchair travellers who never leave their rooms. Then she looks back at the doors. Twenty-seven years. Almost the whole of somebody's working life. Time enough to fall in love, find a home, have children, and time enough for the children to grow and leave. Time enough to walk to your work through sunshine, rain and wind. Time enough to grow old and leave something behind — like these golden doors — that says, here, I did *this* with my time.

So she lingers because it's the least she can do. But it's not just some sense of duty. She feels like lingering in front of them. For the more she looks, the more she sees — the details and skill. And she knows about skill. And craft. She was trained as a milliner. She made, when she was young, hats of remarkable style and colour. All by hand, and all requiring the most extraordinary attention to detail. It was all in the detail. Get the details wrong and the hat was wrong. But hers never were. She always got the details right. So much so that clients came to that small shop in the Block Arcade and asked that the girl, not even eighteen years old, make their hats. So she knows what skill is and she knows it when she sees it. And she's seeing it right now, which is why she lingers.

Beside her and around her the members of the group are looking at these doors. And they're not just doing it because they feel they ought to. There is no sign of restlessness or boredom in the way they look. They, too, are drawn to the detail and the scale of the doors, four times the height of a human, glittering in the afternoon sun. Glittering now and glittering as they would have from the moment they were completed. And it's not hard to imagine locals viewing the doors for the first time and really feeling they were at the gates of paradise. And the look that must have been in their eyes, she imagines, is in the eyes of these bank clerks, tramway ticket collectors and housewives with whom she's travelling. Sheep. *Baaa*, she'd mouthed to Michael as she'd disappeared through the door of international travel. *Baaa*. Sheep. No, too easy. Too easy to laugh. For, at this moment, she's convinced they will take back with them memories of more than just their hotel rooms, their buffets and their smorgasbords. They will, she likes to imagine, go back larger than they left. No, it's too easy to laugh. Like the priest in a book she read before leaving. The priest is English, lives in Florence at the turn of the century, and occasionally takes small groups of English visitors on tours. Pitying them for their reliance on their Baedekers, he relates the story of an American family in Italy. 'Say, Poppa what did we see at Rome?' asks the child. 'Guess Rome was the place where we saw the yaller dog!' says the father. No, too easy. And as she looks from the doors to the group, she concedes once more that she could almost get to like some of them.

In time they all drift away from the doors, from those tales of Solomon and Moses and David depicted on them, and drift into the cathedral. Under the dome groups mingle with other groups, a swirling pattern of figures moving from one point of interest to another, commentaries merging with commentaries, and whispering waves of sound, like a thousand swallows, rising to the ceiling.

So, the afternoon passes. And afterwards they all walk back to their hotel where an afternoon tea is laid out for them. And although all of the talk is about the spread, how good the buffet lunches, teas and dinners are, and how they are so beautifully presented, there are also those moments when no one is talking. The silences in between. And a look in their eyes that suggests they may well be dwelling on those doors, that dome and that ceiling — a look that says they've *been* somewhere. Somewhere beyond the borders and confines of their everyday world, the knowledge of which they will take home with them. A look that says maybe, just maybe, they will return larger than they left. Why not? At least, Rita would like to think that. And even though they may not talk about it all that often (because it's not done to go sounding off about these things), it's just possible that the memory of this day will return to them in moments of silence, sitting alone in their lounge rooms and kitchens or watering the back garden on some still summer evening. The passionfruit vines along the fence will be golden, distant birds will wheel across the sky to nest, and the Gates of Paradise will glitter again for them.

* * *

There's this toff on the television. He's got a tweed tie, and a sort of reluctant smile on his face, and a toffy accent that — not that you can blame him for it — makes you want to turn off the television all the same. But she doesn't. She knows this toff, she's seen him on the television before. In the old house, in the old suburb. And, as much as you might have thought that Vic would have hated the toff, it was a constant source of curiosity to Rita that Vic actually liked him. Every week Vic and Michael would sit in the old lounge room and listen to the toff for the hour that he was on and then talk about the show afterwards. He could surprise you like that. Every week he'd sit and listen to what the toff had to say about art, civilisation and history because he was *interested*. They both were. But as much as Vic might have been interested, he would never have come to the places that the toff talked about. And why was that? He was, after all, interested. And it occurs to Rita that Vic was an armchair traveller. Liked to visit these places for an hour every week from the armchair in his lounge room, but would never have risen from it and taken that twelve-thousand-mile hike to the places the toff talked about and around which he walked as if they all — Paris, Florence, Rome — constituted some sort of vast open-air museum to which he had the keys.

No, he preferred things — golf club, pub, shops — to be within an easy stroll or a short train ride. And so, as much as she might envy those couples who travel together, she knows that if he were here she'd have that constant feeling of dragging him round from one gallery or museum to another like one of bloody Michelangelo's statues. No, he would never have come here, and just as well. But he liked the toff all the same.

Rita is sitting in her hotel room, afternoon sun coming in through the open window, staring at the screen. It's an English show on the television and it hasn't been dubbed, which is unusual. The Italian translation is at the bottom of

235

the screen. And, she notes, it's good to hear English, even if it is oh *so* English.

As much to relax as anything else, she's watching the toff on the television because she's discovering that you need moments like this when you're travelling. And he's talking about civilisation. In fact, he talks about it a lot. The word returns again and again: civilisation and being civilised. But she can't help but feel that he talks about it in a way that suggests he's got it, this business of being civilised, and you haven't. And that's why he's talking to you. And he's not talking to you because one day, if you listen hard enough, you might have it too. It's all a way, she's thinking, of putting you in your place. And that's the whole point of the toff talking to you. Of course, you can't just *put* people in their place. It's not done. At least, not by well-meaning toffs. You've got to say it all as if you're really trying to lift them *up* and *out* of their place — when, all the time, you're really putting them back in it.

But maybe it's just the toffy accent doing that. Maybe he really is trying to lift you up and lift you out. And maybe this is his way of doing it. He looks a decent sort, and she even likes the tie. No, it's good to hear English, and the more you listen the less you notice the voice.

Then the show's over and there's a plump, middle-aged Italian man with two young women in bikinis either side of him selling something or other, and she switches the television off.

Once again she's thankful for having paid the extra to have a room to herself. And she drifts across to her window

236

and looks down on her part of the street, content to watch the people pass, taking in that feeling of being here, on the other side of the world, while taking in the view.

Then she glances down at the itinerary open on the table beside her and notes the following day's activities. Not a big city. Unusual. A town just outside Florence. A fifty-minute bus ride. A typical Tuscan town, where they will spend the afternoon and the night. A taste of Tuscany, the brochure proclaims. Up there in the hills just beyond the city. A bus winds down through the hills … a bus winds down …

She leans from the window, the street below her, the prospect of the hills before her. And she feels a long way from the old suburb, the old street, from the old station and the old ticket office she walked through so often on the way home, showing her ticket to the ticket collector who hardly ever looked because he knew everybody so well anyway. And then she's thinking of Vic, the way she does every day, not a day passes … wondering just what he would have made of all this, if by some miracle she could have dragged him all the way here. But, of course, he wouldn't have made anything of it because he never would have risen from his chair and left the country in the first place. Not Vic. Then again, perhaps he just preferred to travel alone. To go alone, one of those who should never have married in the first place. Because, in the end, he *did* rise from that armchair, took trains across the Western Australian deserts by himself, went down mines, stood on top of giant red rocks — and when he'd finished with all that he travelled over a thousand miles north to that harbour town he moved to and from which he never returned. All without her. Better off alone. Perhaps. There's always a 'perhaps' when she thinks of Vic. As though after all those years, all the laughs and all the fights, she never really knew him at all or what plans he quietly hatched in that armchair of his.

She steps back from the view and lounges on the bed, letting the late-afternoon sounds drift in through the open window before going downstairs for dinner with the rest of the tour group, to a dinner of making conversation with strangers, and suddenly she misses Vic, the best of Vic. Is that possible, to imagine yourself well rid of someone one minute and miss him the next? Perhaps, she thinks, listening to a scooter pass by, it's just that flat time of day before evening that does this: that leaves you feeling flat too. The time of day that has travellers who go away and never come back wishing they'd never left home. She picks up a magazine from the table beside her, flicks through a few pages, and drops it on the floor. Huh! Then again, perhaps she's travelled all this way, over land and sea and through one time zone after another to that elsewhere she's dreamt of going to all her life, just to be bored.

She leans back on the pillow and closes her eyes. The street sounds below become muffled, even distant, as she drifts off. Thoughts of being well rid of Vic, missing him and travelling with the ghost of him; the strangers she's with (some of whom she could almost get to like); the Gates of Paradise and these long, long days of planes and buses and early breakfasts; the toff; scooters, wonder and boredom all jostle for a place until she doesn't know what she's thinking. The tiredness she didn't even know was there settles on her and her crowded mind shuts down and drifts into a deep afternoon sleep.

* * *

'This,' the Italian tour guide at the front of the bus is saying, 'is the house of Amerigo Vespucci. Who left from here to discover the New World in 1491. Who gave his name to the Americas. Amerigo. America. This is where he was born.'

Eyes, Rita's among them, turn to the door of the house in this hilltop town the tour bus takes them through. 'And that,' the tour guide adds, putting the microphone back to her lips, 'is the family crest above the door. The *vespa*. The wasp. The emblem of the Vespucci family.'

She puts down the microphone and gazes upon the door with, Rita imagines, a sort of tired wonder. The gaze of someone who has looked upon this door time and again over the years, with countless busloads of tourists, but who retains a touch of wonder each time. She also speaks, Rita can't help but think, with the kind of pride that says, *that*, that is what our towns and villages are like. You pass through and you think there's nothing there, but look again. Any one of them, that pride says, could be the birthplace of Amerigo Vespucci, da Vinci or Machiavelli. Our towns are like that.

And when they have paused long enough, when the eyes of the touring party have taken in the crested doorway long enough, the bus moves on, leaves the village behind and takes the narrow, winding road through the vineyards and down into the town below. A bus winds down through the hills. A bus winds down …

It is the only town they will stop in during the tour; all the rest are big cities. But, Rita notes, they have chosen well. It is a postcard town. The kind of town that people imagine when they think of this part of the world. Of these hills and valleys.

While everybody is waiting for their bags to be unloaded, Rita looks about the square, noting large colour posters on walls and noticeboards. Even a large drape hanging down from the hotel balcony. And all, it seems, saying the same thing: advertising a festival of some sort — an art festival — and they have landed in the middle of it. There are, she learns later, tents in the park, and galleries here and there, filled with the works of artists from all over Italy — and elsewhere. And as she stares at the posters, she scans a list of names. Mostly Italian, and none of which mean a thing to her — except for one. Not Italian, but English. For some reason, it is familiar. But she can't understand why. There's no reason. And she's puzzled for a moment before she picks up her bag and walks into the hotel — then forgets all about it.

* * *

It is late in the afternoon, or early evening. She can't decide. And while yesterday this time of day felt flat, today it doesn't.

Rita is sitting in one of the small cafés on the main square, watching the changing colours in the sky and on the walls of the buildings as the sun sinks — and watching the people, some from her group who wave as they pass, as well as those who have come for the festival. But the locals are out too. It's that time of day, she's noted during the trip, when they gather in squares and cafés for their drinks. There's a word they have for their drinks, but she's forgotten it for the time being. It's that time of day when, she imagines, the square is at its busiest and everybody mingles.

And at the same time that she's observing all of this she's wondering again what Vic would have made of it. But as much as she tries to imagine him sitting on the other side of the table, she can't. Or, if she can, she can only see him with that sour look on his face (that sour look that so often turned to a sneer), the sour look that always said, why have you gone and dragged me here? I never wanted to come. I said it often enough. But I came. And here I am. Dragged here. Are you happy?

No, she's better off alone. She's also beginning to realise that she could have been here years before. When she was younger and everything would have been different. And when she sees the young girls travelling round with nothing much more than their backpacks, she envies them. What it must be to be young and see these places for the first time. To have the memory of seeing these places with only a backpack over your shoulder, then bringing that memory with you as you grew and returned; your pack, with age, becoming a suitcase. What it must be to have familiar places made different each time you see them because you would always be that much older and different every time you returned.

She reminds herself that nobody travelled then because nobody had the money. At the same time the nagging thought that she could have been here years before, but didn't travel because Vic wouldn't, won't go away. How much of their life worked like that? How often did she not do something because he wouldn't, and she couldn't bring herself to do it alone? And why? Because she always thought in terms of 'him', and, when Michael came along, 'them'. Not her. Because to think of herself would have been selfish. Not that Vic would say that — *she* would. She was, throughout those years, always ready to pass judgement on herself. And did. For as long as she can remember it was always 'us' and 'them' but never 'me'. 'Us' and 'them' were good. 'Me' was bad. And even when he was gone, when he'd left and gone up north, it didn't change. Even when he died it didn't change. For the habits of a lifetime don't change just like that. And as much as she might, even now, tell herself that she was only ever happy living the life of 'us' and 'them', she's also asking what might have become of those parts of her that never fitted in with the 'us' and 'them', and which never had a life.

Suddenly she's tired of dragging Vic around with her. And she never imagined she'd think or say that, but there you are. She is. She's said it. If only to herself. Thirty years. It's a lot of years, a lot of living to throw off. Even if it's only the memory of him (and why only the bad memories at that, most of the time?), she's tired of dragging him around. And she's also beginning to wonder if, throughout those thirty good, bad and nothing much years, they might have only ever been in love for a short time, after all. How do you measure that?

She rises from the table and begins wandering around the square: the wine shops, the grocers and gift shops. Eventually, and after great hesitation because she's still wary of stepping into these tiny shops in case somebody speaks to her, she goes into a stationer's. She is drawn to the writing pads and envelopes, to the rich, decorative writing paper of this area. Something out of another time. Little works of art. The way these people attend to the small, the little everyday things that are so easily overlooked because they're just little and everyday — she likes that.

Outside in the late sun she decides to write a letter. But who to? This is the problem with buying writing paper. It is meant to be written on, not just looked at. But that means having someone to write to. Her few friends (and she's never been good at making friends) don't even know she's away. So she determines to write to Michael and returns to the café she just left.

At first when she sits she is thinking only of what to write. Then, gradually, she becomes aware of a conversation at a table nearby. And only because the conversation is being conducted in English. Not Italians speaking English. No, they are English speakers, but where from? And then she realises they are Australians. The accent is there, but only slightly.

You have to be listening, and she is. And she is content simply to listen. She has no great desire to seek out her fellow countrymen; there will be enough of them when she returns. So she plunges into the letter, noticing as she does that the sun is sinking behind the green hills around the town and that the air is turning cool.

At some point, and she's not sure how long she has been writing, she looks up and notes that the two men are still there, and they look like they've been there for a long time. Talking, she concludes, the way old friends talk. Old friends who haven't caught up for a long time. She stares at the man facing her, his hair parted and combed back in that forties matinee style. The way Vic combed his hair. For they are of the same generation, Vic and this man. And it is while she is staring at him, deciding that it is a handsome face in that ageing matinee style (the hair longer to accommodate the times), that she realises with a jolt that she knows that face. Not the man himself but the face. How can that be? She is sitting in the main square of a small town in Italy. One table removed from where she sits, two men are talking in faint but distinct Australian accents. And she knows one of them. How can that be? And it is while she is contemplating that puzzle that the name from that list of artists at the festival comes back to her, the English-looking name that stood out and seemed oddly familiar. And then she puts the two together, the face and the name, and she suddenly realises why she knows him.

Just before leaving — and it feels like ages ago now — she went to an art exhibition. Not that she goes to exhibitions all that much. Only from time to time, and usually when they bring images of faraway gardens and shuttered houses. But this was an exhibition of an Australian painter's work. A famous one. At home and abroad. Introduced to the wide world, although Rita doesn't know this, by the very toff she was watching on the television the day before. He is one of those who left and never came back because fame found him. But she didn't go to see his paintings that midweek day before she left because he was famous. Or because he was Australian. Or for any of the usual reasons. No, she went because of one painting in particular. Years before, when she and Vic and the weight that would become Michael all lived in a small, industrial dockside suburb, this painter, who sits only one table removed from her right now, painted Vic's aunt. And, for the moment, Rita is both seated at this café table and simultaneously seated in the kitchen of that long ago timber cottage as Vic's aunt Katherine burst through the door complaining of a cheeky young man with a paintbrush.

How do these things happen? Something takes place thirty years ago, lives brush up against each other then go their separate ways until something brings them back together again. A bus winds down through the hills to a town below it. Two men sit at a café table in a town square, talking of old times late in the day. The bus parks, a woman steps onto the square … Like the opening of a story: but it's not a story, it's life. Except that's the funny thing about life. Sometimes it's more like a story than stories. What is that phrase? You wouldn't read about it. And perhaps you wouldn't.

But, all the same, here's this painter from just a few weeks before and all those years ago, sitting facing her, one table removed from her. The cheeky young man who disturbed Katherine all those years before. Aunt Katherine, with her wild, white hair, who lived in a tent on the land that became theirs and who always frightened her. For that is the way she always seems in recollection. Like a force of nature. Katherine, who died in her tent on the land that became theirs; Katherine, who died in that tent but continued to shake her fist at the world after death in art galleries like the one Rita visited just before leaving to come here — to sit at a table, to write a letter to Michael, to pause, to look up and see, seated one table removed from her, the faded matinee figure who was once that cheeky young man. No, you wouldn't read about it.

So what does she do? Her impulse is to leave it at that. To silently acknowledge the coincidence, finish her letter, and leave the two men to their conversation. All the same, life has gone to a lot of trouble to bring them together again. And it seems to her that if life can go to all that trouble then she really ought to acknowledge the moment with something other than silence. And so, in deference to life's efforts (for it seems to her that something with the intricacy of a clockwork mechanism has been set in motion), she puts her letter aside, places the carefully selected paper and envelopes back in her bag, and rises from the table. And, without knowing just what to say when she gets there, Rita approaches their table as the two men look up.

'You're Australian!' she bursts out, and feels as though the whole square heard and is listening. The man with the grey goatee beard looks away across the square, as if dismissing her from his vision as he would also dismiss her from his presence, and the other one stares back at her, his expression one of resignation to what may follow. As if having been in this situation many times before, such is the burden of having a famous face.

'Mind you, I had to listen. You're good …' she adds, as if commenting on a fine forgery.

There is a long silence and Rita looks at the painter with the ageing matinee look, clearly bored and annoyed, and wishes she hadn't bothered.

'We've met,' she continues, but mechanically, her heart no longer in it.

He leans forward, studying her face, as if she were a model and he were about to paint her, then leans back, silent and puzzled.

'More or less. Well, not really …'

She is the only one speaking. They haven't said a word and clearly have no desire to. They're just staring at her, waiting for her to go on, so she can finish and they can be rid of her.

'You painted Katherine.'

And it occurs to her that she should really explain who Katherine was, but who cares?

'She lived in a tent. There was a big picture in the paper. Very embarrassing, well … *she* thought so. You probably don't remember.'

It is then that the painter stares at Rita as if seeing her for the first time and speaks to her with a sort of puzzled wonder.

'Of course I do.'

Rita half-smiles.

'Of course. Nobody forgets Katherine. And it wasn't just the tent.'

The other man with the grey goatee, who has either been staring vacantly out over the square, wishing her away, or looking at her with a bored, blank expression until now, breaks in.

'You knew her?'

Rita nods.

She could go on and tell them she was Vic's aunt and all the rest of it. But she can't be bothered. It was a big mistake. And it is while she is thinking this that she looks across the square and sees some of her touring party — those that she's decided she likes right enough — and notes, in that instant, that she's never been so pleased to see them.

'Oh,' she says, relief in her voice, 'I've got to go.' But she quickly turns to the painter and adds, 'You met her, did you? We were never sure. Katherine told tales.'

And the painter, suddenly animated, nods.

'Yes. Of course. Twice.'

'So you didn't just paint the photograph in the paper?'

'No.'

He then stands and invites her to sit at the table, pointing to a vacant chair.

248

'Please, join us. Sit down.'

She shakes her head.

'Sorry'.

'Must you go?'

She nods. All she wants to do is go. Michael was right not to speak to this painter when he had the chance, for he has told her about attending the same exhibition, seeing this painter talking to the leaning tower of Whitlam, and deciding whether or not to speak to him about Katherine — and eventually deciding not to. Yes, he was right. These things are best left alone. And just as she is about to leave, she glances at her group, now waving to her, and turns again to the painter.

'She died in that tent. She was there for three days. An old farmer found her.' She pauses, now confident, knowing she is leaving. 'Vic, my husband, she was his aunt. He grew up with her. He always said you got her in one go.'

The members of her touring party are now calling and she waves back. After all, they're more her people than these two.

'Sorry to bother you,' she adds upon leaving.

'But, you haven't …'

As she walks away she doesn't look back at the two men because she's had enough of their staring faces. But, if she did, she'd see the painter with the ageing matinee look staring, eyes wide, face almost blank, following her retreating form as she joins her group, his hand still gesturing towards the vacant chair, the offer to join them, although sadly declined, still open.

Rita joins her travelling companions, disappears into the twilit square (the green hills surrounding the town now black), and the two men resume their places. Life went to a lot of trouble to bring them together, but Life, Rita muses, strolling along the now chilly colonnade of the square, needn't have bothered.

* * *

What did they make of her? And what does it matter? The next morning she's back on the bus, winding through green hills stitched with grapevines. Every view a postcard. Not quite real. But all she can think of at the moment is what the painter and his friend thought of her. And she's put in mind of the toff on the television. Did they see her the way the toff would? Probably.

They pass through little towns like the one they've just left, Rita still dwelling on the previous evening and wishing she'd never approached them. And it is while she is brooding (for, like Vic, she is a good brooder), that she suddenly realises the woman beside her is speaking. Happy to be distracted, she turns to her and listens.

It's the hanging baskets she's talking about. The baskets hanging from the flats and houses of the town through which they're passing. And while Rita is happy to be distracted, she's also in no mood to be discussing hanging baskets. Why are they so bright, so colourful? this woman is asking. And she's not asking Rita in particular, or anybody

250

else, for that matter — she's just struck by the brightness of the flowers. Like the greenness of the hills. Why is that? Or does it just look that way because everything's so new to her?

The woman's name is Nellie. Not a name you hear all that much these days. Not many Nellies left in the world. But they'll come back, and the Nellies of the world will be new again. Rita has spoken to this woman before and has learnt something of her. Her children have all grown and gone. Her husband left the world all too young. The children are gone and she's all she's got now. Suddenly, she'd said to Rita, you realise you're on your own. Rita now learns she's a florist. With a little shop. Nothing much, but it does nicely. So she notices flowers. People like flowers, she says. They like to bring them into their houses. Something to marvel at. People need that. Takes them out of themselves. So they buy flowers because you can't wrap up a rainbow and take it home.

The woman falls silent and turns her gaze back on the view. Did she recongnise a fellow brooder in Rita? And was she speaking to Rita because she was trying to take her out of herself with talk of hanging baskets?

As the bus winds down the hill into the outskirts of Florence, the city itself spread out beneath them, the great orange dome in the distance, Rita eyes the woman briefly, her gaze now fixed on the city below, as if it were one vast vase of marvellous things. And, for that moment, Rita is conscious of looking at things through somebody else's eyes and asks herself if we all see different worlds: to Rita it is a cause of wonder that Florence exists; to the bus driver it is a place of congested traffic before he hits the open freeway; and to Nellie it is a vast vase of marvellous things.

A bus winds down through the hills. A bus winds down. The people inside the bus look out; the people outside the bus look in. What do they see?

From Florence the bus turns north to Venice. Morning gives way to afternoon, the sky clouds over and soon the whole bus seems to be sleeping, and Rita leans back and enters that dreamy half-sleep of the afternoon doze, as if in her armchair at home. An armchair traveller, after all.

* * *

What is it about this place? So far away, but so familiar. What is it? Rita is standing on the footpath at the front of her hotel contemplating the familiarity of this place that's not Venice, but … what do they call it? Mestre. They will go into Venice in the morning, but tonight, and the following night, they're stuck here. Out on the edges. Grey apartments. No hanging baskets brimming with life here. The sun is gone but it's still light enough to see. Dusk. And getting darker by the second. For the moment, though, she has a good view of the apartments around her and the street upon which they sit. People are living here, but these apartments have the look of places that nobody really wants to be living in. Not if they could choose. No hanging baskets, no postcard views — just the everyday life behind the postcards. And, once again, she's dwelling on why it should not so much look familiar, as *feel* familiar.

And she doesn't know how long she stands there. Long enough for it to become dark. However long that took. But still, the question persists. Why? Why so familiar? And she's not sure she even wants to know, for there's a sense of dread that comes with the question. That the answer to the question contains something menacing. Not something she can put her finger on, but there all the same; the sense of something out there she'd rather not remember, rolling in with the darkness. But what? And it is then that a child, five or six years old, emerges from the shadows, smiling, eyes wide, arms outstretched, with a handful of crushed butterflies, saying, 'Here, Mum, for you'; then that she sees, and she doesn't want to, her hand reach out in the night and slap the butterflies from the child's hand; then that she watches the crushed wings fall to the ground, sees the smile vanish from the boy's face and once again hears her voice, coming back through the years, its clarity undiminished, demanding to know of the child where the *hell* he has been, screaming that it is dark, couldn't he see, telling him that he's been gone for hours, and that she's been worried sick all the time and why, *why* didn't he realise … and it is then that she sees the frame of her 23-year-old self fall to its knees on the dirt footpath of that dusty frontier suburb and kiss the hand from which she had slapped butterflies, a mess of tears and anger and shame, and afraid to look in the boy's eyes in case he sees the shame in hers.

And it is then that she knows exactly where she is. These frontier places that nobody really wants to live in —

wherever they may be — have that in common, the look that tells you nobody really wants to be here. At least, that's how it looks to Rita, who knows that look because she gazed upon it for years.

Yes, that's where she is. Travel the world and your world travels with you. A bus drops you on the outskirts of a famous place. You step outside as darkness falls on the streets, and straight away everything is eerily familiar. But why? Then a child emerges from the shadows with a handful of crushed butterflies, and the dusty streets, the vacant paddocks, the thistle and the stick houses of that suburb she fought against with all her strength for all those years assemble around the child and she's plunged back into it again.

How is it that the image of the five-year-old Michael comes back with such clarity? And how is it that the dirty, dusty street follows her here? And not just follows her, but pushes in and takes over. Re-assembles all around her. How is it that Vic, with that silly don't-want-to-be-here, never-wanted-to-be-here-in-the-first-place look on his face, has been striding along beside her or following just behind her all through the tour? With that walk that he took everywhere, as if striding into an imaginary wind, a winter walk in summer. The sort of walk you acquire in hard times and never lose. How is it that he's still there? Just as he was. And how is it that the very place she fought against all those years ago is back again, all around her, right now?

Is there ever any end to it? Does it ever let go? Or does it keep you forever in its thrall? And the 'you' that existed then — the you that gave everything she had to that one glorious shot at living that never came up to what it could have been and was never going to — does that 'you', the you that gave and gave and gave until there was nothing left to give, ever step aside, its job done, and let another 'you' have a go?

All her life it's been like this — this giving that becomes a point of pride. All her life has been like this — lived for other people, other people's lives, as if her own were unimportant. Almost irrelevant. As if there were always some greater good to which she readily deferred. A giving that became, in the end, a way of living. No frivolous thoughts, no trams of one's fancy back then. Just this greater good to which she readily deferred and which defined her life. Moulded her. To the point that she can stand here in a foreign street, on the other side of the world years afterwards, and it can still claim her.

But it's while she's turning all this over, the street now dark, the apartments now shadows and outlines, that it suddenly occurs to her that it's *she*, Rita, who not so much allows it to claim her but who keeps dragging it all back. As if the very thing that she fought against all those years she really needed all along. Or grew to need to the point that she misses it. And now that it's gone she misses her pain and calls to it, calls it back, at the same time that she is desperately trying to wave it goodbye.

It is, she imagines, a sort of tug-of-war. Like, and she frowns faintly in the darkness at the front of her hotel, one of those life-and-death struggles. For it is, this tug-of-war between then and now, a life-and-death tussle. And she knows she can't go on calling it all back again and again and blaming it for being with her again and again. When it's not *it*, it's *her*. Let go, let go. Do a little something for yourself. For the 'you' who was denied all those years. And isn't that what she was doing when she jumped upon the tram of her fancy?

For in all those years of giving, the idea of doing something for yourself, and for yourself only — no 'us' or 'them' — became forbidden. Even unthinkable. But now she must do a little something more for herself. Something more than just jumping on the trams of her fancy. She must let it all go and stop calling it back and, finally, become the 'you' that she never allowed a life, whoever that 'you' might be.

And it occurs to her that most of those on the bus are women, and most of them about Rita's age, all possibly doing a little something for themselves — the lifetime of day-to-day struggle in all of them remaining unspoken. For whenever it is spoken it comes out all wrong and sounds sort of laughable: we sacrificed ourselves, we scraped by, we did this all for you, and so on. So the loss and the struggle remain unspoken. Of course. Is that not always the way? A life of giving and giving until there is nothing left to give never makes a fuss. The low, rumbling moan of a ship entering the port rolls in with the darkness. Once, twice, but Rita barely hears. Let our children know, she silently intones, shivering in the salty cold and speaking, if only to herself, that which is not spoken. Let them know, let them all know, that we tried. In our way.

That we grew older for them, that they might not grow old. That we lived the wrong life for them, that they might live the right one. That we suffered for them, even before they were born, that they might not. And if we snapped and shouted and slapped their love away or brought damage down upon them, it was not for want of trying not to. For we tried, in our way. We tried. And if they should ever ask, let them know.

She looks about her, at the flats, factories and smoking chimneys not far off, still shivering in the salty cold. How do you tell those two artists in the town that? And what did they think of her? Not, she reminds herself, that it matters. She concludes, though, that they'd see her as being just like all the other little people they left behind when they left the country and never returned, except perhaps on visits — a bit, she sniffs, like catching up with your mother on Sundays. Yes, they'd see her the same way they see all the others. Square little people in their square little houses, square lawns and square lives. Little people who live and die and never really live at all, with their silly phrases, what do they call them? ... homilies ... like 'doing a little something for yourself', that pass for life's acquired wisdom. Not people but types. The types that they make jokes about on television, or put in books or on the stage, the types that everybody laughs at. Or that become paintings put up on the walls of public galleries so that everyone can come along and gawk. And it's *not* you; it's the way *they* saw you. And that's just it. Once they've pinned you to the wall and caught you the way they wanted you to be caught — once you're there and helpless and pinned up on the wall the way they saw you — *that* is what you become. It's a sort of theft. They steal your life, and all our lives, these people. They're always stealing you, taking what you were and turning you into something else — painting pictures of mad old women living in tents on the edge of the world who were never mad at all. Not mad, just having a shot at living. At getting something out of life while it's still there to be got. But they're always stealing you, and once you've been stolen, that's what you become. That's how everybody eventually comes to see you: a mad old woman in a tent, an annoying intruder at a café table, a busload of sheep going *baaa, baaa* at the passing towns, and a silly housewife who comes all the way to the Tuscan hills and remembers them only for the hanging baskets and completely misses the majesty of the Gates of Paradise. Only, she didn't.

But when they pin you up on a wall or put you on a stage with a tea-pot and some flying ducks in the background, the possibility that there just might be a bit more to it all than that will be washed away by the laughter. And before long you're laughing too. Not that there's anything wrong with laughing at yourself — but in laughing along, you're agreeing with them just a bit. Aren't you? Saying, yes, that's me and that's them — when, all the time there's more to you and more to them than that. And when you laugh at yourself the way *they* see you, you're also laughing away those other parts of you that never get into the picture, because all anybody can see is the you up there on the stage with the flying ducks.

Yes, that's how the two artists saw her. One of those quaint little people from the land of lounge-room feature walls, shadow boxes and ornamental boomerangs, and no hint of her struggle against that dirty, dusty street where dogs howled like something out of the Middle Ages, and no sense of the struggle to create something as simple as a white house with French windows and long curtains in the midst of it all — a house, white, and lighting up well in the night, shining like a touch of civilisation (because the toff's not the only one who knows about that). And no hint of being hounded by the very thing you struggled against all through those desperate years when you lived the wrong life so that your children might not, nor of the emptiness that follows when everybody's gone and the house is deserted. Nor of the question, what now? No hint of any of that at all, just a silly housewife on a stage with her tea-pot and her flying ducks on the wall behind her and everybody laughing.

When, all the time, there was a life inside that laughing-stock figure — and a thousand *more* lives inside her just waiting to be lived. And Rita knows, standing on the now dark footpath of this suburban edge of Venice, that it's time to start living one of those thousand lives. Step out of the painting, step off the stage, and live one or two of those thousand lives that exist out there beyond the frame and outside the walls of the theatre itself. Time to step free of the shadows of that place that she called home and struggled against and that follows her wherever she goes, and which she summons up without thinking. Like a sickness she can't shake because she doesn't want to. Time to say goodbye to it all. For, as much as she struggled against it, she held onto it. All those years. Time to let go. Time to let be.

She's shivering and can smell the sea out there, towards the end of the street. And beyond the red-and-white smoking chimneys, she can see a cruise ship, lit up in the night, coming in to dock. And the blinking lights that guide it in. And as she's staring at the spectacle of the cruise ship and the lights and smelling the sea out there, a child suddenly emerges from the shadows, eyes wide, arm outstretched, with a handful of crushed butterflies, saying, 'Here, Mum, for you.' Time to let go … Let go … And maybe, she tells herself, just maybe, one day when she finally has, when she has let go for long enough, the child's palm will open out, the butterflies will take flight, and the air will be alive with a thousand fluttering wings.

* * *

At the beginning of her trip time moved slowly, everything was new and had to be lingered over; a shop window here, a famous monument that she had only ever seen in a film or photographs there. Now, a two-day stay in Venice done, time has begun to speed up: the days are shorter, the moments have lost that something that made everything special. One city gives way to another — Vienna, Zurich and now Paris. Except this is not the Paris of her imagination — of story-books and pictures. They're out in the sticks again where the bus left them, and a number of the party are demanding their money back. Some are shouting at the tour guide; somebody is crying. And Rita can't help but think that these members of the tour are like little children, who are just over-tired and need an afternoon sleep. They've been like this for days now. And, Rita has noticed, it doesn't take much to set them off — like little children, tired and ready for home.

She exchanges glances with Nellie on the other side of the hotel foyer. She's never had much to do with these members of the party, kept her distance. Just as well. And knowing that there is more to them than this, she, nonetheless, offers a silent *baaa* to the absent Michael and one more silent *baaa* again. It's almost funny. Like the end of a party that's gone on too long. They're tired and ready for home.

This is how these things end. In a hotel foyer that could be anywhere, but which just happens to be in Paris, although you wouldn't know it because they're out in the suburbs that could be any city's suburbs, with a giant freeway running out to the airport beside their hotel. Suitcases, coats and shopping bags are all over the foyer and against the walls. And there's shouting and tears before bed-time. It's almost funny.

And then, when the shouting dies down and the tears subside and the protestors have been given their rooms, the tour guide joins Rita and sits beside her, and lights up a cigarette. 'Who'd do this?' she says, expelling a cloud of smoke with the question. And Rita smiles, for, as well as

Nellie, she has come to know the tour guide a little. And so she smiles when the guide poses the question to her, but in a tone that suggests it's for anybody else who wants to hear. But Rita is no sooner smiling than she's contemplating the idea. Then dismissing it, then contemplating it again. The idea, never having entered her head until the tour guide blew the question out into the hotel foyer along with her cigarette smoke. There are, the tour guide adds, always five or six like them. You get used to them. Besides, we've had some fun, haven't we? Then she takes another drag on her cigarette. She's younger than Rita, but not by much. She worked in a bank before she decided there was more to life than standing at a counter all day saying, 'Next, please.' And, if you weren't careful, you could spend *all* your days like that. So she took a plunge, and it's got its moments, like the cry-babies who wanted their money back, but it takes you out into the world beyond the counter.

And with the word 'plunge', Rita is suddenly seeing that young woman diving into the icy waters of the bay. Once again hearing the splash as she plunged into the sea. And, once again, imagining that what she was witnessing was the splash of life. Like those moments when an animal suddenly has to run. And keep running. All life, no thought. Until something in the animal has run its course. Sometimes you have to plunge if you want to live. And, once again, she's contemplating the tour guide's question.

* * *

During the last days of the tour, in between climbing the Eiffel Tower and riding a tourist boat down the Seine, Rita has more time to talk to the tour guide. Time to ask all the questions she imagines she needs to ask. And on the very last day the guide gives Rita her card and her number. And it is agreed they will talk more. She also tells Rita that, of course, she could do it. She's organised herself for most of the tour, hasn't she? Why not the others? And it's not so bad, it's just that there are always five or six cry-babies.

And on that last night, alone in her room, vaguely watching French television after a dinner at a 'typical' French restaurant, Rita has time to look back over the trip and recognise that they have been twenty-one of the kinds of days that aren't the usual ones. Each day with a story, even those that sped by and didn't seem all that special were: it's just that she didn't notice the special things at the time — a bit like life. And she realises, with that thought, that along the way she has gathered traveller's tales, after all. And she knows already that Michael will particularly enjoy the tale of those last days — the tears before bed-time and those over-tired little children who were missing their sleep. As well as Nellie, who gazed upon the flowers of Provence with the eye of a van Gogh.

She breathes them in, these last hours of the tour. And as much as she pictures herself returning to that life of quiet suburban streets and trams and standing at a counter of the department store all day asking if anybody needs help, something has happened to change the picture. Nothing grand, but something, all the same. A modest picture of a modest life modestly shifts. Nothing grand, but a shift all the same. And the Rita who always gave, who defined herself in a lifetime of giving, and who denied any number of those thousand other lives that we lose in living, feels that shift, as modest as it may be, and for the first time since leaving home, the inevitability of returning to her job when she returns to Melbourne is not so inevitable. She steers her thoughts towards home, remembering those ships that she spent all day watching, coming into the bay from out there on the other side of the horizon before going back again. And the image of Rita, sitting on her bench at the beach, observing it all, comes back with the memory: framed, like a painting. A modest picture of a modest life shifts, and in the corner of that picture, a young woman plunges into the icy waters of the bay and her splash carries to the shore and beyond and echoes around the room in which Rita now sits, taking in the last hours of the tour.

10. Art II

Two men sit at a restaurant table in the town square. Above them, in the green hills that surround them, a bus winds down a narrow road that leads into the town. The sun is low, the sky glows orange and yellow, and the shadows are long across the wide, open square. Those who live in the town and those who are visiting wander along the colonnades that border the square looking for a place to stop and eat. The

264

green hills turn to ochre, a bus winds down a narrow road, two men sit at a table.

Art and Sam have talked for more than an hour, mostly about old times — the people they knew and that city that they couldn't wait to be shot of. And, during that time, the sun has slipped behind one of the hills above the town, the sky has turned purple and yellow, and the bus that was winding down through the hills has deposited its passengers and their luggage at the hotel opposite them in the square.

They finish their drinks, they order more drinks. Talk of old times gives way to talk of what they are doing now. And there is, for Art, a surprising ease to it all. And what might have been an awkward occasion is becoming an enjoyable, even rewarding, one. To the degree that he forgets about the square, the larger than usual crowds for this time of year and the festival itself. He is vaguely aware of acquaintances passing by and aware of them waving and of waving back. But all the while, Art and his old friend (and he is now thinking of him as an old friend, as apart from the distant one he was when he was walking down into the town) are talking about their work and what they are doing now, not what they did thirty years ago.

And the more they talk, the more oblivious they become of their surroundings, and all those people out there. Then Art becomes dimly aware of a presence. A figure hovering nearby. The feeling of being watched, at first a fleeting one, becomes insistent. And it is just when Sam finishes what he is saying that Art looks round in the direction of this hovering figure and sees a middle-aged woman step up to their table.

She doesn't greet them and she doesn't introduce herself; she simply exclaims: 'You're Australian!'

And Art's heart sinks and he notices that Sam instinctively looks away. The conversation and all those matters of work and art have been interrupted. And, what is more, there is a distinct sense of intrusion. And presumption. As if merely being from the same country is sufficient reason to intrude upon somebody else's time and talk. And privacy. And, with no desire to prolong this moment, they both tacitly resolve to say nothing. For in saying nothing they cannot possibly add to the conversation, it will quickly end and they can get back to where they were. And so they let her talk, and stare dumbly either across the square or back at her, clearly waiting for her to finish.

She has, Art imagines, a familiar look. A look that carries with it what he can only call a sort of insularity. The very thing they strove to get away from all those years ago. And she seems to be travelling in some sort of package tour, for her companions are waving from across the square and she waves back. And it is then that she looks at Sam and announces that they've met, and Sam turns his gaze back from the square and examines her face with no sign of recognition. They met, she adds, more or less. Well, not really. And the two men now look impatient, for there seems to be no reason for this intrusion. They have much to discuss and years to catch up on. And she is in the way. The glow is leaving the sky, the hills become a darker, shady green. They are losing time.

She talks, and neither of them is listening with any great attention and both are resigned to letting her talk run its course until she sees sense and goes back to wherever she came from. And it is when they have almost ceased to listen at all that they register — and it is a delayed response — the words 'woman' and 'tent'. And it is at this point that the expression on Sam's face transforms. There is not so much recognition in his eyes as understanding. And Art knows exactly why. They had, among all the things they were talking about, talked of this not long before. For Sam had painted an old woman just before they all left their city and went out into the great world. An old woman who lived in a tent out on the fringes of the city. Countryside that must surely now be a suburb. And he never sold that painting, but kept it with him. For there was something about the old woman and her tent, hovering there on the canvas between one world and another, that some deep instinct in him told him not to part with. It has been returned after the tour of Sydney and Melbourne and is now stacked against a wall in his studio in Kent with his other paintings. It is, he'd only just remarked to Art, a sort of touchstone. And he looks at it regularly, as a way of judging the distance between then and now, of there and here. A sort of reference point. And now, as if summoned up by their talk, this woman appears, approaches their table and pronounces the words 'woman' and 'tent' in such a way that leaves no doubt that she knew both the woman and her tent.

And suddenly both Sam and Art are standing and inviting this woman to sit at their table. There is a spare chair, they say, for her. But she says no, and Art can see in her eyes that she imagines she has intruded upon them and stayed long enough. Worse than intruded, she has transgressed. They are one world; she is another. And we don't mix, do we? Our types. Except when the accident of a grey-haired old woman and her tent brings us together, and our paths cross. However briefly. And this is clearly what the woman means when she says they have met — more or less. And as much as they insist she stay and join them, for there is clearly much to discuss and much to ask about the old woman, she backs away. I've intruded. I won't do that again. And as they continue to gesture at the vacant chair, she continues to retreat. We must all know our places, the action and the look on her face say as she continues to draw away. But not before offering up the very information they had been puzzling over. The old woman, whose name was Katherine (of course, Sam's nod seems to say, how could I forget), died in that tent not long after Sam painted her. Died and lay in her tent for three days before anybody found her. And there is sadness, Art notes, in this fate, but a fitting sadness. She hovered between two worlds, that old woman, but she was never destined to pass from one (what was) into the other (what they have all become, this post-war world). For she *was* that moment between the two worlds, one of those discernible intervals when history pauses, before gathering itself and moving on.

And just as she is about to turn and leave, she asks Sam if he recalls meeting Katherine, for they say now that the painting was all taken from the newspaper photograph that so embarrassed the old woman's sisters and family. And Sam nods emphatically. He did meet her. Of course he did. Twice.

'Yes,' she adds, 'you don't forget meeting Katherine. Frightening, wasn't she?'

Sam laughs, as does Art, and it is clear they want to talk more. But the woman, whom they had silently defined as the very thing they sought to leave all those years ago, slips from them and retreats into the twilit square — for at some point during the encounter, the glow went from the sky and the hills turned black. And they watch, hands quite possibly still pointing to the vacant seat, as she merges with the crowd and joins her travelling companions.

And so, the woman gone — and they never caught her name — they sit once more and attempt to resume their conversation, but neither can recall the point at which they left it. There is a vacant chair beside them that will remain vacant, and a space in the conversation that will remain a space.

As Art sits down at the table, he concentrates on the woman now on the other side of the square with her travelling companions. Just anybody. The very thing they fled. But he feels a curious sense of connection to her. She is tugging at him, or so it seems. Look at me, look at me properly. I am your subject, this tugging figure seems to say. Almost apologetically. And I wish, oh I wish I could be more interesting. But I'm just me, aren't I? And I can only be just me. The thing you fled. A disappointment. Poor you. All the world has such subjects, doesn't it? Grand and exotic. From grand and exotic places. And *such* names: Karenina, Bovary, d'Urberville. But perhaps, if you look closely, you might find something more. Something that you didn't know was there. Something that *I* didn't know was there.

But, Art notes, when they invited the subject to sit with them, the subject declined. The subject would not sit, and the subject declined their offer, just as it had defied easy definition. Now she is gone, leaving a space at the table that wasn't there before, and a look in both men's eyes that seems to say, now, where were we?

* * *

Every morning now, with autumn quickly slipping into winter, Art lights a fire in the studio, which is cold and smells damp like a cave until the fire warms it and takes away the damp smell. He has worked all morning in this world that he disappears into each day, the lost domain of his birthplace that he is reconstructing, brick by brick, building by building, street by street. And all morning his mind has been moving between then and now, from those streets and buildings he left years before to the woman at the table the previous evening, and back again. The woman being both someone he met just yesterday and, at the same time, one of those nameless faces that walk the streets that he spends every day resurrecting. For it is almost as though she has stepped out of one of his paintings, stepped out of one of those anonymous peak-hour crowds, either going to or coming from work, and entered his studio, offering the nagging observation, 'No, no, you haven't got me right, have you?' And it is a disturbing, disruptive thought, for it undercuts the very confidence required to finish the task he has set himself. Almost as though she is wandering about with him, looking over his shoulder — and rarely approvingly. A self-confessed disappointment who is, in turn, disappointed at his failure to look more closely. And why should he care? After all, she is one of those from whom he fled. But he does care.

It is while he is contemplating this question, and in a slightly annoyed manner, that he sees the figure of Sam appear at his studio window, tapping on the glass.

The studio door opens onto the road that winds down into the town, a winding, dirt road that the tourist buses never take. And so when Art opens the door, Sam steps straight in off the road and into the warmth of the studio. They greet each other and Sam goes to the fire, puts down a large bundle wrapped in newspaper, which he has carried under his arm, and warms his hands.

He takes his coat off and rubs his hands vigorously. And when the cold has melted from his fingers, for the day has a wintry bite, he looks around at the studio, at the paintings stacked against all four walls, then turns to Art as if to say, well, let's have a look at them.

And as much as Art knows that a painting has got to be seen sooner or later — in the same way that a book is meant to be read — he resists, for a moment, the instruction in his old friend's eyes. But his old friend has travelled a long way — not just over land, but time — and who knows when he will be back. He deserves, at least, this much.

And as they stroll around the stone studio, Art selects which of the canvases he will put on display, then stands back and observes Sam's responses. The process takes about an hour — for Art and Sam have long agreed that an hour in a painter's studio or an art gallery is all the mind can accommodate. After that the viewer is not seeing, only looking. And Sam's responses range from staring intently at scenes to nodding or smiling at a familiar building or pub, sometimes remarking on forgetting all about such and such or so and so until the painting brought it back. And when he is finished and they have exhausted their hour, he looks at Art and nods. It is a knowing nod, a thoughtful one, but, above all, it is a nod of approval. And it is followed by the simple observation, 'They're good 'uns.' And he nods again. 'Good 'uns.'

Sam, Art knows full well, is not one given to grand statements about the work of fellow artists or his own. We leave that, it has always been tacitly acknowledged, to others. And so that slow, thoughtful nod of approval and those few simple words matter, and Art nods back as the two old friends return to the fire.

All talk of paintings ceases, which Art is happy with, and when they reach the fire Sam looks down at the bundle wrapped in newspaper that he carried with him.

'I've got a surprise,' he says, then instructs Art to pull up a chair by the fire and close his eyes.

Art is reluctant — closing his eyes is too close to being blind, which, he has always been convinced, would mean the end of living. But the generosity of his friend's nod and those few words of approval are still fresh and, once again, he concedes that he owes him at least this much. So he sits. And he closes his eyes.

The room becomes sound: Sam unwrapping the bundle. Rustling and snapping sounds, over and again — and, eventually, the crackling of flames. For he knows from the sudden burst of warmth that something has just been placed on the fire and that flames and, no doubt, sparks are leaping into the air.

And then the first wafts of scent reach him, strong and unmistakeable, and gathering in potency as Art continues to breathe in the scent coming from the fire. And from the moment the scent reaches him — still keeping his eyes closed, for he is suddenly discovering the power of smell — the scene in his mind, his mental picture of the room, changes. From studio to landscape; from the closed and internal to the infinitely open. Trees, hills, dusty roads, yellow grass, pale blue skies and a dazzlingly bright, unrelenting sun all appear before him. The places they went in their youth, the countryside they escaped to on those days when the sun sent you to the brink of murder and the only course left was to get out to the country or the sea. The smell summoned it all up. All back, all there with such a heady immediacy that he could now almost be sitting again in that countryside he left all those years ago. For he knows, still without opening his eyes, that Sam has just placed the leaves and tender shoots of a gum tree on the fire. And the rustle he heard was the dried leaves, and the snapping sound the breaking of twigs — and the landscape, the countryside that immediately appeared to him, has been conjured up by the magic of the eucalypt.

Sam is not the first to bring the scent of the bush with him to Art's studio. One of those visiting academics had brought the scented leaves with him once. It is a sort of ritual offering to some. Which, in the past, Art has always thought of as a clichéd one, too. Like the offering of a jar of Vegemite. But not this time. Perhaps because the offering comes from Sam, one of that tight circle of artists from their home city, one of the select society of those who were there, and thereby possessing all the credentials required to get away with an offering such as this, the offering of a cliché. Perhaps because the time is now right: that he is now at the age where such things matter, whereas earlier in his life he would have sneered at such an offering. But not today.

For it is not simply the immediacy of the scene that hits him — and the impact of the scent is as powerful as being physically hit, or so it seems to Art at this moment — but something else. Something unexpected. For with the scent and the scenes that it conjures up comes an aching tenderness for the place, that he could never have imagined having. For, like the summer stink of vomit in pubs with tiled walls (which were hosed down at closing time) and the wide un-peopled city streets upon which the sun beat down on summer days, the countryside, too (bare, dusty, spindly gum trees and half-dead shrubs), was part of the thing he couldn't wait to leave. It was always an unattractive countryside to Art. Even alien. But here he is being moved by it, even possessive of it. Responding to it with a sense of ownership that only those who were there could possibly assume. And he realises there and then, with a sudden jolt as he finally opens his eyes, that what the smell has unlocked is something that he never felt himself capable of; something that he had, and with relief, assumed he would never feel: nostalgia.

Sam's face is smiling. A big, open smile that says, yes, I know, you don't have to say a word. The room is smoky and the smell of the gum fills Art's lungs and he is floating. As if inhaling some sweet drug that brings with it the unmistakeable ache of nostalgia: the very nostalgia that he swore was never within him to feel now conjured up (albeit with the faint, residual feeling of succumbing to a cliché) by the gum leaves.

* * *

Soon afterwards he is watching Sam walk back into the town along the dirt road. From time to time Sam turns and waves, and Art waves back. Then Sam follows a bend in the road and disappears, and Art turns back to his studio door, taking in the village opposite as he does. Did Amerigo Vespucci, after the thrill of setting out, after the thrill of adventure had faded, succumb — on the long journey to the New World — to the drug of nostalgia? Did he long for these green, rolling hills and those long summer evenings that pour gold and vermilion twilight over the land? Did he ever look out over the rolling waves and see these hills instead? And were there times when he wished he'd never left home?

Nostalgia. They'll tell you — all the dictionaries and all the books — that it's a longing for home. Or the past. But Art, with the scent of the gum leaves still in his nostrils, has had time to think about this and he's not so sure it's either of them. It is true that from the moment he inhaled the scent of the leaves he was filled with a longing that he could only call nostalgia. But for what? Had he really discovered a longing for the place the leaves brought with them — or something else?

The smell of the leaves conjured up a place and a time, and with that came an aching desire he *chose* to call nostalgia. But what if that wasn't it? Or, rather, what if the feeling needs to be redefined? And is nostalgia not so much a longing for a place or a time as a longing for youth itself? Home merely the place where youth is lived. The place where it is played out, and where, on that inevitable day of departure, it is left. All destined to be consigned to the distant past. Until somebody uncorks the magic potion that brings it all back.

He knows, and he has told himself this often enough, that if he were to go back he would not find the place he'd left. It would not be there. His city, his place, his home, existed once upon a time. And that time will not return. So how could nostalgia be a longing for home, when going back to that place called home would neither ease the ache nor satisfy the longing? That place which was home lives in another time. To go back to the place as it is now — and he is not seriously contemplating it anyway — would achieve nothing. He would merely be a stranger in a strange place. For there is no place to go back to. No, the longing is for the place as it was, the time that was, when they were younger and older, older and younger than they knew. A longing for that lyrical age of youth that never comes again.

And just as well, Art tells himself, as he enters his studio, just as well there's nothing to go back to. Because he can't go back anyway. You may not be able to go back into the past or to a place that doesn't exist any more, but you can re-create it. And this is exactly what Art has been doing all these years. Art has been re-creating that sunken city. So that if it were ever to be rebuilt as it was, it could all be done from his paintings. And if someone were ever to ask, 'What was it like?', they would only need to walk through these paintings to know. But, and Art knows this full well, the whole enterprise sits on mythic memories — not fact. And the success or otherwise of the whole pursuit relies on preserving those mythic memories. To go back to what now exists, he is convinced, would destroy them.

No, nostalgia is not the longing for home or the past — it is the longing for youth itself. And the object is not to ease that longing by returning, but to bottle it and, in so doing, preserve those memories.

Did Amerigo Vespucci succumb to the same longing on those long, lonely days on the open sea, sailing to the New World — and, if so, did it draw him back or drive him on, knowing full well there was no going back? And at what point does the adventure of setting out for New Worlds become an exile?

Art wanders about his studio, the smell of the gum leaves still heavy in the air, putting the canvases back into place, stacked where they were before Sam's visit. All put away for the time being, the sunken city in the process of being re-created — brick by brick, building by building, street by street.

And it is as he is wandering around the studio that he turns one of the paintings round — an old painting, one he did when he first came here. It is an interior study, one of those paintings that take you through the front door and inside a house to its interior life. It is, in fact, the kitchen of the house he grew up in, on the day he left. Art and his parents are seated at the kitchen table: his father in his singlet, newspaper opened in front of him and a big cup of tea (even in the January heat), his mother in her apron, tea, too, in front of her. There is a cake and special plates and dessert forks on the table. A typical kitchen scene, except for the cake and plates and cutlery. It is these things that tell you this is a special occasion. Nobody appears to be talking. His father stares at the newspaper, blank-eyed. His mother looks directly at the viewer, puzzled. And Art, at the end of the table, removed from them as if already having left, has that unmistakeable look of someone who can't wait to leave.

It never occurred to him at the time that his father, a Tramways mechanic, and his mother, a shop assistant, were

278

well aware that they were not simply saying farewell, but goodbye. But the blank eyes, the puzzled look, the silence and the sliced but untouched cake all tell you this without need of it being said. They were, his parents (like all of them in that cluttered workers' suburb by the sea in which he grew up), no-fuss people, and so nobody in the painting lets on that this may not just be a trip to foreign places, and a farewell, but goodbye. The Art in the scene is all impatience, his mind elsewhere, on imagined horizons, barely registering the kitchen or what his parents may or may not be thinking.

Art had already left home anyway, already been married and separated (quite young), and only ever came home on Sundays, and reluctantly at that. Small. Smallness. Suburbs as closed as mediaeval villages. Suffocating. Depressing, maddening. This is how he thought of it all then, and how he still does. Small lives jammed together, lived and ended within the walls of that cluttered little world that rarely looked outward, and when it did, did so with suspicion.

His mind in that scene is on imagined horizons, for he is going out into the great world. The world that the likes of his parents would never venture into, and not only because of the expense but because *this* was their world. All they were given, and all, in the end, they asked for. A world of 'cuppas', 'white with two', of calling each other 'Mum' and 'Dad', of drawn blinds and dark rooms in summer with the front room always shut and only ever opened on special occasions. A world of defined comings, goings and rituals — work, pub, Sunday leg — that would never change because they were beyond change. A world that constantly sought to draw you in, to make you one of them, so that it would, this world, go on and on … As if there were no other way, as if it were their and *your* natural condition. And the more they drew you in, the more the naturalness of this condition became confirmed and, therefore, beyond questioning. To seek more, to seek out the world's edge, to set out after new and uncharted lands, was not only a betrayal of all this but an insult.

But none of this was spoken that day. The only thing to be done with that world was to leave it. Impatience defines him in that scene, and it was one of the first paintings he completed when he settled here, to remind him, should he ever need reminding in the years that would follow, why he left in the first place.

And it was only after news reached him of the death of his parents a few years later, one after the other, that he remembered the occasional trembling of his mother's lips that day as she smoothed the tea cosy, and her occasional sighs that spoke of things they didn't speak about. That, and the fifty pounds his father placed in his hand as they all stood and made their way to the front door: the fifty pounds that proudly proclaimed, never let it be said we don't look after our own; that and the brief, no-fuss farewell that the sadness in their eyes betrayed.

These impressions were only finally registered as the years passed, but are not visible in the painting, for his youthful impatience to be shot of that house and the city framed the whole scene.

He puts the painting, face in, back against the stone wall of the studio with all those other stacked works that will eventually comprise a complete portrait of that sunken city. He then turns to the door, the smell of gum leaves still in the air, and remembers the thrill of setting out as he stepped onto the boat later that day and watched the port recede and heard the squawk and cry of the great world beckon.

Outside, he closes the door of his studio, for it is too late in the day for further work, and stares across the green valley, to the hill on the other side and the village that sits on it.

His father had placed the envelope filled with pound notes in Art's hand in such a way as to suggest that the matter was settled. No protests. But he knew from the moment that he took the envelope that it contained a large sum. No doubt a substantial part of their life savings. And he almost spoke, almost protested, but the look in both his parents' eyes reminded him that they were no-fuss people.

And he can see that house now as clearly as he can see the village opposite. That house and all those small box houses surrounding it, and the street that ran all the way down to the bay that flowed out into the open sea, the smell of which reached him and called to him from where he stood that last day.

That bay-side workers' suburb has now become, his friends tell him in their letters, a home to the new rich. For the sons and daughters who make up that post-war generation that grew up in the frontier suburbs of the city are now returning to those cluttered inner-city workers' suburbs their parents fled and are making them their own. They're renovating the suburbs their parents came from. Renos, they call them. And, often enough, these letters tell him, their marriages fall apart under the strain of these renovations, but the houses themselves emerge re-invigorated and re-created. And History, its job done, throws its tools and ladders and lunch-boxes into the back of an old ute and moves on. And what *was* is re-invented, though still discernible, for those looking, under the new paint and new colours of a new age.

And there is an odd sense of possessiveness that comes with this knowledge, the conviction they have no right to do it, this young, rich generation that once sang and danced for this Whitlam of theirs and once dreamt mountainous dreams and which now does renovations and repossesses those inner-city suburbs that the likes of Art once called home. And with the word 'home', that ache like a longing returns — and not, he realises, not just for his youth and all their youths, but for the place itself. An odd pity for the place. What have they done to you; what have they turned you into? A smart young thing, no doubt, street after street of smart young things, where there once lived no-fuss people.

And it is then, staring out over the green hills and valleys around him, that this longing, summoned up by the magic of gum leaves, becomes not simply a longing for the lost domain of youth but for the lost domain itself — for the place that makes you and never leaves you. And with that comes the recognition that there will always be this reluctant possessiveness, even resentment for those who occupy the space you left on departure and who transform the place you once called home into something else that they call home, because they've no right to. But, of course, he knows that it is unstoppable History that drives those utes and that the new, young rich are simply History's agents. Just as he knows that History, wearing the khaki overalls of Progress, will always be throwing its tools, ladders and lunch-boxes into the back of an old ute and moving on. And on. An individual's longing we call desire. But the longing of a whole society we call progress.

But it is, he also acknowledges, a longing that cannot be satisfied. For the drug of nostalgia works most powerfully in exile, preserving those mythic memories that his return would only renovate.

And he's left, as the hills begin to take on a late-afternoon glow, to contemplate that blurred zone, that no-man's land that you cross without knowing and which leads from adventure to exile, and which, having been crossed, makes return impossible. Not because you won't, but because you can't without giving up that lost domain itself, so perfectly preserved in the aspic of memory. And this is all you need, and all you want, until some bastard comes along and waves the drug of nostalgia under your nose, and a part of you is left wondering what on earth you're doing here so far from home after all these years. And it's a lonely thought that leaves you, for a time, looking out over the hills and valleys as if they were some foreign place you've suddenly woken to. Damn Sam. Damn bloody Sam and his bloody gum leaves.

PART THREE

Election Day
Saturday 10th
December, 1977

11. The Shadow Line

The uncertain weather is gone. It is a humid day. Light cloud will come and go. The sun will sparkle on the steeples of St Paul's and St Patrick's alike, on row upon row of suburban rooftops and country towns, then pass into cloudy shadow. It is mid-morning and still cool, but the day will slowly warm to its task and reach a top temperature of twenty-six degrees. There is a light wind, with an afternoon sea breeze predicted and the possibility of a late-afternoon shower. It is, in short, a typical early summer day.

The winds that rioted through the park in spring have exhausted themselves. And even when the afternoon sea breeze arrives it will pass over the city like the gentle breath of some pagan god whose brief it is to blow the air into sweet, refreshing movement. The sun will light the streets where cars stalk Saturday-morning parking spots outside cafés, markets and parks, and shine into open doorways where people will look up to the sky questioningly and quickly decide that the revolution of spring has passed and that the stability of settled weather and settled days is upon them, chaos has given way to order, and the day, where cats stretch out on lawns and nature strips and birds walk the footpaths untroubled, holds no surprises.

Michael is driving to a suburban park to see his old band play. Already he thinks of it as his 'old' band, even though it hasn't been long since he left. But almost as soon as he did, music, the band and all those songs that anybody could make up all receded, almost instantly, into a completed, distant past. The Michael, the self that he was then, already taking on the appearance of somebody else, the way old selves do.

Churches, schools and public halls along the way are draped in banners proclaiming them polling booths for the day. Men and women stand on the footpaths holding how-to-vote cards; photographs of Whitlam here, Fraser there, stare back from fences and walls, both in these streets that he is now driving through and all over the city. Over all the cities, the towns and the countryside beyond, they stare back with steady eyes that say, I will give you days like these that hold no surprises — for you have felt the upheaval of spring and desire now only long, summer days, and I will give them to you, the joyous days of blissful indifference. Days that are indistinguishable from one another, and which are calmly taken for granted; days, months, years, that roll across an untroubled sky from dawn to dusk. You desire only the lost paradise of settled times, and I shall return paradise lost to you.

There are queues along the footpaths, early voters honouring their duty and so clearing the day for cricket, golf or the garden. And the smiles on the faces of those waiting patiently in lines and on the faces of the men and women handing out their party flyers, and the laughter (inaudible from the closed compartment of the car in which Michael sits) all create a festive air. As though it could just as easily be a school bazaar or a church fete as an election.

They are everywhere, these makeshift polling booths, all along the streets that lead Michael to the suburban park where his old band will soon play. Smiling faces, inaudible laughter, posters of candidates promising more days like these — all come and go like the sun through the trees or the waves out there on the bay where the high-water mark will be reached by two in the afternoon and the low by nine that night when everything will have been decided.

Somebody, in some local council, had the bright idea of harnessing all that festive spirit, and putting on a free concert in the park for the people on this people's day. And so his old band was hired. And it occurs to him, as he turns into the street where the park is and hears the familiar echoes of a sound system being checked, that these may well be the last days in which rock 'n' roll and politics are thought of in the same breath. The whole decade has been defined by music and politics, politics and music, but the decade, which found its voice in the music that shakes things up, the music that smashed art but which will soon become art, is leaving its radical past behind and coming to a close. The seventies will become the eighties, the difference between being in your twenties and being in your thirties. And in time, no doubt, the children of this decade will look back upon their long hair, their flared jeans and those interminable songs they danced to until the early hours of the morning and pronounce them all silly. The sort of thing youth does before growing up. And all their young marriages, which came and went with the explosive brevity of the Whitlam government itself, will be thought of in the same way. An experience. A youthful one. A sort of growing up. For the decade is closing and its explosiveness is all but exploded.

Michael thinks of it like that because he is re-reading his Johnston. Not Samuel, but George. Who said something similar about his earlier explosive times. Johnston, who travelled (as Michael will the following week), who lost himself and found himself in his travels, and left the record of his journey in his books. Johnston, whom he discovered at university, who turned Michael's city of boring milk bars and familiar, ordinary suburban houses into something new. Johnston, whom he carries now in his coat pocket, and who has been his touchstone these last few years, in the same way that those jingle-jangle songs of earlier times were to the younger Michael. Times explode, times settle. Explode and settle. It is the nature of things.

As he reaches the park, noting with relief that there *is* a crowd come to listen, as apart from a few scattered drinkers doing their best to look like a crowd, the band starts. And it occurs to him that it's probably the first time he's actually heard them. For when you're in the midst of a sound, you don't hear all of it; not really. Not the way the crowd does.

Now he is in the crowd and feels as though he is hearing them for the first time. And they are good. Their imitations are good, their copies — the test of all cover bands — close to the record. But there is also that lingering feeling of disquiet in the fact that they *are* a cover band. That he ended his jingle-jangle days in a cover band, which wasn't the way it started. But was, nonetheless, the way it ended.

As much as he thought there may have been regrets in coming here, that seeing his old band would prompt regrets about leaving, there are none. As he watches them he is reassured about the rightness of his decision. Any earlier and the time would not have been right. Any later, and he would have missed his new calling, his new self, the self that will soon walk out of this decade and into the next. No, the timing, for once, was right. And so he listens, noting that they are better than he ever realised, and noting that the crowd is a happy crowd, enjoying the gift of someone's bright idea to provide music in the park, and enjoying those last days in which politics and music would be thought of in the same breath.

As the crowd builds, for the very sound of music draws a crowd, he moves to the front and, catching the eyes of the band, he waves. And they smile and nod back, the singer calling out, 'It's Joyce fucking James!' in between lines as he waves; the drummer, too early in the day to be drunk and so secure on his stool, twirls a drumstick of hello and goodbye. For it is, they know and Michael knows, goodbye. Simple. No fuss. A farewell to those jingle-jangle days that promised so much and led you to believe that anybody could do this when all the time they couldn't, a farewell to those days of politics and music, music and politics, those times which, no doubt, the crowd will come to think of as part of the silliness of youth with its long hair and flared jeans.

* * *

Mr Whitlam has that goodbye look in his eyes, his mother is saying on the telephone. And she doesn't think it's because the way she looks at him on television and in the papers and posters. No, she's not giving him that goodbye look, he's just got it. And, when pressed, Michael says that may or may not be the case. But he hasn't called to talk about that.

It's late in the afternoon; the shadows are long on the cricket field in the park opposite his flat. The voters voted early, then put on their whites and became cricketers for the afternoon. And there they are, timeless white figures on a green playing field. And for a moment, while his mother's voice continues on the telephone, he's remembering those endless hours in his youth that he spent in the nets pursuing speed and the perfect ball, and those long summer Saturday afternoons that were never Saturday without becoming a white figure on a green playing field and replicating the feats of the great Lindwall. And then remembering how he simply left those fields of play one late afternoon like this, with the shadows long across the ground, and never went back because there were other things in the world to distract him, like the jingle-jangle world of jingle-jangle songs. And it prompts the thought that we are never one life, but a succession of lives; never one self, but a succession.

He reminds his mother that he's leaving in a few days, and she says she knows, but when exactly. He says he's already told her, and she says he hasn't. And because this could go on all afternoon he just names the day early in the next week. And she is surprised it is so soon, and her surprise annoys him because he's told her and she already knows. But is her surprise really just a way of saying, yes, I knew, but hasn't it all come around so quickly? Like growing up, and then leaving home and then leaving the country. Hasn't it all come around so quickly? And there's a hint of loneliness in that surprise, the realisation that sooner, rather than later, she will have to make do without the only thing she's got left in the world. For however long it takes.

So they must have a farewell dinner and this is why Michael has telephoned.

'When?' says Michael. 'What day is best?'

'Any time. I'm just here.'

And he likes the way she says this. She's never been one of those people who pretend they've got something to do when all the time they haven't. She's just there, and hasn't she always been? Too easy to forget that she was always there, for all those big and little things that mattered so much at the time. And still is. She knows no other way. And they agree on the night before he goes. Somehow it seems best to say goodbye, and then be gone the next day. No hanging about.

And he knows full well as he thinks this that it is the wise child speaking again.

And so, the day fixed, they return briefly to the goodbye look in Mr Whitlam's eyes, and she tells him, almost in a by-the-by manner, that she plans to leave her job and work for the travel company. And how that should be fun. And, who knows, she might just land on his doorstep over there one day or night. There's a brief silence, then she goes on. Does he think she's being reckless? And he replies that she's already told him about this and she says she hasn't. And to cut things short he says *he's* hardly one to speak. That he, too, has just resigned his job and will soon be taking off. Must run in the family. And they both have a laugh about that. And a laugh seems a good way to end the call. And so, telling her he'll telephone either the next day or the next, they hang up. And among all the other concerns of the day, he's left pondering the possibility of his mother landing on his doorstep one day or night, and concludes that it's a possibility but a slim one.

At some point during their conversation the white figures left the playing field and the shadows are now stretched across the oval. The birds have returned to their trees, the cricketers retired to their clubhouses; the ground now green, gold and slowly slipping from shadow to darkness.

He rises from the couch and switches the television on, and pictures of polling booths, people and politicians fill the screen. And he thinks that somewhere in the background, everywhere in evidence but nowhere to be seen, Peter will have his feet up, his mind ticking over, with the mill horse of his art still going round and round, grinding out the language of Power, day in, day out. No rest.

* * *

The late showers never came. The afternoon sea breeze cooled the air and the high tide came and went and the low-water mark followed, more or less, on time.

It is late to be arriving at a party, almost ten. But Michael preferred to stay in his flat and watch events unfold on the television by himself. For it seemed a fitting way to farewell the mountain of Whitlam. For the mountain has lost and will soon speak to the cities, suburbs, countryside and farms to say that it is withdrawing from the landscape. And its withdrawal will be noted and not noted. The mountain will be remembered or forgotten. For we have few mountains, and it would be easy to imagine, once it has gone, that this is the way it has always been. And will be. But even as Michael tries to imagine this, the mountain forgotten to the extent that it never existed, he can't. For the years they have just lived through were, indeed, mountainous. And the memory of that may be dulled by time, but surely never erased.

He is parked at the front of an inner suburban house belonging to friends of friends. It is large, with a garden and lawns. Coloured party lights are strung across the veranda. The sea breeze carries in from the bay and ruffles the wind chimes at the door. His window is wound down and he hears the faint tinkling of the chimes, music from a stereo and the sound of talk and laughter. Mountains withdraw. But this is not to say that the mountains are forgotten. Old music gives way to new, old jokes find new laughter, old dances give way to new moves. Life goes on. But, occasionally, someone stops and notes that something is missing, remembers for a moment what it is, then resumes the dance, drawn back into the rhythm of the years, which has a life all of its own, and through which we move, a succession of selves.

And it is while he is contemplating the chimes and the music and the coloured lights strung across the front of the house, imagining, as he always does, that lights and lanterns somehow transform houses into barges, and lawns into lakes, that he sees two figures emerge from the doorway. Two young women. They speak, but softly. And he can only hear the sound of speech, not what they are saying. And as they make their way along the path to the front gate he realises that the young blonde woman on the right is Mandy.

His impulse is to wind his window up, not because he doesn't want to be seen, but because Mandy doesn't. Not by him. The last few weeks have made this plain. But the two women are absorbed in each other's company and don't even notice, as they pass directly in front of him, that the car parked in the shadows, removed from the street light, has somebody inside, watching them as they pass. They do not notice him because he does not concern them. He is just something else in the world. And this leaves him free to observe, to note that she is happy. He doesn't know how he knows this — but he is sure he is right — for she neither smiles nor laughs. No, this is not the happiness that announces itself through smiles and laughter. She is, he concludes, happily calm. There is something almost serene about her. And when she speaks he notes that the sound of her voice is soft and soothing, like chimes. And he is pleased to see her happy. And that the wrong, to this extent, has been righted, and that it did not require his presence or intervention for this to occur. No, this newly acquired serenity seems to say, your Mandy is not your Mandy any more, she doesn't need you to put things right and will see things through in her own way without you.

The two women pause at Mandy's car, the car that he, too, has sat in, and for which, at the moment, he feels a certain possessiveness. Then Mandy, in fluid, almost trance-like movements, opens the driver's door, slips onto the seat and leans across to open the passenger door. The young woman with her, brushing her fringe back, slowly slides onto the seat. And there is a faint thud as she closes the door. The engine starts, at first loud then settling to a low hum. Lights come to life with the engine, and the car draws out from the kerb, slowly drawing away from him, then turns from view, leaving him to the street, the faint tinkle of the chimes and the music of the party with its insistent rhythms. She was happy. The wrong, to this extent, has righted itself. And as the car drew away from him he knew, without doubt, that she was driving into another life. And that she had, without knowing, farewelled him as he had farewelled her.

* * *

As he steps onto the floating barge of the party, music — a gust of sound that makes talking impossible — rushes to meet him. A couple is dancing in the hallway, others in the lounge room where the stereo is pumping such levels of sound into the air that everybody is relieved of the courtesy of speech and the ritual of greetings. There are few dancers, they are widely spaced, and the lounge room has the look of a sad café. An unpopular one. Or, rather, one that was once popular, but which has fallen into disfavour. There are parties all over the city, all over the country. Some celebrations; others — like a wave from the ground offered to a departing plane that has already disappeared — just for the record.

There is a colour television on in the corner. The sound may be up or off — it is impossible to tell. The mountain of Whitlam is speaking, surrounded by three or four sombre companions. But nobody has bothered to turn down the stereo, so his lips are moving but his words are inaudible. The dancers occasionally look over and take in the spectacle of Whitlam; a couple even stops dancing and stares for a beat or two, then resumes the dance. They understand without the words. The mountain is departing. See, it withdraws (without waving). Then it is gone, and for a moment the screen is empty, the room itself more emptied than filled. Shadows step rhythmically this way and that, twirl, then resume their steps.

So the dancers dance, the music plays and at some stage between the end of one song and the beginning of another, Whitlam departed. He came and went. Observed only by the one or two dancers who paused for a couple

298

of beats. Reluctantly. Like looking back when you've told yourself not to. And is there something else in that reluctance to look up? Did the early evening belong to another phase of life? The night was young, and so, too, were the dancers. But not any more. And there's a touch of saying goodbye to your childhood in that realisation and watching the departing Whitlam, who will always be synonymous with the wild days of youth. Did the dancers know this, and is this why most of them chose not to look up — because they knew that at any moment, one or another of their steps would take them over the line from what they were into what they will become? And is it best not to look up or be aware of it when it happens?

The night was young, and so were the dancers. But their world has moved on and they, too, have been carried forward with that movement. A past has been created. The before and after of their youth, what they will soon call the Whitlam years, is now defined and the line, the shadow line, dividing one from the other, is now visible.

Michael looks out into the yard, blue under the party lights, and sees a familiar face here and there, but feels no desire for company. The party can go on without him. The dance without him. He has not yet been seen by anybody he knows and it is not too late to slip away. To slip back into the street as if he was never here.

Outside, the house is once more a floating barge lit by lanterns and the lawns are lakes again, and he concludes, as he slips into the driver's seat and switches on the engine, that houses and party lights on nights such as these are best observed from the street. A before and an after have been created and it seems that all of them, Michael and his kind — whether knowing or not knowing or even wanting to know — have crossed that shadow line that divides what they were from what they shall now have to become.

12. The Sword of Damocles

When did they teach us to think in hand-me-down metaphors? Or didn't they have to? Has it always been like this? The same words, going round and round and in and out of each other down through the centuries and the years, the days and the nights such as this one, their meanings determined before they are even thought, uttered or written — to the extent that the words write *us*. When did they teach us to think in hand-me-down metaphors without us even realising it?

Peter is sitting in his kitchen observing the party all around him. And he's thinking of the same old words and the same old symbols and hand-me-down metaphors, because at some stage during the night the sword of Damocles came to mind. And he's fallen into thinking about it: Damocles and the sword suspended above his head by a single hair, ready to fall at any moment. Damocles? Who taught him that?

And why is Peter, rather gloomily and on a night of victory, which should be a night of celebration and happy thoughts, dwelling on the sword of Damocles instead?

Because the poster is still up there on the kitchen wall. And as much as he would love to tear it down, he knows he can't, because that would confirm his wife's pronouncement that it means something, and that he, Peter, knows what that something is. And so, the poster stays. And stays. And has now become something of a fixture. Permanent. At least, nobody has expressed any wish to remove it. Neither he nor his wife. It has become a sort of unspoken battle of the wills. A test. Of who will be the first to break. Who indeed? Not his wife, it seems, and certainly not him. And so it stays. A fixture.

Furthermore, it has become a conversation piece. For almost everyone here tonight has paused in front of this poster and discussed it. Sometimes briefly, sometimes at length. But nobody has ignored it. And, as often as not, the discussions are light and clever. Party talk that everyone enjoys. Well, almost everyone. The poster inspiring wit and laughter. Or what passes for wit and laughter. Occasionally, it inspires more serious discussion. And these are the lengthy ones. And it is surprising to see who dismisses it with passing quips and who stays longer to dwell upon its blunt message. But the fact is nobody has ignored it and the poster has become exactly what his wife said it would become when she pinned it up on the kitchen wall.

And so as much as he would love to tear it down, he can't. If it were to be removed now, it would create a space. Even a vacuum. And people would notice, and note, that it was gone, as much as they now note that it is there.

And at some stage during the evening Damocles came to mind. And why Damocles? Because there is a touch of Damocles to the poster. More than a touch. For the poster contains a threat. And the possibility of the threat becoming real and fate falling on him is always there, suspended by a single hair. The sword will fall. It has to. He doesn't know when — but he knows that one day or one night the hair will snap and the sword will plummet onto him. Onto them. Onto the house.

Perhaps someone, some visitor from the capital or a member of the party, will pass it one day and casually remark, in the presence of his wife, that they'd seen just such a poster in Beth's place. You remember Beth? Poor Beth; what a business. Perhaps it will happen as casually as that, for he wasn't the only contact Beth had (and the poster isn't *that* common). Surely, from time to time, others had sat in Beth's armchair, sipped the same whisky and noticed the same poster. Even discussed it. So perhaps one day any one of them, just passing through, will notice it in Peter's kitchen and remark upon the coincidence. Or perhaps it will happen differently. Perhaps one day, in an unguarded moment, *he* will inadvertently refer to the original owner, and let slip her name. Wonder out loud where on earth Beth found it. And his wife may well conclude that this Beth (whom she never met, but read) was the grubby little affair at the heart of the matter, and he will be forced to deny it. And in denying it, may also be called upon to explain things. All the result of an unguarded moment. Such things happen. Or perhaps one day one of them or both of them will finally snap; the tension, at last, too great, and the game, the test of wills, will get serious. Heated words might follow and the truth be blurted out. And Kate will finally know what the handkerchief and the poster mean, and what he did, and quite possibly look at him at that moment and forever after as if she never knew him at all and had married a stranger. And he would remain a stranger to her, and she to him: strangers to each other living in a strange house they call home. Who knows what form the threat will take when the hair by which it is suspended snaps, but he is convinced the sword will fall all the same.

And, as much as it is a threat, it is also a constant reminder of what took place — the whole sequence of events that at first he controlled, but which very quickly assumed a life of its own and eventually controlled him. To the point that 'events' have now entered his house, his marriage and his daily life — up there, permanently, on the kitchen wall. A constant reminder that says: I am your works; look upon me and know that this is how our works return to haunt us. For we must all choose wisely when we do works and send them out into the world, or they will come back to us, to you, as I have.

For Peter, rightly or wrongly, with reason or without (it doesn't matter), has become convinced that what is suspended by a single hair is nothing less than that which he calls his life: wife, family, house — and all the ingrained rhythms and routines that define that life, without which he would be lost. And it won't go, this threat. And it is not distant like the memory of Pussy Cat is now. Nor does it fade graciously into the past, like the view from a rear-vision mirror, Pussy Cat's sad, wise eyes absolving him as he leaves. No, it's up there on the wall every day.

Then, as if having been silenced by his thoughts, the noise of the party suddenly returns: explosions of laughter, the constant rumble of talk and, under it all, low music. And now a hand is slapping his back. A familiar voice is speaking. Good work, it is saying. Good work. Cheers, drink up. Here's to us. And Peter smiles and their glasses clink as they toast themselves.

Then Whitlam appears on the screen. And in the same moment in which Michael observes the dancers at the party, the blue party lanterns lighting up the house and the yard outside it; in the same moment that sees the headlights of Mandy's car light up a pathway to a new life; and in the same moment that Rita eyes a box of travel mementoes beside her — in that same moment Peter turns to the screen and watches the farewell minutes, the last moments, of this Whitlam of theirs, who was once his. For soon he will be gone, banished from the scene. And Peter feels neither joy nor triumph. Nor is it indifference. And while he is contemplating just what it is, he notices his wife, not talking to anyone, separate from the groups around her, with a puzzled and puzzling sadness in her eyes as she, too, stares at the television. And it is then that she turns to him, a look that seems to say, yes, it's a party, and, yes, we won, but I watch him leave and I feel something leave with him. And what is it? And what's happened to *us*?

304

And why aren't things good any more? And, as much as he would love to answer the unspoken questions in her eyes, the answers remain suspended in the air with the cigarette smoke hovering over the lounge room.

And, at the same time, that sense of threat hovering over the kitchen acquires unexpected poignancy. And suddenly (the thought springs upon him like some animal in the night) *everything* seems suspended by a single hair, not just one person's life, not just his and theirs, but life. Everyone here, everyone out there across the city, under party lights strung up all across the country, and beyond. Everyone who has ever been, or is or will be. All of it. The thing itself.

And as the thought springs upon him from the dark, his wife stares at him from the other side of the room with the same puzzled sadness still in her eyes. And he is contemplating her eyes and wondering when he last *really* looked at them and, as he does, he realises with a jolt that everything he calls his life, without which he would be lost, started there, in those eyes and with that face, back then in the last of their student days, when they were older and younger, and younger and older than they knew. And what they were and what they have become merge. One and the same. Peter stares at his wife: the memory of what we were and what we had is so easily lost; the wonder that we *are* at all is so easily ignored and taken for granted. Until moments such as these, when we look up and see this Whitlam depart: this Whitlam of theirs who was once ours, who stood over the years of our youth, and who was wise like us and silly like us. And as he departs, that wise and silly, silly and wise youth departs with him, and his departure is registered in the questioning eyes of his wife, staring at him across the smoky room, asking, What's happened to us? And why aren't things good any more?

How long, Peter asks himself, has it been since he's been moved by that face and by the ordinary 'us' that they became? How long since that love has moved him? And do we have to be shaken to our foundations to see it and remember it?

Whitlam departs; the party, and Peter is only vaguely aware of it, continues all round him. The occasional hand slaps him on the back. Good work, good work, they say. Glasses are raised, victory toasts proclaimed. Loudly and with laughter. Whitlam departs, victory is proclaimed, but all he is mindful of now is the look in his wife's eyes — and those days when they were older and younger, and younger and older than they knew. When they knew spite that had no limits and love that knew no bounds. Days that fused them together all the same, and which were all but forgotten but have suddenly been returned to them. Whitlam departs, but something is regained in that moment of television departure that takes Peter's breath away and renders everything and everyone around him, these strangers in his house, so much passing show. A distraction from the real living. And do we have to be shaken to our foundations to see it? And can that ordinary 'us' that they became be won back? Or when we have the distance to see it fully for what it is and to understand just what we have lost, is it already too late?

And it is then, still holding his wife's eyes, that Peter nods to the backyard. And Kate nods back, sadness and smiles, and together they give them all the slip — the party, the house, their children (long put to bed and asleep upstairs) — and meet by the garden shed in the yard. And, standing close, just close enough to lean on each other, without speaking or feeling the need to speak, they take in, from the gentle hill upon which the house sits, the sights and the sounds of all the yards and all the streets, all across the city and beyond, all part of one constantly moving, constantly evolving miracle. All suspended by a single hair.

13. Mandy's Silence Breaks

The party lanterns cast a blue light over the yard and the lawns. It's a blue world unto itself. And Mandy, and all those around her, are the inhabitants of it. And once again, as she did in the hospital, she is floating through space as much as she is standing alone beneath a plum tree, observing the groups around her, all absorbed in their talk, their laughter and their circles of friends, leaving her free to watch. And it's something she's noted about herself lately: she watches more. As though there was this game she used to play — laughter, love and couples — but doesn't any more, and which she is content to watch from the boundary line.

But at the same time she gradually becomes aware of someone watching *her*. And she's not sure who or where from, but she knows she's being watched all the same. And then she sees her. There is a woman standing beside a group near the line of lanterns, staring at Mandy. The distance is not so great, the light not so dim, that she can't tell. How long has she been watching? All the time that Mandy, content to stand alone, was observing these people — friends (who know to leave her alone because she wants it that way) and strangers — in this suburban backyard, the television and all the events of the day playing in the background, she herself was being observed. For how long? And even when Mandy returns the stare, more in curiosity than anything, this woman doesn't stop.

Then the woman smiles. As if to say, look, we are the same, you and I. All these people, all these groups and couples, and we choose to stand alone. And this woman's smile assumes a puzzling familiarity, as if they already know each other, which they don't. And it is while Mandy is contemplating all of this that the woman strolls towards her and Mandy is able to see her better: a sharp fringe slanting across her forehead, the lightness and spring in her step like a fox and, Mandy notices as she nears her, eyes to match.

Then she is standing in front of Mandy.

'You don't like trooping off in a gang either.'

It is not so much a question as a statement. Mandy nods, but her eyes are puzzled, as if to say, don't I? And if I don't, how do *you* know? And answering the implied question, the woman adds: 'I've been watching you.'

As much as Mandy ought to feel uncomfortable, she is not. And it is all in the way it is said. I was not spying, the woman's tone implies. Nor, I hope, was I intruding. And it is not that you draw my interest because you are alone, as I am, and don't like trooping off in gangs either. Or that you looked lonely. Or that I was lonely. No, it's none of that. I was drawn to you. Do I need a reason? And, once again, Mandy has this feeling of standing in a blue world unto itself, and that at any moment she might just float off into blue space. Mouths move silently on the television screen, visible over this woman's shoulder in the lounge room of the house; the music is distant; the dancers, shadows.

And it is at this moment that one of Mandy's friends (the very friend who took the call from Michael) approaches and smiles, pleased to see Mandy has found a friend.

'I see you've found each other.'

And Mandy stares at her, puzzled, as her friend continues.

'You have a room in common.' Then, waving a hand, Whitlamesque, in the direction of the television, she says, 'Isn't it dreadful?'

Then she is gone. The question implies its own answer. Yes, it is dreadful. The woman who has just joined Mandy watches her friend go, then turns back to Mandy, a glint in her eyes, and a slight, conspiratorial smile.

'I don't care.'

And straight away Mandy's eyes light up.

'No.'

'I did once.'

'Yes, didn't we all?'

'But I don't care any more.'

'No.'

And this woman, who, it seems, just plunges in and says whatever she wants, sips from her drink as she stares at the house then turns back to Mandy. 'Perhaps I will again. But I'll never care the way I did.'

'No, you can't. You can only care like that once.'

Mandy is wondering where the words are coming from, and with such an ease that both delights and puzzles her — like those dreams in which we perform the most extraordinary feats with a naturalness that we take for granted, but which, all the same, leave us thinking, no, this can't be real.

But it is. And implied in their exchanged words, and in that conspiratorial glance that passed between them, is the assumption that you and I, we understand each other. We have known things, such things as pain and hurt and loss; we share this, and in sharing this we can speak frankly. Life is short. Shall we plunge in?

The words flow, and all with a dreamy ease that both amazes and delights Mandy, but which also leaves her thinking, no, this can't be real. But it is. How long do they stand and talk? What do they say? Words, words of release, liberating her from a silent loneliness she'd begun to take as her natural condition and which she'd begun to take for granted, flow from her with dazzling ease. Words made new by that silent loneliness she willingly entered, and which has now broken. Has she ever spoken like this?

310

Has she ever felt free to speak like this before? Not asking herself if she is saying the right thing or the wrong thing, or wondering what everybody will think; if she's being silly or putting her foot in it, or asking herself what Michael and all the other Michaels she's ever known are thinking. And it's not as though she's even speaking her mind. She's left her mind, the mind of the old Mandy, behind her and is speaking, more or less, without thinking. Words are just welling up like water from a spring and flowing from her. It's all deliriously mind*less*. And, as much as the words and the talk, Mandy is also conscious of the woman's voice: soft, and as soothing as the blue light of the lanterns in this blue world she has landed in. And how long have they been standing here beneath the plum tree? It is impossible to say, for it would need to be measured in blue seconds, blue minutes and blue time.

And it is while Mandy is contemplating blue time, when she is lost in thought and this woman, too, has stopped talking, when there is a silent pause that drowns out the music, the surrounding talk and the occasional shouts and car sounds from the street that tell you there is a world out there after all — it is in the midst of this silence that Mandy watches, with a fascination that leaves her a spectator to her own self, the woman's hand fall slowly through the air, and land upon the inside of her forearm, with breathtaking sureness, stroking it in slow, circular motions, offering up, as she does, the words Mandy has longed to hear, like the last words of a dazzling dream that have miraculously lingered on beyond dreaming and which have waited all this time, for just such a night, to fall upon her in the same way that this woman's hand just has: 'You are beautiful. More beautiful than you know. Have you never been told?'

And it is not an affront. It is not presumption. Nor intrusive. No, it is none of that; it is simply the recognition, and registered by both of them, perhaps in an instant and with absolute certainty, that something momentous has happened.

And Mandy watches, spellbound, registering the faint touch of the woman's fingertip, now on her palm, as she continues to stroke her in slow, circular motions. This woman, all the time, speaking the words that have been travelling towards Mandy through blue time and have now arrived, going round and round in circles like her finger: You are beautiful. More beautiful than you know ... And I will not hurt you. Or harm you. But love you.

And when she has finished she takes Mandy's hand, enfolds it in hers, and holds it in silent compact. It is breathtaking. Direct. As if to say, there isn't a minute to lose. Life is brief and moments such as these pass from us far too easily, and happiness is too often lost in the blink of an eye. But you and I, we have known pain and hurt and loss, and we will *not* let this moment pass. And, as breathtaking as it is, Mandy is also registering, with astonishing clarity, that she trusts her completely. Not simply trusts this woman whom she has only just met but trusts the moment itself — that it is not only something momentous that has happened but something true — and that the silence into which she withdrew, calm as the Buddha, cradling that six-week-old gift in all its infinite loneliness and wisdom, has broken. And she has, for all the world, the distinct sensation of being born anew. Oh good silence, true silence …

You enter a party with no expectations, then step under the blue light of party lanterns into the spell of a blue world and everything changes. The woman is still holding her hand, silent for a moment, allowing her words to sink in, then she speaks again with utter certainty.

'Shall we leave?'

And Mandy nods, just nods. Without hesitation, for she accepts the certainty of things as naturally as she accepts her hand.

'But I don't even know your name.'

They are walking towards the back door. The woman releases Mandy's hand and turns her head towards her as they approach the door.

'My name's Theresa. But everybody calls me Trix.'

Mandy passes through the doorway and stares at her. Of course, Trix. And it is the rightness of the name that she is registering, as if the rightness of her name were confirmation of her trust. Trix, of course. Who else?

They pass through the house, leaving the music, the dancing shadows and the lanterns behind, and stand at the front gate. Trix. Her sharp fringe slanting across her forehead, her eyes clear, nimble and mischievous. Her whole body ready to spring at any moment. Ready to pounce upon life. A fox, eyeing her from the carefully trimmed nature strip at the front of the house; a fox, wild and *untrimmed*. The wild, untrimmed part of us all. Which Mandy had lost, and has now recovered. And will never lose again. Her fox has come and summoned her back to life.

They stroll towards Mandy's car, the house and all its lights floating away, the faint tinkle of chimes fading in the still street. It is after ten, and out there in the bay the waters have passed their low tide and are once again rising. The sea breeze has dropped; the late showers never came.

They are vaguely aware of a parked car behind Mandy's and of someone, a dark shape, sitting in it, possibly listening to the events of the day on the car radio. They are aware of this dark shape but pay no more attention to it or the car than they do to the trees, the moon, or the cat perched on the garden fence beside them.

Mandy unlocks the car, then two doors shut, faint thuds in the night, and the headlights cut a path along the street, illuminating a closed milk bar, a shop here and there, converging at some distant point out there in front of them. Then they pull out from the kerb and follow the twin beams, towards that point of convergence.

The house, the party lights, the yard and that blue world they had entered recede behind them with the parked car they barely noticed, the tinkle of the chimes, and the cat, still perched on the garden fence, watching the comings and goings of the street with animal indifference.

14. Whitlam's Eyes

Is it all accident? Is it all luck? What chance have you really got? Then again, maybe everything comes round in the end and everybody gets their share. Rita is sitting in a tea-room in the city. It's a famous tea-room. At least, in this city. The world changes around it, but it doesn't. The cakes, the sandwiches, the teas on the menu have been there through war, depression and more war. And sometimes she feels she's been coming here for a hundred years, and other times she still feels like she's the youngest customer in the place. This tea-room has that effect. It never changes, or never seems to, and all the selves you've ever been are all here waiting to greet you when you walk in.

But what was she thinking about? Yes, accident and there only being so much of the world and everything coming round in the end. These are the sorts of thoughts that come to you when you're waiting for someone. And Rita is. She's been back from her trip for a few weeks and she's meeting the woman who led the tour. The guide. The woman who said during the tour that Rita could do this. Mainly because Rita, as often as not, went her own way. Could organise herself. And so why couldn't she organise others as well?

So, here she is. Giving it a go. And while she's been waiting she's remembered a day in her travels when she watched two young women in Paris. They were sitting at a table and talking quickly. In French. And then they switched to English. For no apparent reason. And listening to them, she could have sworn they *were* English. Then they switched back to French — and they were French again. Then English. And French. And they did this all through the conversation.

And it was this that got her thinking about accident, and things eventually coming round to everyone — or not — because there's only so much of the world. She, Rita, was born in this city in the distant decade of the 1920s to a mother who was always working and a father she never knew. But it didn't have to be like that. Did it? She has a history, but that history didn't have to be hers. You live the life of Rita, but you could easily have been one of those two young women sitting in a smart French café, jumping from French to English and back to French again without pausing for breath. And looked at like this, history becomes a kind of accident. A sort of game. A throw of the dice. And, for the moment, her whole life seems like a sort of accident or chance, something that resulted in the Rita that she is. But it didn't have to. So often we look back and everything seems as though it could have been no other way. That we have lived the life we were destined to live. That we love our life. And that we wouldn't want it any other way. *Can't* have it any other way. But we can. And she may well have gone along with everything had it not been for the surprise impulse to jump on the tram of her fancy one morning.

Rita looks up at the clock, wondering where on earth this woman is, when she suddenly enters, apologising for being late — voting, queues, damn election.

Half an hour later the woman rushes from the tea-room as quickly as she entered, leaving behind a small pile of

316

brochures and forms containing, Rita has been assured, all the information she needs. And when Rita has gathered it all together and placed it in her bag, she pays at the cash register and steps out into the gilded arcade that runs quietly through the city. And when she finally emerges into the glare of the street, her steps take her automatically up the hill towards the department store where she worked for half her working life for one last look.

Odd, to think of everything still in there. Everything and everyone still in their places: perfume, lingerie, coats, shoes and so on. The wives of distinguished newsreaders and prime ministers, and the odd dame, will continue to shop here while their drivers wait outside. They may even be in there now, while Rita stands on the footpath in the last minutes of the morning, knowing that everybody will be watching the clock. And she can picture all their faces, the lips that smile and form polite greetings, the eyes that stray to the minute hand that strains uphill towards the destination of midday, the feet and calves that ache from standing all morning. And, somewhere in there, Rita's place at the perfume counter, to which she has promised to return, is being held for her. But she will not take it. It will become somebody else's now, and Rita will wear the weight of being a disappointment to them all for a while. The store will go on and the marvel of commerce will continue without her. For the woman, the tour guide who arrived late at the tea-room, brought with her an entirely different promise altogether. The possibility of living differently. A sort of new life. An uncertain one. And possibly a foolish one. This is what you get for jumping on the tram of your fancy. It leads you to fanciful notions, and fanciful new lives that could leave you looking foolish. And as she stares into the glass doors of the store, picturing that neatly ordered world behind it, everybody in their places, levels of power and importance rising from street level to the fifth floor, a picture of how the world ought to be, stable and ordered, she can imagine no one foolish enough to follow her fancy and throw it all away. Nobody foolish enough to look at her life and conclude that she didn't have to turn out the way she did, or stay that way. To think that she could be different. No, she can imagine nobody, at any of the numerous counters in the store behind those glass doors, foolish enough to follow her fancy. And just as well. For the world can only accommodate so much foolishness before those carefully constructed levels of place, power and importance start to tremble.

She turns around and walks to her tram stop. And a few moments later, while she's standing there, she hears the town hall clock strike the precise second, minute and hour that liberates all the shop assistants, the salesmen and women, the floor supervisors and their managers, from their posts and duties, and knows that soon the stops will be crowded, the trams into which they will all pour will be filled and, soon afterwards, the city will become a ghost town. Its doors shut, its streets and footpaths all but empty. It's the hour that the town hall clock once struck for her, and it's odd to be looking at the spectacle through the eyes of the fanciful, who may well look foolish one day.

318

When she leaves her tram she walks to the local primary school, now draped in the banners and posters and colours of a polling booth. And as she enters the school, the representatives of all the parties, and there seem to be so many, push their leaflets upon her. And she takes them. She always does, so that nobody is left out. Posters of Whitlam and Fraser have been fixed to the fences and gates. There is the smell of a barbecue, and music somewhere. It could be a public holiday, or a church fete. And when she looks at the poster of Whitlam, he has, she notes — for all the grandeur of his bearing, and he does have that look of grandeur, one of those who's not frightened of thinking big or jumping on the trams of his fancy — that goodbye look in his eyes.

And she notes, at the same time, that he was always *theirs* really. This Whitlam of theirs, Michael and his kind. He was always theirs more than hers. All part of their youth, like long hair and beards and young women wearing overalls. But now he's got that goodbye look in his eyes, and all of them, Michael and his kind, have cut their hair and the young women aren't wearing overalls any more. And what does that mean?

She votes, she leaves, weaving through the queues inside the hall and out into the festive playground, the smell of barbecues and hotdogs, the sounds of music and talk, receding as she walks through the school gate, the eyes of Whitlam staring at her, even following her, from a poster wired to the fence.

* * *

The late-afternoon glow is fading and she switches on the lounge-room light just as the telephone rings. She guesses it's Michael, because of the time and the fact that, really, she receives few telephone calls. It's usually Michael, and it is now.

She tells him about the look in Mr Whitlam's eyes, and he tells her that he's called to remind her that he's leaving in a few days. So soon? And he may be away for some time. She knows that. And she has had time to think about it and adjust to it. But, in the end, it's possibly not so much the time he may be away as the distance. That and the nagging thought that sometimes they go away and never come back — except for visits to a place they once called 'home'.

They make a night to have a farewell dinner, the night before he leaves. And then she tells him she plans on leaving her job, then adds quickly that it won't just be the ducks on the wall flying from now on, but your mother as well. And, somewhere in there, she says that she might just land on his doorstep one day or night, and there's a bit of a silence before she goes on. And that gives her smile, because she well knows that you don't travel the world to have your mother land on your doorstep. Do you? Certainly not Michael — or his kind, for that matter.

We're all gypsies, she adds. And they both have a laugh. And a laugh is a good way to finish a call, and they hang up. And in the silence that follows she wonders if she just might be being reckless, after all. But she also has the feeling that something has been set in motion and, for better or worse, she's now set on a course and will see it through, to whatever or wherever it leads her. A modest picture of a modest life changes. Splash!

That night, as she lounges on her couch, commentators, journalists and politicians are talking about the day's events on the television. They talk of this seat, of this candidate, and of something called the mood of the country. Which is puzzling, but only mildly so, because she's not really listening.

She is recalling the posters of Whitlam she saw that afternoon at the polling booth. And how, for all his grandeur, he had that goodbye look in his eyes. The sort of fragility behind all the front, she imagines, that only a mother or a wife might see. And at some stage during the evening, no doubt, that goodbye look will become goodbye words. And there's something moving in that, which, to Rita, is more interesting than talk about the mood of the country. He was never 'her' Whitlam in the same way that leaders of the past, of *her* past, belonged to her. Belonged to her in a way that they almost became one of the family. Like a sort of uncle or brother-in-law. And, of course, Vic never tired of telling her that Joseph Benedict Chifley, prime minister, was once an engine driver. That he grew up firing engines and learning, word for word, *Bagley's Guide to Locomotive Engine Driving*, or whatever guide they studied in that foreign country of New South Wales. Joseph Benedict Chifley was hers in the same way that he was Vic's. But not Whitlam. Not really. For although she has lived on into these times, she knows that they are not her times. Our times, the times we call our own, she imagines, only last for those years that it takes to marry, have children and watch them go out into the world — and into *their* times. So he has always been 'their' Whitlam — Michael's and his kind's, with their smart university talk, and that look in their eyes that says they know something you don't (and never will), and their bottles of wine, not beer. So why should the goodbye look in the eyes of this Whitlam of theirs be moving?

She thinks about this while the commentators on the television talk more about the events of the day and the mood of the country and, in the end, all she can say with any certainty is that when the goodbye look in Whitlam's eyes becomes goodbye words, it will mean that a time is over. But not hers — Michael's. And she realises with a shock that what it really means, at least to her, is that Michael will no longer be young. Young in the way that she has always thought of him as young. For how could he be any other way than always young? The eternal child. But when Whitlam says goodbye, he won't be any more. And somehow, just to think of Michael and that whole generation that Rita and all the Ritas gave birth to as no longer young is more difficult than thinking of herself as no longer young. We can bear the fact of ourselves growing old, but not our children. Why is that?

And so, when she looks back to the television and watches as the goodbye look in Whitlam's eyes becomes goodbye words, she is barely listening. The election has been lost and won, or won and lost. But it doesn't concern her, not

322

at the moment. It's the thought of Michael and his kind not being young any more that not only distracts her but absorbs her until she's left sitting on the couch, still and quiet, as she would at the end of a film with a particularly sad ending: not wanting to talk or be disturbed. The job of bringing their children into the world, however well or not the job may have been done, is over. Finally. Irretrievably. It seems to her that the reality of this is only just sinking in. That she knew it, but didn't *want* to know it. And it is this, this farewell to the youth of their children, *all* their children — to Michael, all the Michaels and all his kind — that she now draws into her, rocking back and forth ever so slightly on the couch as she does. The job is done. However well or badly. Finally. Irrevocably. Done. Let them know, if they ever ask, that we tried. In our way. Let them know.

The face of Whitlam fades from the screen, the mountain from the landscape, and the commentators' talk returns once more to the mood of the country. Rita slowly stops rocking gently back and forth and gradually lets the thing go that she drew into her. For now.

On the couch beside her is a box containing bits and pieces from her trip: museum tickets, menus and postcards. And the names and addresses of people she travelled with over those twenty-one days of adventure. The sheep. *Baaa.* And she smiles to herself briefly. Such as the woman who owned a flower shop — Nellie — whom she has promised to stay in touch with. Just as Nellie has promised to stay in touch with her. It all seems long ago and far away. Not weeks but years. And it occurs to her that for most of those on the coach, that twenty-one-day tour may be the first and last time they will ever venture out beyond the borders of their world. Into unknown lands. And they will all, no doubt, have a little box of bits and pieces that they will take out from time to time for their own amusement or the amusement of others, to re-trace the bus route through the Tuscan hills, or the walk from a bus stop to a public monument, or from a hotel lobby to the Gates of Paradise. And those golden doors will gleam once more for them, as if they were standing in front of them, until the telephone rings or the doorbell chimes and everything is put away, back into the box.

When she looks back to the screen again, the commentators have gone — having examined the events of the day and measured the mood of the country — and there is a variety show on in their place. She rises from the couch and switches off the television and the room is silent. A flat silence. Like something's gone — from the room, from everyone — which may or may not return. Depending, and here she smiles briefly to herself, on the mood of the country.

Michael will call tomorrow (or he said he would) and she will learn something of how his night went, but only something. For he never tells her everything. Not now. Of course not, it's been years since he did that, when she was a young mother and he was impatient to tell her everything. *Everything.* A life distant enough to be another life altogether, yet not distant at all. A five-year-old hand reaches out in the night … tell them we tried.

It's a quiet world out there beyond the lounge-room curtains — a hushed world of houses, villas and sheds. Of morning radio and evening news. Home and not home. Native and alien. Enough, and not enough.

In a few days she will hear from her new employers and learn that in the New Year she will take a tour group, much like the one she was part of, to America. More specifically to California and the mid-west. And she will, for a moment, be disappointed, for she has acquired a taste for Tuscan hills and Paradise gates. But there will come a time in that American tour when she will stand and marvel at the sheer wonder of the Grand Canyon out there beneath her (which she never in her wildest dreams expected to see) and the wonder of the Rita inside who led her there.

And that, in the end, among all the uncertainty and questions of 'Should I?' and 'Shouldn't I?' and 'What will everybody think?', may very well be what you get for leaping on the tram of your fancy, and being foolish enough to go where it leads you.

15. A Good Day for Work

The spirit of Amerigo Vespucci is indoors today. The rain falls softly on the hills and valleys. It has all morning and will all day. This is no morning for setting out. The New Worlds can wait. The spirit of Amerigo Vespucci isn't going anywhere. Let others lend their name to the Americas. He's sitting by his window watching the rain, as is Art. And as Art watches the rain fall, he is calm and content. It is a good day for work.

Over the valley, the hills, the seas and the continents, over in the land of eucalyptus leaves, the events of the day have been decided. At some point in the afternoon, somebody will telephone him and deliver the news, and when they do they will add, 'Isn't it dreadful?' And he will agree, looking out over the hills and the rain. And they will add that he is better off away from the place and, once again, he will agree. They may even go on to say that they may well come and join him, that their impulse is to leave the country (how often has he heard that?), but he knows full well they won't. No, it takes a certain type to leave their country. And neither a more adventurous nor a bolder type. Just a different type. Those who were always leaving. Who are better off out of it all.

It is a good day for work. He rises from his chair and leaves the rain to fall without him. A painting, half-finished, is propped up against a wall: a portrait of that café they all went to with the Russian-sounding name that nobody could ever remember, but, all the same, one of those places that made you feel you were somewhere else, and which had to do until somewhere else was possible. Someone is standing in the doorway of this café, leaving; someone else is waiting to go in. Their faces are broad brush strokes of colour, familiar and unfamiliar. The café, the scene, is one of those constituent parts, one of those details that make up the whole, of a place and a time that once existed and which only exists now in this room, in this studio — a place and a time, he'd like to imagine, that could be rebuilt, if only mentally, street by street, building by building, brick by brick, from here.

At some point in the day the telephone will ring, and one of those friends who still ring and write will say that something has gone from them. That once they pushed their tables and chairs back up against their lounge-room walls and danced all night, but not any more. Not that they won't dance again, they will — but it will be a different kind of dancing. You only dance like that, they may well add, once.

And when they say, 'Isn't it awful?', he will agree. But what he'd like to say is that the events of the day will pass. That outside his window the rain is falling softly on the hills and valleys, and that it is a good day for work. And when he hangs up the telephone, when talk of the day in another time zone, in another world, has exhausted itself, he will return to the café with the Russian-sounding name and immerse himself in the scene.

And wasn't it always like this? These three or four hours of oblivion: *this* is where he is alive. The events of the day will pass, and he will watch them pass from here as he has for years now and will continue to. For as long as he has those three or four hours each day, they can't touch him. Nothing can. And so, the brush poised in the air, he is ready to resume. Over the hills and the valleys, the seas and continents, to that city he once called home and which is his life's work, certain events have come to pass that will, themselves, pass. He is a still, silent figure, his brush hovering over the canvas, the fire taking the chill from the air of the old mill house. Outside, the rain falls softly on the rooftops and towns, the valleys and hills. The spirit of Amerigo Vespucci is indoors. It is a good day for work.

PART FOUR

France,
late December, 1977

It is a living toy-town. The houses, buildings and streets are like one of those model towns that correspond to some reality out there beyond the model itself. At least, that is how it looks from the vantage point of the top floor of the town hall in which Michael is sitting, facing a wide window almost the length of the wall, which provides a panoramic view of the scene.

The postman on his rounds, the café owner in the doorway of her café, the town doctor in his red sports car, now turning into the square where the bus driver finishes a smoke in between one stop and another — all under a still blue sky, with low white clouds, blown in from the Atlantic, looming over the tree-tops of the nearby forest — could all just as easily be model figures as real people. All as still as the morning air, caught in perpetual greeting: the postman waving to the woman in the café door, the bus driver holding up the three fingers that indicate the time until departure to an old woman carrying her shopping basket, the doctor's red sports car paused at the corner, waiting for the stationer to cross into his shop. A toy-town caught in perpetual morning.

Michael has been here a week, and every morning about now (just after nine) he calculates the time at home. It will be evening. A summer night. Friday. And all the rituals and activities that he was once part of or observed will be starting again. The five young women who most nights, in that vast, outer suburban hotel, perform their ritual dance to the scattered patrons of the pub will be sitting at their table, eyes blank, waiting for that moment when the band finishes and their cue, this song about a place called Nutbush, will activate them and they can once more line up on the dance floor and give those scattered patrons the feeling of company and comfort that they came for. And his old band, in between sets, will either notice or not, so familiar is the ritual. And Peter — the mill horse of his art retired for the weekend — will be sitting at the dinner table, having just flown in, bringing news of the capital with him: the minister said such and such; the PM thought otherwise. But what Michael doesn't know is that while Peter speaks, his thoughts will be elsewhere, distracted by the memory of the poster that has just been taken down from the wall in his kitchen and wondering whether it is too late to regain those simple things that are so difficult to find and so easy to lose. And Mandy, with her newly acquired air of serenity (which he was thankful to have witnessed), will be going about that new life that he's sure she drove into the last time he saw her, whatever it may be and wherever she may be going about it. And his mother, probably in her lounge room, the television on, with that which passes for the news informing her that the mountain of Whitlam is retiring from politics and will soon leave the political landscape. All of them, going about their lives through morning and afternoon hours that have already passed there and are yet to unfold here, just as in a few hours it will still be today here but tomorrow there — everything, Michael fancifully imagines, occurring simultaneously. Stay in a jumbo jet long enough and you become the eagle that looks down and sees no difference between any of it.

And it is while he is idly turning these idle morning thoughts over in his mind, seated at a makeshift desk overlooking the town, his typewriter, notebooks and reference books all arranged with a neatness that won't be there in few weeks, that he becomes aware of an insistent sound coming up from the street below. A loud, whacking sound. A crack that cuts through the stillness of the morning and shatters all his idle thoughts about the neat divisions of time — of yesterday, today and tomorrow, and the eagle's view that makes no distinction. Curious, he rises from his seat and opens the window, the sound rising to meet him — louder and sharper — as he does. And as he looks down, his curiosity is satisfied.

Directly below him, on the opposite footpath, a stout and strong-looking woman has brought a rug out into the street to clean it. She is shaking the rug, and every time she gives it a good shake this loud snapping sound cuts through the still morning and dust rises into the air. At first it is a pleasant, vaguely amusing sight, for she has strong arms and looks as if she could shake up some unfortunate troublemaker as easily as a rug. But as she continues to shake the rug and the sharp, cracking sound returns again and again, it becomes vaguely disturbing. Something is happening and he doesn't particularly like it. But what? The woman shakes the rug, and every shake creates this sharp, cracking sound. A sound like what? And it is while he is contemplating this, as the woman with the rug pauses for a moment to allow a neighbour to pass, that he answers his question. A sound like what? Like a slap.

And immediately he is standing at the doorway of his parents' room all those years ago. And his father is shouting at his mother in a drunken rage, telling her to shut up. Just shut up. And every time he tells her to shut up he brings his hands together, making a loud slapping sound, showing her just what he could do if he chose to. And in that same moment the stick houses and the dirt street that he once called home come back as clear and sharp as the cracking sound of the rug being shaken out below him on the footpath. And as they do the image of three people standing on that dirt street in front of a vacant paddock, one long-ago summer evening, returns as well. And as they assemble, their eyes turn to him in sad question. How long must we continue to assemble here? And when shall we be released? Must we continue to return? Forever? To this spot, to this dirt street and this vacant paddock, ears tuned to the horizon, just beyond the flour mills and railways tracks, for the sound of the setting sun as it drops to earth? A summer stroll without end, always pausing here in front of this paddock? And they continue to stare, eyes in sad question — Vic, Rita and the twelve-year-old Michael that he was — frozen there on the dirt street, their night of immortality leaving them forever where they stand. No escape. No setting of the sun, no waning of the moon. No fates to be met because nobody is going anywhere. *They are walking down the old street again* ... They will always be walking down the old street. And always, always poised at this point, staring back, eyes in sad question, like those gods who tire of forever and yearn for mortality.

The woman on the footpath has gone inside, the rug dusted. Michael closes the window and returns to his makeshift desk: typewriter, notebooks and reference books all neatly arranged, awaiting the first words of the morning. The toy-town below twinkles in the morning sun, the blue sky above them is still, clouds blown in from the Atlantic a few miles away loom over the tree-tops of the nearby forest. But the trio — his father, his mother and the twelve-year-old self he once was — linger on, reflected in the glass. *They are walking down the old street again* ... They will always be walking ... What else can we do, they say. You call us, and we come. Every time. To this spot, and this place of stick houses, dirt streets and thistle paddocks. You call us and we come. And so here we are, walking down the old street again. His mother's eyes stare back, a look direct and imploring; his father offering an apologetic shrug suggesting, What can I say? What can *we* say? Only this. Tell our children, *all* our children, if they should ever ask, that we tried, in our way, and that if we ever hurt them it was not for lack of trying not to. That we were damaged before we came to them, and if we failed to keep our damage to ourselves it wasn't for lack of trying. Tell them how it was, behind the flying ducks and the laughter; behind the quaint feature walls and shadow boxes and ornamental boomerangs; tell them how it *really* was, if they should ever ask. That on these dirt streets and in these stick houses we lived the wrong life that they might live the right one. Tell our children, *all* our children, if they should ever ask ...

* * *

A sudden gust of wind lifts the bare branches of the trees just beyond the town, flinging birds into the sky. The wind comes without warning. The birds are flung upwards, float on the wind, then settle back on the bare branches from which they were thrown. They are flung, they fall. Clouds roll in from the sea, the forest is moving. The pace quickens on the town's streets beneath Michael's window. Street vendors, shoppers and townspeople hurrying to work look up. The forest heaves, the wood's in trouble. The wind is indifferent. It tosses us — blossoms, birds and lives — into the sky and we are thrown back. We land and look about — earth, wind and sky — before picking ourselves up. It is us, we are it. The thing itself. It worlds, it is worlding.

Acknowledgements

Many thanks to the following for their help during the writing of this novel.

The Australia Council for a two-year fellowship in 2012.

To Shona Martyn, Catherine Milne, Denise O'Dea and Amanda O'Connell at HarperCollins, Jo Butler, and my agent Sonia Land and all the gang at Sheil Land for their support and enthusiasm.

Finally, my special thanks to my partner, Fiona Capp, for her constant support, suggestions and advice, not just in the writing of this novel, but all of them. And to Leo – the lion-hearted boy.